THE
ONE
WHO FELL

BOOKS BY KERRY WILKINSON

THE JESSICA DANIEL SERIES

The Killer Inside (also published as *Locked In*)

Vigilante

The Woman in Black

Think of the Children

Playing With Fire

The Missing Dead (also published as *Thicker than Water*)

Behind Closed Doors

Crossing the Line

Scarred for Life

For Richer, For Poorer

Nothing But Trouble

Eye for an Eye

Silent Suspect

The Unlucky Ones

A Cry in the Night

THE ANDREW HUNTER SERIES

Something Wicked

Something Hidden

Something Buried

SILVER BLACKTHORN

Reckoning

Renegade

Resurgence

Kerry Wilkinson

THE ONE WHO FELL

bookouture

Published by Bookouture in 2023

An imprint of Storyfire Ltd.
Carmelite House
50 Victoria Embankment
London EC4Y 0DZ

www.bookouture.com

ISBN: 978-1-83790-052-7
eBook ISBN: 978-1-83790-051-0

ONE

Millie Westlake was in the cheese aisle when she realised she was being watched. She was in the middle of a difficult choice, what with all the cheeses and everything. Was the mature cheddar better than the sharp cheddar? What about the *extra* mature, or the *extra* sharp? Was there an extra sharp mature? Or maybe she'd get a nice blue cheese to crumble into the toastie she had spent the night before thinking about? She could buy both, of course. Double-cheese it.

The boy watching her was ten or eleven, his hair shaven at the sides, with the leftover bit on top slicked forward into something swooshy at the front. He was in front of the Babybels, staring at her in much the same way that Millie had been staring at the packet of 'carrot-infused Brie'. The carroty abomination shouldn't be with the cheeses – and the boy clearly thought Millie shouldn't be out in public.

'What's wrong?' Millie asked.

One of the boy's eyes twitched. 'Huh?'

'You're staring.'

There was a gulp and the boy checked over his shoulder, to where there was nothing except a row of milk.

Millie remembered that sort of glance from when she'd been more or less the same age. That quick look to make sure there were no adults around.

She flashed back to HMV in the old days, ensuring no one was watching, then stuffing a CD into her jacket's inside pocket and striding confidently out of the shop. Millie wondered what kids nicked from shops nowadays. Surely petty theft hadn't gone out of fashion? She wasn't that old.

The boy was back to looking at her again. He licked his lips and took a breath, psyching himself up for his big moment.

As soon as Millie had noticed him watching her, she'd known why. Sometimes it was the groups of mums sitting in café windows, their prams shoved to the side, blocking part of the pavement. One time, it had been a pair of six-foot-something rugby lads walking through town in their kit, their studs click-clacking on the tarmac. There were always children, too: younger ones all the way through to the teenagers. They'd stare, sometimes even stop to do it, as if Millie had grown a second head. They would all be thinking the same thing, although very few were brave enough to actually ask it.

This boy was brave enough.

'Did you kill your mum and dad?' he asked.

He spoke quickly and with a bit of a stumble. The sort of hesitance a slightly older boy might show when asking out a girl if he wasn't confident of a positive reply.

'Why would you ask that?' Millie replied.

The boy checked over his shoulder again, though there was still nobody there. Just Millie and him, alone in the dairy aisle, surrounded by the gentle hum of the giant fridges.

'My mum reckons you did,' he added.

He sounded less confident second time around. As if the girl had mumbled a reply, forcing him to ask again.

Millie thought for a moment, wondering if she might know the boy's mother. He was around the age that meant there was every chance she'd been at school with at least one of his parents. Not that it mattered. It sometimes felt to Millie as if everyone in town knew who she was. It was that sort of place.

'Your mum sounds pretty stupid,' Millie replied, calmly.

It took a moment for it to sink in. The boy goggled at her, his cheeks puffing out like an inflating balloon, mouth slowly opening.

'She sounds like a proper moron,' Millie added. 'A great, big thicko.'

The boy was frozen for a second more, before he took a half-step backwards. He glanced to the Dairylea triangles – quickly realising they would offer no support – then back to Millie, before moving further away. It felt as if he wanted to say something, though the words seemed stuck. Another moment and he spun quickly, tripping over his own feet as he hurried away, disappearing off towards the cereal aisle.

Millie watched him go, wondering if he'd be back, his mother at his side. Him and his stupid mum.

She waited a couple of beats, until she was sure nobody was coming, then turned back to the cheese. She snatched the mature cheddar, blue cheese and mozzarella from the display, before dropping all three into her basket.

It was a triple-cheese kind of day.

TWO

Millie could still taste the greasy goodness of her cheese toastie for one as she eyed Bill's egg-shaped head. With his silly ginger goatee, rosy cheeks, and uneven eyebrows, he was quite the odd-looking man.

'Is it a she?' Ingrid asked from across the table.

'No,' Millie replied.

Ingrid was almost ninety and already slightly hunched – but she leaned forward and slowly flipped down five plastic characters on her board.

The *Guess Who?* set at the nursing home was old-school, from a time when apparently only white people existed. Mainly white men. It was the same set of characters with which Millie had vague memories of playing when she'd been a girl.

'Does yours have dark hair?' Millie asked.

Ingrid shook her head. 'Nope.'

Millie flicked down a third of the faces on her board as Ingrid reached for her tea. The cup rattled on the saucer as Ingrid's hand trembled, before she lifted it to her mouth and sipped.

Around them, the nursing home's rec room was a carpeted

calm of soft voices and low, shaded light from the windows at the back. A television was pinned to the wall in the furthest corner but the volume was muted as subtitles flashed across the bottom. A crescent of four or five people were watching, while others were swiping on iPads, or tapping at their phones.

In the other corner, Millie and Ingrid were sitting across from each other at one of the tables. They were a short distance away from Alan and Mick, who were – as usual – playing chess. A couple of other tables had been pushed together, as another pair of residents worked together on a giant puzzle of some bridge.

'Is yours ginger?' Ingrid asked.

Millie glanced at the Bill card, with his pointed, red beard. 'Yes,' she replied.

Ingrid let out an excited 'ooh', before starting to flip down tiles.

'Did you hear about Elsie's daughter?' she asked as she continued knocking down characters until there were only four left facing her. She spoke with a hint of a smile: a *you-really-want-to-hear-this* glee.

Since starting to volunteer at the nursing home, Millie had discovered that the residents were gossips on an industrial scale. They made teenage girls in American movies look like hushed nuns when it came to tittle-tattle.

'No,' Millie replied.

Ingrid glanced up from her board and checked both ways, before lowering her voice. It had to be good stuff. She spoke quickly and excitedly. 'Elsie's daughter's husband was supposed to be at some weekend training course for his work, something to do with insurance, or banks: that sort of thing. Anyway, Elsie's daughter got an email from Netflix saying there'd been a new login to her account from Harrogate, except her husband was supposed to be at a conference in Manchester. She did something to trace the login from the email back to this hotel on the outskirts, so she phoned them and asked for her husband's room – and they put her right through.'

'What did he say?'

There was a shake of the head and another check sideways before Ingrid continued. 'He didn't pick up – but, because she knew he was there, she drove up to Harrogate. She was waiting in the lobby as he came in from dinner with some woman from his office who was half his age!' Ingrid finished with a gleeful flourish.

Millie had discovered that this generation talked about sex easily as much as those half their age. Perhaps a *quarter* of their age. It was, admittedly, usually about which resident's children, grandchildren, or great-grandchildren were getting up to no good. Millie found herself easing into the currency of gossip. She could often hear the same rumour spread three or four times across a few days, usually with added embellishment.

Millie risked a sideways look towards the chess players, figuring Alan and Mick were probably listening in.

'What happened then?' she asked, curious.

Ingrid leaned in and sipped her tea, relishing the moment. She enjoyed spreading gossip more than Millie enjoyed hearing it – but one of the reasons Millie started volunteering was to give the residents someone to talk to. It just so happened that many wanted to speculate on the relationship status of other residents' relatives.

'They had a row in the lobby,' Ingrid replied. 'A proper barney, apparently. First she was shouting at her husband, then at the other woman; then the other woman was shouting back and the husband had to separate them. Then he got back into it with his wife. All the while, there's a wedding going on in the next room. The mother of the bride came out to ask them to keep it down, then she got involved in it all.' A pause, followed by a beaming grin. 'Great fun. What a hoot.'

It did sound like quite a lot of fun for anyone actually involved.

'What does Elsie think of it all?' Millie asked.

Ingrid bit her bottom lip momentarily and gave a small shrug, as if to say she'd not thought about it. 'Oh, she'll be fine. Her other daughter married some sort of talent agent and he's loaded. He took Elsie off to Dubai the other year.' Ingrid angled in a fraction. She winced slightly from the movement but her eyes twinkled with wicked enjoyment. Her voice was a croaky whisper when she finished. 'Lucky cow.'

Millie swallowed the half-smile. There was a camaraderie around the home in that the residents appeared to stick up for one another against anyone from the outside. If one resident was treated badly by their children, or someone else, they would get unending support. That support didn't stop them all bitching about one another when there was nobody else around to hear it though.

Millie gave Ingrid her moment and then looked back down to her board. 'Does yours have facial hair?' she asked.

Ingrid was instantly focused back on the game. 'Nope.'

Millie lowered three of the characters on her board. She was going to lose and it was going to be a massacre.

Ingrid knew it. Her grin widened and Millie pictured the older woman playing her own children at games or sports years before. She was obviously the sort who'd never let them win at anything. The Monopoly player who ended up with more than half the board but wanted to keep going to the bitter end.

'Is yours bald?' Ingrid said.

'Yes.'

Just two tiles remained.

'Does yours have blonde hair?' Millie asked.

Ingrid let out the merest of winces. 'Yes.'

Millie knocked down her characters until there was only

three remaining. She'd barely finished before Ingrid eagerly
continued.

'Yours is Herman,' she said.

'Nope.'

One character remained on Ingrid's side.

Millie had a one-in-three chance of guessing correctly. It
was either Anita with her red bows, Eric with his stupid blue
hat, or Joe with his massive bum chin.

'Is yours Joe?' she asked.

Ingrid slumped in her seat, head drooping. 'This is a
robbery.'

She held up her card to show Joe, as Millie revealed Bill.

Ingrid squinted in at Millie's card. 'I used to know a man
who looked like Bill,' she said. 'Ran the local am-dram society
and always played the lead. He fell off the stage one year; broke
his hip, or his knee, something like that.' She paused momentarily, humming to herself as if trying to retrieve a memory. 'Got
sent to prison in the end,' she added. 'I think he was fiddling his
taxes.'

Millie blinked at the story. Ingrid was full of similar matter-
of-fact reminiscences and rarely expanded on the bare bones of
the story. As she eased further into her wheelchair, a man
passed along the back of the seats, carrying a phone-charging
cable towards the other side of the room. He caught Millie's
gaze and rolled his eyes, having apparently heard the end of
Ingrid's tale.

Jack was Millie's friend and the person who'd invited her to
volunteer. He'd said that he reckoned most of what Ingrid said
was made up, exaggerated, or misremembered – but, to Millie,
the truth was largely unimportant. Who cared if a man that
looked like a *Guess Who?* character once got caught doing some
dodgy accounting? The important thing was that a woman well
into her eighties enjoyed telling the story.

Ingrid wriggled in her chair again, wincing as she did so.

She tried to sit up straighter but then grunted as she fought with her body. When she next looked up, there was something glassy about her stare, as if she'd accidentally looked at the sun and she could now see only stars. She opened her mouth and closed it again, then the wrinkles in her forehead deepened.

'Do you know when Gordon's coming?' she asked.

Millie took a breath. Gordon was Ingrid's husband, who'd died more than twenty years before. When Ingrid had first mentioned him, Millie thought he was another resident and she'd gone around asking for Gordon. It was Jack who told her that Ingrid sometimes thought her former husband was still alive. It was like there was a switch, where Ingrid could jump from the present into the past with almost no change to the way she spoke. Jack had explained that, for Ingrid, the present and past blurred into one. Half a century could be perfectly clear in her mind, while that morning would be lost. Some days, she'd be stuck in her own history; others she'd be as alert as anyone.

'I think he'll be here soon,' Millie replied.

'Because he said he'd be here at one and it's now quarter-past.'

Millie looked across the room, towards where Jack was plugging in an iPad for one of the other residents. It was rare but Ingrid could sometimes become so distressed by Gordon's lack of appearance that she had to be taken back to her room.

'I'm sure he said two,' Millie said softly. Jack had told her that it was always better to go with things, rather than point out that Gordon was dead.

Ingrid's head snapped up. 'Two?'

'That's what I heard.'

Ingrid remained sitting upright for a moment, her nose high, as if sniffing the truth. For a second or so, it felt dangerous, as if she might start shouting. Her glee at the game felt long-forgotten.

And then she allowed herself to sink back into the chair. 'I guess that's all right, then,' she said. 'I wanted to tell him about the girl.'

Jack had finished helping with the iPad and was heading back across the room. Millie almost flagged him down, except he was hurrying in a way that meant there was likely a mini-emergency in another room.

'What girl?' Millie asked.

'The girl on the roof last night. Looked out my window and she was right there.'

Millie returned her full attention to Ingrid. 'There was a girl on the roof?'

Ingrid sounded exhausted when she replied. Her voice was more of a sorry sigh than it had been before. She waved a hand in vague direction of the back of the home. 'Right there on the roof. All in white.'

Millie thought for a moment. It was probably another memory from the past, though it was hard to tell.

'Which roof?' she asked.

Ingrid suddenly lurched sideways, almost toppling out of her chair as the wheels rocked. Millie lunged to catch her but the older woman was already righting herself as she tried to turn.

'I'll show you,' she said.

She'd already started wheeling herself towards the doors when Millie caught up. Millie took the handles at the back of the wheelchair and guided Ingrid through the corridors, following directions until they were outside the door to Ingrid's room. Nothing was locked, so Ingrid opened up and shunted herself inside as Millie followed.

There was a bed covered with blankets on one side of the room, with a step protruding from the side. A series of handles were connected to the wall, leading towards the darkened shower in the corner. A small television was on the other side, sitting on top of a large dresser, alongside twenty or so framed photos.

Ingrid ignored all that, racing across the room until she was in front of the window at the back. She pushed the net curtain across, holding it wide so that they both had a view of the valley beyond. Mossy green stretched into the distance, with a bushy hedge interrupting the grass, before the land dipped down towards a house in the middle distance.

'*That* roof,' Ingrid said.

Millie stepped closer to the window, taking in the scene. There was a skylight in among the reddened tiles on top of the house's roof, though little else of note.

'What was she doing on the roof?' Millie asked.

'Don't know – but someone pushed her off.'

The bottom half of the house was obscured by the hedge but Millie could count the three floors of windows. 'That would be a big fall,' she replied. 'Nobody's making that without breaking their legs.'

A shrug. 'I guess she broke her legs then. Shame about the dress. It was this lovely white thing, like the one my Simone wore at her wedding.'

Millie was mindful of everything Jack had ever told her about conversations with the home's residents. When it came to shaky memories, it was better to say nothing, or play along, than to deny something.

'Are you sure she was pushed?' Millie asked.

'Definitely.'

'When did it happen?'

'Late. It was dark.'

'If it was dark, then how did you see her?'

Ingrid was quiet and Millie wondered if the older woman would end up moving on, as if the conversation had never happened. It wouldn't be the first time.

The reply took a while, but then it came, as clear as the

other details. 'The moon was bright,' she said. 'I could see across the whole valley, right out to the woods.'

She poked a finger, emphasising the point as Millie followed Ingrid's look, towards the trees in the distance.

'All in white,' Ingrid repeated. 'Lovely blonde hair, like my Simone.' She paused for a moment and then pointed towards the houses. 'Right there on the roof. Pushed.'

THREE

Millie was on her way out of the staff toilets when Jack finally caught up to her. He was hurrying along the corridor, arm half into his coat as he fought with the other side, as if trying to get out of a straitjacket.

'I've not had time to chat,' he said. 'I had to work through my break because there was a big mix-up with the laundry. We were supposed to get everything delivered but then...' he tailed off, realising it was the sort of work story nobody wanted to hear. 'Do you want to nip out back?'

Millie retrieved her own coat from the staffroom and then met her friend in the smoking area at the back of the home. As she pulled her jacket tighter and settled underneath the overhang, Jack was vaping something fruity into the chilly, bright skies. He held the device with one hand, while using his other to pull a slightly flattened Cadbury's Caramel from his pocket.

'I sat on it,' he said, as he started to unwrap the chocolate.

'Why'd you do that?'

'It wasn't on purpose.'

He ripped off the top of the foil and bit away the first chunk, before offering the bar to Millie. The chocolate was cracked and mushed, with hardened caramel spilling from the sides.

Millie waved it away. 'I don't want to eat something that's been up your arse,' she replied.

'It didn't go *up* my arse, more to the side of it. It still tastes the same.'

'I'm not eating anything that's been in the vicinity of your bum.'

'Just my bum?'

'Anyone's bum.'

Jack smiled as he juggled his vape pen and the chocolate, before dispatching the former into a pocket. He bit off the second rectangle and then started to chew.

'Is that really your lunch?' Millie asked.

'More of a pre-lunch.'

'Didn't I see you eating a scone at about eleven?'

'That was a pre-pre-lunch. It goes breakfast, after-breakfast, pre-pre-lunch, pre-lunch, then lunch. This is basics, Mill. Didn't you learn anything at school?'

Millie momentarily wondered how her friend remained so thin, given the amount he seemingly ate. It was probably the vaping.

'You're supposed to have it little and often,' Jack added.

'Are we are still talking about food?' Millie replied.

Jack gave her the side-eye as he finished chewing. His lips curled but he didn't quite give in.

As he ate, Millie turned to look out across the valley, where the grass glistened with a dewy glow. The sky was silver, with angry dark clouds on the horizon. It would be raining before long.

Millie pointed down towards the house in the distance, waiting until Jack was looking in the same direction. 'Ingrid says she saw someone on that house's roof last night.'

Jack took another bite from his chocolate as he thought on

it. It took a short while for him to reply. 'You know I'm not trying to be mean but...'

He didn't finish the sentence. Didn't need to.

'It didn't feel as if she was talking about the past,' Millie replied.

Jack craned in and then back. 'If someone was pushed off the roof, there'd be an ambulance. Police. People would have seen the lights across the valley. It'd be on Facebook.'

'Not everything's on Facebook. And she said the girl was pushed.'

'Everything important is on Facebook.' He paused for another bite and then spoke with his mouth partially full of chocolate. 'Just because you're not on it.'

Millie ignored the gentle jibe. Jack was always trying to get her back on social media for some reason.

He was right about the house, though. The roof seemed high from Ingrid's room but it was even taller from the smoking area. The house towered over the hedge at the edge of the field. Two full storeys were visible, with another shielded behind the green. If one storey was the height of a seven-foot man, the fall would be a minimum of twenty feet. Six full metres. With the angle of the roof, it was even higher.

Ingrid had specifically said the woman in white had been 'pushed' from the roof. Except that would mean not one but two people being that high. If that was somehow true, whoever fell would almost certainly have broken a bone or ten. Or worse.

'It's a really precise thing to remember,' Millie said. 'It wasn't *just* a woman. It was a woman she says she saw on that *specific* roof. She said she was wearing white and had blonde hair.'

'Why would a woman in a white dress be standing on a roof in the middle of winter? On the outskirts of Whitecliff? Why would someone push her off?' Jack sounded tired. The tone of a man who'd heard all sorts of improbable nonsense over the course of working in the home.

'I don't know...'

'Ingrid probably saw something similar on TV last night. Last week she told me how one of her daughter's friends crashed his car back in the day and broke his leg. Then Jacqui said the exact same thing happened on *Emmerdale*.'

Millie thought on it for a moment. She was never sure where Ingrid's true memories ended and her imagination began. Perhaps it was nothing?

Jack finished his chocolate and lobbed the wrapper towards the bin. It missed, bounced off the nearby fence, and landed in a puddle. He sighed as he crouched to pick it up.

'You're losing your touch,' Millie said.

Jack ignored her. 'What are you up to later?'

'Pot noodle and *Judge Judy* repeats. You?'

'Quiet night in with Rish. It's our anniversary.'

'I've seen your "quiet nights"...'

Jack smiled, though he didn't reply. 'Is it your weekend with Eric?' he asked.

Millie gave herself a moment, as if she needed to think about it. As if those few days of custody with her son weren't permanently etched in her mind. Of course she knew... but, even with her best friend, she didn't want to allow the desperation to show.

'Not this one,' Millie said, breezily. It would be a full week until she saw her son. She pushed that thought away before it became too dark.

Not that Jack noticed. 'Are you back tomorrow?' he asked.

Millie looked across the valley, to where the darker clouds were rolling ever closer. 'Probably. It's not as if I have anything better to do.'

FOUR

Millie parked her car a little past the faded, old-fashioned, red phone box. A good forty years before, a little before Millie was born, the phone would have been shared by everyone in the local area. She could vaguely remember being four or five, crammed into one of the phone boxes on the seafront with her mum. Her mum was struggling to find change as she tried to get through to her father for some reason.

It felt like a different age, for more reasons than the obvious passing of time. Millie was still in awe of her parents at the time, as she assumed most children that age were.

As the memory flitted in and out of her thoughts, Millie stopped momentarily and took in the phone box. There was moss growing around the bottom and the glass panes were either cracked or no longer in the frames. There was a scratched metal panel inside, with a phone receiver resting on a chunky-looking box that had a keypad. Squiggled remains of obscene graffiti were written in black marker across almost every visible surface. She wondered why it was still there. It surely didn't work any longer

Millie turned across the road towards the house she'd seen

from the nursing home. It was on its own plot, though not as isolated as Millie had first thought. The house was at the start of a short street which connected to the coastal road that snaked out of town. As well as the first house, there were another seven or eight spaced apart from each other.

It was hard for Millie to know why it had all been bothering her. In some ways, it didn't. Someone fell, or someone didn't; someone was pushed, or someone wasn't. It didn't affect Millie and, within a day or so – perhaps even by now – Ingrid would have forgotten it herself.

Except...

As Millie had told Jack, she had nothing better to do. It was why she was volunteering in the first place. She could go home and stare at a wall, or mooch around the market and be stared at herself. Or, maybe, Ingrid *had* seen something...?

A wind whipped and fizzed between the houses, as Millie got out of her car. One of the freezing sea breezes that gave no regard to how many layers a person might be wearing. Millie shivered and clasped her coat tighter, before crossing the road. There was no pavement and it was only as she reached the gravel on the far side that she realised she was being watched. A man was in the garden at the front of the house, his phone held high in the air. He was in jeans and a vest, apparently unconcerned at the temperature.

Millie well knew that phone pose, as did anyone who lived in Whitecliff. A phone signal was like a waiter in a busy restaurant. Nowhere in sight when needed, omnipresent when not.

There was no fence and the patch of gravel led directly onto the grass, where the man slowly lowered his phone and then narrowed his eyes to take in Millie. There was recognition that he knew her, though couldn't quite place who she was. It was a look that Millie knew well. There were days when it felt as if everyone in town knew who she was. She'd learned to ignore it and continue on.

'Do you live here?' Millie asked.

The man pursed his lips as he pushed his phone into a pocket. 'Who's asking?'

'I know this sounds like a weird question but is there a chance someone fell off your roof last night?'

Millie kept the specific 'push' part to herself.

The man turned to look up at the house and Millie followed the gaze. It felt a very long way to the top, the sort of distance she couldn't imagine falling without serious injury. Not only was the house as tall as she'd thought, the roof angled steeper and higher.

When she looked back to the man, he was frowning at her. 'Why would someone have fallen off the roof?' he asked.

Millie suddenly felt very silly. Of course nobody had dropped so far. Ingrid was confusing the present with the past, or real life with TV. Jack was right.

She found herself stumbling over a reply. 'I, um, work at the nursing home,' she said, waving a hand in the vague direction of the large building up on the hill. 'One of the residents says she saw a girl fall from your roof last night. I told her I'd ask, just to put her mind at rest...'

She tailed off, hoping the man would jump in to offer an explanation. Instead, he stood with a hand on his hip, frown deepening until he eventually replied.

'I live on my own,' he said.

'Oh, uh... sorry for troubling you. I'll tell her it's nothing.'

Millie took a step away, except that the man now wanted to talk. 'What did she see?' he asked. 'Or *think* she saw?'

'She said she was looking out her window and there was a girl on the roof. She reckoned the girl fell – but it's obviously way too high for that.'

The man nodded along. 'You'd break your legs,' he said.

'That's what I thought – but I told her I'd check. I'll tell her tomorrow it's nothing to worry about.'

The man was still nodding, eyes narrow, perhaps still trying to figure out who Millie was. It was another look with which she was familiar.

All of a sudden, he thrust a hand in Millie's direction. 'It's Dean,' he said. 'Feel free to bring her down here if she wants to check for herself.'

Millie couldn't think of a way to turn down the handshake without being obviously rude, so she offered her own. Dean pulled it into his mitt. His fingers were chubby sausages and he squeezed hard as Millie attempted to pull away. He let her – but only after he'd left a whitened imprint of his fingers on her skin.

'Millie,' she said quickly. She tucked the hand behind her back, trying not to show him that he'd hurt her.

Her name was the prompt he needed. 'You're that news-reader's girl, aren't you?'

His accent was strong and local, with the Rs over-pronounced. It was as if there were two or three in a word, instead of one.

Millie took a step away, craving the safety of her car. Dean stretched towards her but she was already far enough away that he couldn't reach, even if he wanted. By the time she was on the other side of the road, Millie wondered if that had been his intention at all. Perhaps he'd been trying to scratch his arm or his leg? When she glanced back, he was lifting his phone towards the sky in an elusive search for signal. He wasn't even looking at her.

Millie fumbled with her bag and keys, struggling to get back in the car and wondering why she'd locked it in the first place. She didn't fancy doing a three-point turn while being watched, so, with a grunt of the engine, Millie lurched away. She continued on the deserted coastal road, even though it was the opposite direction to where she wanted to go.

Wind buffeted in from the sea, rocking the car from side to

side on the crumbling roads. Millie checked her rear mirror, though there was no one on the road behind. It was half a mile or so until a turn appeared. Millie took it and then found herself doubling back towards the town. Minutes later and she was again on the street where Dean lived, though at the other end.

She parked and sat, peering along the lengthy road towards Dean's house. There was nobody in the garden any longer and no one else in sight. Each home was different to the next. There was a sprawling bungalow with no yard, next to a place with a football pitch-sized empty plot, with a caravan at the back. Dust and sand skitted across the gaps in between houses as the wind continued to fizz.

Millie got out of her car and headed into the alley that ran along the rear of the properties. It was a dirt-gravel track, with four junked, rusting cars at the back of the caravan and a battered, grey wheelie bin on its side. Millie crunched along the lane, passing three spaced-out houses until she arrived at the back of Dean's place. The high hedge on one side blocked her view of the nursing home, while, on the other, Dean's house towered above. She shivered in its shadow, looking up, unable to see the roof itself above the overhang.

She should let it go, Millie knew that. It felt impossible that Ingrid could have seen what she said she had.

She *should* let it go, except...

There was a mound of rubbish close to the house. An old TV unit with a hole in the back and a door hanging loose sat next to some dusty wooden flooring. There was a rug covered in grimy grey muck, a table with three legs, and a smashed-up microwave. It looked as if someone had cleared out a house and tipped it. Either that, or Dean had dumped it himself.

Millie stepped away, ready to head back to her car, when she noticed the reddy-brown square on the ground, close to the hedge. She crouched and picked up the shard of thickened clay. The edges were sharp, from where it had shattered.

It was a tile.

The same sort that was on the roof of Millie's own place.

She edged further towards the hedge, craning up and trying to see if there was a gap on the roof, except there was no angle that would give her the view.

Millie couldn't see any other tiles among the rubbish. The rest was mainly furniture.

Just one smashed tile.

Millie dropped it into her bag, feeling the weight of the tile pull on her shoulder. She turned back towards the other end of the lane – and her car. Millie had already taken a couple of steps when she felt something prickling the back of her neck, as if somebody unseen had scratched a nail across her skin.

She turned quickly, eyes searching across the empty alley – except the feeling hadn't come from there. Standing in the window of the house, watching her with a curious, gnarly stare was Dean.

They locked eyes for a moment and she wondered if he'd seen her pick up the tile. Wondered if he'd been watching the entire time.

And then Millie turned, pulled her jacket tighter again, and hurried back to her car.

FIVE

The roof tile was in the middle of Millie's kitchen table as she sat across from it, twirling her fork into her Pot Noodle. In the background, Coldplay, or Ed Sheeran, or somebody else instantly forgettable was seeping from the radio. It was the same radio that had sat in the corner of the kitchen for as long as Millie could remember. Her mum would listen to Radio 4 in the morning and then, by the time Millie got home from school in the afternoon, it had become Radio Two.

That was twenty-five years ago, yet, somehow, Millie had inherited the same habit, without meaning to. It was more the comfort of the background noise that mattered, as opposed to the station itself. The same voices, the same cadence, sometimes the same music. Childhood into adulthood.

Thinking of her own childhood had her thinking of her son, and how he wasn't with her.

Millie blinked away the thought of Eric, the empty house, and of turning into her mother. Those thoughts of her son never left her, but she couldn't let herself wallow while she was alone, especially not in this house. She would end up in too dark a place.

She scooped another forkful of Beef and Tomato noodle into her mouth. The king of flavours. Always had been, always would be. That was one thing her mum certainly wouldn't have been seen eating.

Millie was considering boiling the kettle to make herself a second pot when the doorbell sounded. Jack would have messaged if he was on his way over, and nobody else ever came to the house, so Millie was hesitant as she headed along the hallway. It was dark but she could see the shadowed shape of someone tall bobbing from foot to foot on the other side of the rippled glass. It had to be a man. His wide shadow jerked across the illuminated white of the security light that triggered itself if anyone stepped on the driveway.

Millie paused on the doormat. 'Who is it?'

The man's voice was part-mumble, part-cough. 'It's Guy.'

'Guy who?'

Millie didn't catch the reply – but she knew who it was a moment after she'd asked. It was a name she hadn't heard in a while, even though there was barely a day in which she wouldn't think about the man on the other side of the door.

She couldn't think of a reason why he'd be knocking.

Millie unlocked the bolt at the top of the door and then unlatched the main lock, before pulling it open.

The man on the other side puffed out a long plume of steam as he shivered.

'I don't want to talk to you,' Millie said.

A part of her wondered if he'd come to apologise, except he didn't seem particularly interested in her. Instead, he was looking over his shoulder, back towards the road.

'Have you seen the panther?' he asked.

Millie found herself staring at the twisting, turning shape of the man who was comfortably six foot. He would be almost seventy by now. As she looked up to him, Millie considered how it never felt quite right when someone that age was so tall. His big shoulders were squeezed into a wax jacket that had a hole in the side. His thin hair was billowing back and forth across his head. He flicked away a strand as he looked between Millie and the street.

'The what?' Millie asked.

'The panther.'

Millie eyed him, wondering if there was some sort of joke she was missing.

'What do you mean *panther*?'

Guy stopped shuffling and turned to face her properly. 'There's a panther on the loose.'

He spoke as if telling her something as obvious as the day, or the time.

Millie's scepticism must have been clear because he quickly added: 'Well, maybe not a panther...'

Before Millie could reply, he thrust a hand into a jacket pocket and pulled out a phone. The screen lit up his reddened, pimpled face as he jabbed at it while continuing to speak.

'There's been two sightings now. Your neighbour over the back says he took this photo by the dividing line to your house.'

Guy continued thumbing the screen while mumbling under his breath. He scolded the device like a primary school teacher telling a five-year-old not to paint the floor.

'Not you,' he said, then: 'It's somewhere here...'

Eventually, he turned the device around and thrust it towards Millie. There was a fuzzy photo on the screen: something black and long against a dim green-grey background. It looked like the phone had been moving when the photo was taken, as the black object was blurred and unclear.

Millie squinted, then tilted her head. Guy let her take the phone and she moved it closer to her face, then further away, before handing it back.

'That's a *panther*?' she said.

Guy poked a finger towards the screen. 'Those are the legs.'

Millie angled in once more. 'Looks more like a bin bag,' she replied.

Guy turned the phone around and glanced at it, before stuffing it into his pocket. '*Could* be a bin bag, I suppose...' He mulled it over silently and then continued. 'There are two sightings, though. This one last night.' Guy looked up to Millie, taking her in for what felt like the first time proper. 'I was wondering if...'

Millie slammed the door on him.

Well, she tried to. It would have had more effect if she'd been able to fling it closed, except it didn't quite fit in the frame and she ended up barging it back into place. The soft, wet *whump* wasn't quite in the same league as the satisfying *thunk* she'd imagined. There was a moment in which Millie stood still, slightly shocked by her own actions. Then she crunched the door back open, to where Guy was still standing where she'd left him.

'You ruined my life,' she said.

Millie hoped for a reaction, *craved* one. It wasn't said flippantly. She'd wondered for a while what she might say to Guy were she ever to see him on the street. She'd had lengthy self-monologues in which she'd say something to Guy, then he'd reply, which would lead her neatly into a sharp comeback. Sometimes, she thought she'd be angry with him, perhaps shout and swear. Other times, she thought it would be better to stay calm. She'd tell him that he'd ruined her life but she wouldn't show anything that would let him see how furious she was. He was the reason little boys in cheese aisles stared at her.

She'd always pictured running into him outside the supermarket, or on a petrol forecourt. Somewhere public – except here he was on her doorstep.

And none of that happened.

Guy took a quarter-step towards her and squinted, as if peering over the top of non-existent glasses.

'You're right.'

He spoke with a softness that Millie wouldn't have expected from such a large man. In all of her imaginary back-and-forths, Millie had never once considered Guy would agree with her.

She stared back at him, bewildered at what to say. All those daydreams had been useless.

And so she closed the door again.

This time, Millie moved away from it, shuffling along the corridor until taking a seat on the second stair from the bottom. She stared at the floor, sensing the shadow move from the door, rather than seeing it.

He had quite the nerve to come to her door after all this time, especially considering his first word wasn't 'sorry' but some nonsense about a panther.

Millie grabbed her phone and angrily poked at the screen until she had the browser open. She searched 'Whitecliff + panther', expecting there to be nothing. Except there was a list of results. The first was from Facebook the week before, where someone had posted a photo even blurrier than the one Millie had been shown. There was a smudge of something dark against a field, with a hint of a bluey sky above. The caption read 'Is this a panther?' – and underneath were a series of replies that ranged from scepticism to outright mockery. Millie had to scroll to find the first response that took the post seriously. Someone said they'd seen a big cat a decade or so before but hadn't got a photo. She'd told her friends and parents but nobody believed her.

Back on the main page of search results, Millie pressed to read the next. It was a news story from seven years before, where a man had told the local paper he'd seen a big black cat while mowing his lawn. He lived on the edge of town, in one of the big houses that needed ride-on mowers, and he reckoned he'd seen the animal on the furthest side of his land.

Millie returned to the front door and opened it to reveal an empty space. She took a step outside, into the cold, then another. A car was idling on the opposite side of the road, underneath the street light. Guy was sitting in a battered Volvo, the sort that always had its headlights on and that Millie didn't really remember existing any time outside of her childhood.

She had a vague memory of being crammed into the boot of a similar vehicle, along with a bunch of other children. She'd have been five or six and there'd have been seven or eight children packed into the various spaces of the car. They'd have been on a trip to the safari park, or a theme park, all organised by a single parent in the summer holidays. It was the sort of all-in-one trip that had died out by the time Millie had become an adult. Health and safety, and all that. You couldn't even cram eight kids into a car boot without seatbelts these days.

Guy was tapping something into his phone as the light above the passenger seat flickered above him. Millie found herself moving without thought. Before she knew it, she was already at the end of the drive, next to the security gates that she never closed. She could see Guy more clearly now, with the light from his phone screen illuminating the underside of his face.

Millie was suddenly at the side of his car and she knocked on the window. If things had been reversed, Millie would have jumped so high, her head would have banged into the roof – but Guy barely reacted. He turned calmly towards her and then wound down the window with an old-fashioned handle. The glass squeaked in protest and then he was looking up to her, almost as if he'd expected her to come out.

'What's this about a panther?' Millie asked.

SIX

Guy's bag had exploded across Millie's kitchen table. He'd asked if it was OK to use the surface and then some sort of detonator had gone off and there were papers everywhere. She'd not even been given a coded warning.

In the space where the roof tile had been moments before, there were now lined pages full of wide, scrawling shorthand squiggles and a ripped Ordnance Survey map. In various spots around the table, chairs, and floor, there were pens, rubber bands, a stapler, a highlighter, nail clippers and a slightly torn copy of *National Geographic* dated from the mid-nineties.

Guy seemed untroubled by the mess as he fought his way from his coat and dropped it over the back of a chair, before honing in on the map of the local area. As well as the elevation circles, there were hand-drawn red lines and arrows spaced across the town and the word 'HERE' written in untidy capital letters close to the road where Millie lived.

Millie stared at it, getting her bearings from the location of the ocean, as the town sprawled and then collided with the green of the map which signalled the woods that ringed the town.

Guy pointed to a spot at the edge of the woods, in between the house at the back of Millie's and near to the trail that went into the trees beyond. 'There was one firm sighting here,' he said.

'Of a *panther*?' Millie replied, not bothering to hide the doubt from her voice.

'Exactly,' Guy answered, either not catching her tone, or not caring. 'Then another sighting here.' He prodded a finger at a spot a little further away, on the other side of the woods. It was near one of the newer housing estates that hadn't existed when Millie was young.

'When were the two sightings?' Millie asked.

'Six nights ago and then again last night.' He started shuffling through everything that had come from his bag. Then he picked up a cardboard wallet, which he passed across. 'There were reports eleven years ago about a panther on the loose around the area. There were tracks found and a good eight or nine sightings. I think a few more people kept quiet because they didn't want to sound like fantasists.'

He nodded towards the folder that was now in Millie's hand. She flattened it on the table and then opened it to reveal a series of yellow-brown newspaper cuttings. The headlines all had something about a panther or big cat sighting in the local area, along with a photo of worried-looking residents. In one, a man was crouched and pointing at a large paw track in the ground, while another had a woman jabbing a finger towards the shed at the back of her empty garden.

Millie scanned the articles, which had been printed across three months of a summer. She was living in the town when the stories had been printed, yet it had all passed her by.

Each piece largely said the same. Lots of pointing, but not much in the way of an actual panther. All the articles had the byline 'Guy Rushden'.

'Nothing ever really came of it,' Guy said. 'I'd narrowed it down to the woods at the back of your house and was pretty sure that was where the cat was living – but the sightings dried up and everyone moved on.'

Millie pressed the articles back into the folder and returned it to the rest of the muddled mound.

'What now?' she asked.

Guy puffed out his cheeks and dropped into the seat that had his coat on the back. He grunted and held his back, then mumbled something about it coming to Millie one day.

'I wonder if the original big cat had cubs,' Guy said. 'It's unlikely the cat from eleven years ago would still be around – but perhaps there was more than one back then...'

Millie found herself gazing through the back window, towards the darkened garden – and the woods beyond.

'Wouldn't someone have noticed?' she said. 'If there were jaguars, or panthers roaming around, surely there'd be proof?'

'It's only recently that everyone has a phone with a camera. If people had seen anything, they might have assumed it was a dog – plus the whole point of big cats, panthers especially, is to *not* be noticed. There are farms around the town and always the odd lamb going missing. Lots of wildlife through the forest, too.'

It sounded as if Guy had considered quite a lot of scenarios before he'd even knocked on Millie's door.

She glanced towards the folder that contained the newspaper clippings of the stories he'd written.

'Weren't you made redundant?' Millie asked. 'I'm sure I heard something.'

'Nine months ago,' Guy replied.

'Shame it wasn't a few months earlier...'

Guy ignored the jibe, though he didn't seem particularly bothered by it.

Without the response she wanted, Millie continued: 'If you don't have a job, why are you looking into all this?'

Guy wriggled in his seat, reaching into one of the pockets of his jacket, before pulling out a business card that he slid across the table. Millie picked it up and read 'Guy Rushden' at the top. Underneath was a mobile phone number, an email address, and a website.

'I run a news blog for the town,' he said. 'Things don't stop just because nobody wants to pay to report it any more.'

There was a twinge of bitterness. The first time Millie had heard such annoyance, even though she'd been pushing for it. She took a few seconds to relish it, before continuing.

'Why did you come here?' she asked.

'I was hoping you might let me look around your garden.'

'What for?'

'Tracks.'

Millie waited for a follow-up, perhaps a punchline, but it never came.

'You've got some nerve coming to *this* house,' she said.

That didn't faze him, either. 'I've always been the sort who figures that if you don't ask, then you don't get.'

Millie sighed and looked towards the contents of Guy's bag, which were still occupying what felt like the majority of her kitchen. 'Did you make all this up as some sort of excuse to come here...?'

Guy thought on it for a moment, taking longer to reply than he had to any other question. It felt as if this was one for which he wasn't ready. 'Of course not.'

Millie thought over all the things she'd wanted to say to him and felt that crinkling swell of anger somewhere around her stomach. The idea of letting him into *her* house, *her* space, was unfathomable – and yet here he was. A slightly bumbling old man, trying to do a job he no longer had, and obsessed with something that was obviously a fantasy.

The anger seeped away, even as she craved it. He was no threat. It was pathetic more than anything else.

But there was something more; something that Millie found surprising.

As with Ingrid's girl on the roof hours before, she was curious. It was something new in a life that had been short of anything fresh.

The panther *was* a fantasy, she had no question about it, and yet there was some sort of mystery. Besides, it wasn't as if people in the town were queueing up to have conversations with her. There was Jack and those at the nursing home – but, around Whitecliff itself, she was more likely to run across people like the kid in the cheese aisle that morning. She didn't have much in the way of *actual* friends.

Millie crossed the kitchen to the back door and unlocked it with the key that she always left in the lock. When it was her parents' house, her dad would always bang on about invalidating insurance policies if keys were kept close to doors – so now Millie left the key in the door more to spite him than anything else.

She opened the door and pushed it wide, before looking back to Guy. 'Come on then.'

Millie snatched the torch from the top of the fridge and then waited as Guy stood and looked curiously towards the roof tile that now sat on her draining board. He pouted his bottom lip, raised an eyebrow that asked a silent, unanswered, question, and then ambled across the kitchen to follow her out to the back.

As Millie trod onto the path, she remembered what Ingrid had told her about seeing the girl on the roof. She said the moon was bright enough to light up the valley – and it was the same now. Despite the angry clouds earlier in the day, the sky was now clear black and cool white moonlight stretched across the lawn towards the back. Shadows clung to the hedge at the back and the fence along the side.

Guy followed as Millie edged onto the grass, swishing the light back and forth, into the crannies of gloom. Millie had kicked on the pair of sandals that she kept next to the back door – and her bare feet were instantly soaked from the dewy grass. She ignored the chill and pressed on slowly across the lawn, not sure what she was looking for. There were dimples in the lawn and small mounds of dirt. The gardener who'd last cut the grass at the beginning of October said he thought a mole was living underground – and Millie had put those mounds down to him or her ever since.

Definitely not paw prints.

Guy was looking at the floor, and occasionally crouching until they were at the back of the garden, where it was much darker. Millie stifled a shiver as she swept the light slowly across the shadows while they walked the hedge line together. It was only as they passed a shard of damp wood that Millie remembered the planters that used to sit towards the end of the garden. Guy squatted and picked up the wood, before holding it up for Millie to see and then putting it in his pocket.

'Mum used to grow strawberries down here,' Millie said. 'Dad bought her planters as a birthday present one year.'

'What happened to the strawberries?'

Millie started to reply and then stopped. 'I don't know.'

She didn't know why she'd brought it up in the first place – but Guy had already moved on. He was almost underneath the hedge when he knelt in the dirt and arched down until he was near enough on all fours. She heard the creak from his back, or his knees, though he didn't seem to have noticed himself. When he twisted around, he was grinning.

'Look,' he said.

Close to his knees, pressed into the dampened soil, was a dimpled imprint of what looked like a large triangle, with a smaller one next to it.

'What is it?' Millie asked.

'A claw print.'

SEVEN

Millie was up early the next morning. She didn't feel as if she'd slept properly since moving back into the house in which she'd grown up.

That had been a little over a year ago.

She was in the routine of ambling down the stairs barefooted and setting the coffee machine gurgling. Usually, she'd play a dumb game on her phone waiting for it to brew but, this time, she spent a good minute staring at the roof tile that sat on her draining board. When she was done with that, she went back outside and had a good stare at the triangle Guy had been so excited about the night before. In the calmer gaze of daylight, it looked to Millie like... a slightly rounded triangle. The mark was so close to the hedge that she couldn't walk around it – and, with only one angle, it was impossible to see anything but the simple shape.

After Guy had left the night before, Millie had googled panther tracks, which had shown a picture of a paw print containing something close to one big triangle and four smaller ones. The dimple in the earth of Millie's garden *could* be a partial paw print, in much the same way that Millie *could* run a marathon. There was a small possibility buried underneath a mountain of the inherent unlikeliness. If anything, in the daylight, it looked less like a paw print than it had the night before. She took a photo of it with her phone and then walked the hedge line to see if there was anything more.

By the time Millie had finished finding nothing, she headed back inside; the machine had finished doing its thing. Millie poured herself a mug of black coffee. She sat at the table, staring at the card Guy had left, before picking it up and typing the web address into her phone.

She expected something cheap and ignorable. A mess of photos and unformatted text, probably on a black background. She was almost disappointed to find a website that was largely professional. There was a clean Whitecliff News banner, and then a series of headlines and intro paragraphs spread around the page. Guy's contact details were at the bottom and there was a link to a profile, which Millie found herself clicking.

Guy Rushden has been a journalist his entire adult life. He worked on the Whitecliff Journal for a little over 40 years, culminating in his redundancy at the age of 67. Instead of retiring, Guy launched the Whitecliff News website, where he continues to report on his home community.

Millie returned to the home page, where there were stories about a council meeting from the week before, a woman who'd been mugged outside the local Co-op, staff cuts at the leisure centre, and a local mum who was planning a hundred-mile coastal walk for charity. It was the sort of stuff Millie could picture a local newspaper reporting, though there was nothing about a panther.

She almost closed the site – but then saw the search box at the top. Before she knew it, she'd typed in 'Millie Westlake' and pressed go. She realised she was holding her breath in the millisecond it took the page to refresh.

There was nothing about her on Guy's news blog.

Millie typed in 'David Westlake' and then 'Karen Westlake' – but neither of her parents featured either. Their names would get hits in other places, of course, primarily on the news website for which Guy used to work.

Millie almost went to the site to do her weekly doom-scroll of reading the same articles over and over. Except, this time, she found herself drawn to the roof tile on her draining board. Then she decided she'd spend her morning in a better way.

Jack was in the smoking area at the back of the nursing home when Millie found him. His vape flavour had something choco-latey about it as he slumped in the plastic seat that had been shoved underneath the canopy. When he spotted her, Jack momentarily looked up to take her in, before slumping some more.

'Never *ever* mix wines,' he said, largely to the floor.

'I thought you were having a quiet night?' Millie replied.

'We ordered a curry – and had that with a bottle of Prosecco that Rish had left over from his birthday. Then he opened a bottle of red and we ate cheese. Then we ran out of cheese, so he ordered more on Deliveroo – and we ate that while drinking a bottle of white that was hidden at the back of the sofa.'

It was a lot to take in as Millie processed what her friend had said. 'Are you absolutely certain this isn't a cheese hangover?'

Jack groaned his head up from the slumped position as he returned his vape pen to his pocket. 'I've not had a hangover like this since I turned thirty.'

Millie considered bringing up why there'd been a bottle of

wine hidden behind Jack's sofa – but there were bigger questions.

'What did the driver say when he turned up with a packet of cheese?'

'He was a bit confused. The Tesco Local has started on Deliveroo, mainly for delivering booze – but there was cheese on there. Rish ordered a four-kilo wheel of Brie.' Jack held his stomach, which Millie could hear gurgling from a couple of metres away. 'Maybe it *is* a cheese hangover,' he added.

'Four kilos?!'

'We didn't eat it all.'

'I can't believe you got cheese delivered.'

'It seemed like a good idea at the time.'

'I'll give you both one thing: you know how to do romance.'

Jack heaved himself up until he was standing. He leaned against one of the wooden posts and they stood together, staring across the valley towards Dean's house. The sky was clearer today, with the burbling bluey-brown ocean rippling in the distance, out towards the horizon.

'I'm too old for all this,' he said.

'Cheese?'

'That too.' A pause. 'How was your night?'

Millie pictured Guy ringing her doorbell and the hunt around her garden that now felt more like a dream than something that had actually happened. She couldn't tell anyone in all seriousness that she'd spent the evening looking for big cat tracks. That and the roof tile that was in her kitchen. Two mysteries for the price of one.

'Ate a Pot Noodle,' she replied. 'Almost had two.'

That got a smirk. 'I've never had you marked down as the Henry the Eighth type. What next? *Actual* Coke, rather than supermarket own brand?'

Jack paused a moment and cleared his throat. He pinched

the top of his nose and then shook his head. When he next looked up, there was more clarity to his gaze.

'You should come over,' he said. 'Rish was saying how he's not seen you in ages.'

'Was that before or after the first kilo of cheese?'

A laugh: 'Definitely into the second.' Jack stretched and touched Millie momentarily on the shoulder. 'Seriously. Come over. We've not seen you properly in months.'

Millie suddenly felt a shiver, that she hoped Jack didn't see. She didn't think it was his touch. 'I've been really busy,' she lied.

Jack took the reply at face value. 'With your dog grooming business?'

'I've got another dog coming tomorrow. An Aussie shepherd.'

Jack nodded along, although Millie knew he had no idea what that breed of dog looked like. He stared into the distance, then caught her eye before glancing away again. She knew what he was going to ask a moment before he asked it.

'Are the reviews still there...?'

Millie nodded.

'You should start again with a new name,' he said. 'Pretend the old business doesn't exist.'

Millie turned to follow his stare. She focused on Dean's house, looking for a gap where the roof might be missing a tile. It was too far in the distance to see.

She had thought of restarting her dog grooming and training business with a new name. She'd almost done it on at least three occasions when a new series of one-star reviews had arrived from someone for whom she'd never worked.

'It's harder from zero,' she said. 'At least with things as they are, there are still good reviews. I'm hoping people can figure out what's real and what's fake.'

'I wouldn't hold your breath.'

It came out harsher than Jack had meant and he caught her

eye once more to tell her so. That was all it took between them. They could say so much more with those little sideways glances than they ever could with words.

'I've got to get back,' Jack said, nodding towards the inside. 'Elsie's lost a bracelet and I promised I'd help search her room.'

'She just wants to see you on all fours crawling around.'

Jack had already turned towards the door but he stopped and winked over his shoulder. 'Not if I throw up Brie all over her floor, she won't.'

Millie felt drawn to Mick as soon as she entered the nursing home's recreation room. He was sitting by himself but, after spotting her, he waved Millie across to the tables near the bay window.

Regardless of the day, weather, time, or anything else, Millie had never seen the man wearing anything other than a suit.

He stood as she approached and waited until she was sitting before he sat again.

'Sure you don't want to play a proper game?' he asked.

Millie looked down to the chessboard that was between them. 'Not really my thing,' she replied.

'I can teach you the rules.'

'I know the rules – I'm just not very good. I think *Guess Who?* is more my thing.'

Mick mulled on that for a moment. 'I'll convince you one day.'

Millie waited, wondering why he'd called her over. It wasn't long before he continued.

'Have you heard the latest about Elsie's daughter?'

There was a sparkle to his eyes, much like Ingrid had the day before.

When she'd first started volunteering, Millie used to pretend she was above the gossip – uninterested, even – but it hadn't taken long for her to realise she wasn't kidding anyone, least of all herself.

'I heard something—' Millie replied, though she barely finished before Mick was cutting in.

'She's chucked out her husband,' he said. 'Did you hear about everything in Harrogate?'

Millie almost told him that he knew she had – because he'd been sitting on the next table when Ingrid had told her the day before. Instead, she nodded.

'Anyway,' Mick continued, 'Elsie's daughter had gone there in *her* car but had the spare keys for their *main* car – so set off in that. That left her husband in Harrogate without a way to get back because he didn't have keys for the other car.'

'What did he do?'

'He was calling Elsie's daughter over and over, asking her to come back and get him, but she ignored him and drove home. His fancy woman, don't know her name, ended up giving him a lift back – and that caused another massive row. Elsie's daughter – don't know her name, either – chucked all his stuff out on the street. His suits, his games thing, everything. Then it started raining and it all got wet.'

He spoke with the assuredness of someone who'd re-told these details every few minutes since he'd heard them.

'What happened to the car that was left in Harrogate?' Millie asked.

Mick thought for a moment. 'Don't know.'

'What happened after everything was thrown on the street?'

A shake of the head. 'Don't know that either – but I reckon we'll find out later. Elsie's been on the phone half the morning. She's lost her bracelet, too. Not having a good day.'

Mick relaxed back into the seat as Millie realised how much of a soap opera it all was for the residents. Scriptwriters were busy banging out TV dramas – but they weren't anywhere close to the saga of Elsie's daughter.

The two of them sat quietly as the silence was swallowed by the low chatter from the other side of the room. Some of the residents were watching the auction show that seemed to be on TV every hour of every day.

Millie was about to push herself up and continue around the room to see if anyone else wanted help, or a chat, but then Mick reached forward and put his hand on top of hers. His skin was wrinkled and warm, his fingers covered in small brown freckles.

'I never told you how much I loved your dad on TV,' he said. 'Before Helen died, we'd watch the local news together every night.' He took a moment and gulped. 'Feels strange saying it like that. We both got home from work at the same time. When we sat down to eat, your dad would be on.'

He released Millie's hand and pressed back into the chair, staring through the bay windows. At the front of the home, someone was making a hash of reversing into a space. Millie wanted to escape the conversation about her father but knew it was politer to sit and nod. Maybe give the odd 'uh-huh', or 'yeah, I know' along the way. She'd done plenty of it.

'I met him once,' Mick added, 'back when the boys were young. Your dad was opening the summer fete on the park. He'd done a piece on the news that week about some bloke who made these wooden cabinets – and my lad was thinking about getting into carpentry. Your dad took his name and said he'd try to put him in contact with the cabinet bloke.' Mick paused again, thinking.

Outside, the person had managed to get themselves into the parking space – but was so crooked that the driver's door was barely a few centimetres from the car at its side. The driver opened the door a fraction, then closed it again.

'I don't think it worked out in the end,' Mick said. 'But it was nice of your dad to listen in any case. My boy was talking about it for the rest of the weekend.'

Millie fought the urge to tell Mick that his son's details would have either gone in the bin as soon as her dad was away from the fete, or been left in his pocket until the next time he came to wear the clothes. Either way, the chance of that name and number being passed on were zero.

She managed a watery-sounding 'thanks' that Mick took to mean something it wasn't.

'Didn't mean to upset you,' he said softly.

'It's fine,' Millie replied quickly.

It didn't happen so much recently, not after what had happened, but Millie was used to hearing these sorts of stories about her father. He'd been a newsreader on the local TV channel for decades, certainly as long as Millie had been aware of what he did. In a place like Whitecliff, and in towns across the country, perhaps the globe, local newsreaders were celebrities. They'd open fairs and carnivals. They'd give talks in schools and make guest appearances at youth groups, or adult classes.

When Millie's father drove her to school, it was always in a sponsored BMW with his name on the side. He was the patron of the local youth theatre company. The cricket club had a bench with a plaque that had his name on it. The TV channel for which he used to work had started an annual bursary named after him that would go to a journalism student from the area.

Millie's dad was everywhere, even now, and everybody seemed to know who he was.

Because of what had happened, everyone also knew Millie.

She realised she'd been staring out the window, vaguely watching as the person drove out of the parking space, did a seven-point turn, and then drove in front-first. Like some sort of savage.

'...terrible what happened to your mum and dad,' Mick said.

Millie realised he'd been talking to her, yet she'd blanked it all out. She nodded along, as she always did when someone wanted to talk about her parents. She'd found it was better to let them talk and throw in the odd 'uh-huh' along the way. It was about *them*, not *her*. She could let them have their moment.

Except, from nowhere, Millie suddenly *was* distracted. She'd turned from the car park and was watching along the main hallway, towards the front doors.

And there, walking out of an office, the nursing home's manager at his side, was Dean.

EIGHT

The man who ran the home was the sort of middle manager that Millie had spent much of her adult life avoiding. He even had that annoying *because-I-said-so* voice about him.

The walls of the home were papered with laminated pages of meaningless, unenforceable, rules that could only come from the mind of someone with far too much time on their hands. Someone who delegated all the real work to underpaid, over-worked staff, so that he could spend his days locked in his office browsing the internet in private mode.

He didn't mind Millie volunteering but she assumed that was largely because it didn't cost him anything.

The residents didn't think much more of him. Wheelchairs were frequently left underneath signs saying no wheelchairs should be left in the corridors. Someone had used a marker pen to scrub the word 'no' from the 'please speak no louder than a whisper' sign that was outside his office.

But now Millie watched as Dean turned and shook hands with the manager. The two men were talking, though too far away for Millie to hear.

Worse than talking, they were *smiling*, even though the only time Millie had seen the manager smile was when a parcel had arrived for him at reception. He'd squirrelled it away into his office, making sure to open it when nobody else was around. Residents had speculated on whether it was some sort of extremely graphic, barely legal, Eastern European pornography or a collection of model railway magazines. Millie wouldn't be surprised by which end of that spectrum he swung towards.

'Who's that guy?' Millie asked.

Mick had been saying something, probably more about her dad, but he stopped and followed Millie's gaze along the corridor.

'Don't know his name but he came round just after breakfast,' Mick replied.

Millie glanced at the clock. It meant Dean had been at the home for a good three hours.

'What's he doing here?'

'I heard he's some sort of handyman touting for work. Alan reckons he was offering to do jobs around the place for a reduced rate.'

Millie watched as Dean and the manager finally stopped acting like they were old friends, which made Millie wonder if they actually were.

Dean stepped away, said something final, and then turned to head back outside. He stopped when he spotted Millie along the corridor. It was only a second, probably not even that, but he was taking her in from a distance.

Millie forced away a shudder as she felt that sixth sense kick. The same one she sometimes felt if she was out at night, walking into the shadows between two lamp posts. The one that told her the bloke standing outside the pub had clocked her, even though she'd been walking the other way and paying him no attention.

It was there – and then it was gone.

Dean continued turning and it was as if the momentary

pause had never happened. He marched through the doors, out of sight, leaving Millie gazing along the now empty corridor.'

It might have been nothing, except...

'Do you know him?' Mick asked.

Millie had almost forgotten where she was. She turned back across the untouched chess board towards him.

'He looked like he knows you,' Mick added.

Millie hadn't imagined it. There really had been something in Dean's stare that wasn't quite right.

'Sometimes I feel like everyone in town knows me,' Millie replied.

It was true, sort of, but that wasn't it. Mick wasn't to know that, though.

He started to nod. 'Aye. I'd not thought of that...'

He tailed off, not sure what to add. In the moment that followed, Millie realised something else that wasn't quite right. She turned and took in the room, before looking back to Mick.

'Have you seen Ingrid today?' she asked.

A shake of the head. 'I heard she's not well. I assume she's in her room.'

Millie pushed up from the table. 'Do you mind...?'

'Of course not.'

Millie's role as a volunteer at the home was loose, to say the least. The manager didn't seem that bothered about what she did, as long as she got through some background check and he didn't have to pay her. Broadly, she'd spend time in the rec room with the residents, checking in on them and keeping them company if they wanted. This allowed the actual paid staff to get on with the general day-to-day duties of cleaning and running the place. She had no set days, and no set hours, and was allowed to liaise with Jack about when she came in. There were a couple of other volunteers, both older than Millie, who did basically the same thing.

One thing that had never been made clear was whether there

were boundaries within the home. She was often in the rec room, or staff areas – but the wing that housed the residents' rooms had never been mentioned as a place she should go by herself. On the other hand, it had never been specified as a place she *shouldn't* go.

Millie headed past reception and out the other side, following the corridors into the other half of the home. The carpet was threadbare and the wallpaper peeling. There were no windows, only a dark white light trying to shine through dusty shades above. There were names on each of the doors, numbers too, and Millie continued walking until she reached Ingrid's, next to an ominous-looking '13'.

Millie knocked twice. She checked both ways as the echo bounced around the long, narrow space. It felt as if she was doing something wrong. There was silence from the other side of the door and then a gentle 'come in'.

Millie emerged into a gloomy room, where the only light was coming from a small gap in the curtains. It felt so much darker, in more ways than one, compared to the day before. She found Ingrid lying in her bed, wrapped in the covers, her eyes barely open.

'It's Millie,' she said gently.

She could feel Ingrid searching for her in the dark as she approached.

'I heard you weren't feeling well...'

There was a croak of a sore throat and then Ingrid replied gingerly. 'I'm all right, love. Just old.'

Millie pulled across a seat and sat at the side of the bed. Ingrid had turned to face her, though her features were grey and almost lost to the dark. There was a shuffling of covers and then Ingrid's hand appeared. Millie gripped the cool fingers in her own, squeezing them gently.

'Are you sure you're all right?' she asked. 'I can get you something to eat, or drink, if you want.'

'No.'

There was a paperback upside down on the nightstand, with a bookmark hanging from it.

'Would you like me to read to you?' Millie asked.

'Oh...' There was a pause and a low cough, before: 'That'd be nice...'

'I'll have to turn on a light, or...'

'Open the curtains.'

Millie let go of Ingrid's hand and did just that. She didn't open them all the way but silvery light spilled into the room and, when Millie picked up Ingrid's book, there was enough to let her see the pages. It was a biography of someone Millie recognised from one of the TV dance shows and she opened it at the bookmark and then began to read.

It wasn't long, barely a couple of minutes, until Ingrid was snoring gently. Millie stopped reading and replaced the bookmark, then waited. There were flowers in a vase on top of the dresser, though they were wilting from the heat of the room. Millie went into the bathroom and filled a cup with water, before pouring it into the vase.

She waited, wondering if Ingrid might want anything more, though the snoring had become louder and longer.

Millie crossed to the window and stared across the valley towards Dean's house.

It couldn't be a coincidence that he'd appeared in the home the day after she'd visited him. What had started as Millie asking a question on Ingrid's behalf, mainly because she had nothing better to do, was now something bigger. If there had been nobody on the roof, if Ingrid was mistaken, why would Dean turn up the next day?

There was no movement at Dean's house, nothing anywhere, except for the rolling ocean in the distance and a vague flutter of what was probably seagulls over the cliffs.

Millie leaned in, squinted, *stared*, but the house was too far away.

With Ingrid peacefully sleeping, Millie was about to leave the room when she suddenly had an idea. She took out her phone and loaded the camera, before zooming in as far as she could on Dean's house. The magnification was so intense that tiny movements of her hand sent the focus rocking wildly from side to side, making it difficult to make out much of anything.

But Millie was only searching for one thing – and, even as the screen flashed back and forth, there was enough time to hone in on what she wanted.

There was a gap on Dean's roof, a little below the skylight. A gap where there was, unquestionably, a single missing tile.

NINE

The cottage sat on the cliff, overlooking both the town of Whitecliff and the bay itself. The wind fizzed across the crags and the moss, biting through Millie's jacket, into her skin. It felt like the sort of place where the wind would howl without end, where even the warmest of summer's days would be accompanied by a blustering gale.

The gate was barely on its hinges as Millie lifted the latch to let herself into the garden. The wood was sodden through, like gripping a damp sponge, as she carefully dropped it back into place. The rest of the fence around the cottage was in a similar state, seemingly on its last legs in a battle against the elements. Like a boxer wobbling on the ropes in the final round.

Even though Millie had never visited the person who lived in the cottage, she knew who lived up on the cliff, in the same way everyone else did. It was part of his mystique, almost his calling card, she supposed.

The Volvo that had been parked outside her house the night before was on a gravelly drive and, as Millie got closer, she could see the moss growing in the seals around the windscreen.

The driver's window was partway down and Millie was only half-surprised the keys hadn't been left in the ignition.

There was a series of notices pinned to the front door, each written in faded pen on lined paper, then taped to the frame.

No estate agents!
No lawyers!
Not for sale!
No solicitors either!

Millie smiled at the last one. The type was newer and clearer and she wondered if someone had knocked and tried to claim they weren't a *lawyer*, they were, in fact, a solicitor – and so the notice didn't apply.

She rang the doorbell and waited. There was no sound from the inside, only the distant rustle of the ocean far below.

Millie waited and then rang the bell a second time. There was still no sound and she figured it was the sort of place where a non-working doorbell wouldn't necessarily be spotted.

With that, she moved back and then rounded the house until she reached a window. It was a single pane, with chipped paint peeling from the frame, flaking onto the gravel. She could hear a man's voice and Millie shielded herself from the glare, peering through the glass, into a gloomy room.

She could just about make out Guy's hulking frame pacing back and forth. He was holding a phone on a cord to his ear and stopped moving when he spotted her. Millie instinctively stepped away but Guy was suddenly in front of her, separated only by the flimsy glass. He waved, beckoning her into the house and, before Millie could ask how to actually get inside, he was gone again.

There was no sign of him at the front door but, this time, Millie didn't bother with the bell. She turned the handle and felt it give, before she creaked it open and stepped into the house.

The hall was clammy, with the sort of thick air that Millie associated with old school changing rooms. The ceilings were low, with wooden beams zigzagging across the cracked plaster. There were piles of books and papers stacked from floor to ceiling. Millie shimmied around them, following the voice until she reached an open door near the end of the hall. She was barely through the door when she realised Guy was talking to her.

'There's been another sighting!' he said.

Guy was no longer on his phone, instead he was hunched over a desk that was covered with the map he'd brought to Millie's the night before. The room was a mess of browning newspaper piles, plus hundreds of books and notepads. As Millie moved inside, she felt a crack underneath her boot and looked down to see a newly snapped pencil. There were plenty more pens, pencils, and pads strewn across the wooden floor, to the point that there was barely a free space among it all.

Not that Guy was bothered about that. He was marking a new cross on the map, still close to Millie's house, somewhere in the fields on the other side of the trees.

'Sighting of what?' Millie asked, fearing she knew the answer.

'The panther,' Guy replied. 'Someone saw it on farmland this morning. No picture but I've just been talking to them. They saw it across the field and were certain.'

'How do they know it wasn't a big dog?'

Millie's negativity didn't appear to rock Guy, who shrugged. 'Would be a bit of a coincidence, given the other sightings.'

'They could all be seeing the same dog.'

Guy mulled on that for a moment, biting his lip and sinking into an office chair that had yellow foam spilling from the side.

'True...'

He motioned towards a second chair that was partially buried under a pile of newspapers.

Guy was suddenly back on his feet, beckoning Millie into the chair in which he'd been sitting. He swept the newspapers from the other chair onto a different stack of papers that were on the floor, next to a crusty bowl of potpourri.

That done, Guy plopped himself into the new chair and then rotated slightly from side to side.

'What's with the estate agent sign?' Millie asked.

Guy seemed momentarily confused until Millie pointed towards the front door.

'People have been trying to get me to sell for years,' he replied. 'Something about building a hotel and resort up here. There's always someone knocking, trying to change my mind. Reckons there are buyers lined up. Developers. All that. They keep offering more and more.'

Through the window, Millie could see the gate swinging open, banging into the post and bouncing back again. Up above the window, a creeping, spindly web of mould was etched into the ceiling, battling for space with actual spiderwebs.

The house felt much like Guy's Volvo. The sort of place, the sort of car, that was on its last legs.

It was as if Guy had read her thoughts.

'They keep adding zeroes but it doesn't matter,' he said. 'What good is their money to me? I'm nearly seventy. What would I do all day if I retired?'

'I dunno... go on a cruise?'

'A cruise?!' Guy laughed loudly. 'Sit in some tiny cabin, where the highlight of every day is waiting for the night-time entertainment from some comedian I thought had died twenty years ago? Or some ABBA tribute band? Come on...' He tailed off momentarily, before adding: 'I'll die in this cottage before I sell.'

Millie didn't clock what he'd said properly until his eyes widened and his overgrown eyebrows shot up.

'Sorry,' he said quickly. 'I didn't mean...'

It took Millie a moment to realise what he was on about. *Her* parents had died at home.

'I know what you meant,' Millie replied.

There was a moment of truce, where it felt as if everything that had happened nine months before hadn't really happened. It was Millie's choice to come to the house after all.

She took a while to compose herself, taking in the rest of the room. As well as the area map of sightings on the desk, there was a bigger one that took up a quarter of one wall. There was a chart of tide times next to it, then another for sunrise and sunsets. A handful of articles were blu-tacked to other parts of the wall, with no apparent pattern or link between them.

Other than that, the room was a cluttered mess of newspapers, pens, pencils, pads, and who knew what else. It was as if Guy owned a series of bags that had all exploded across the room.

'What can I do for you?' Guy asked.

As Millie turned back to him, she realised he'd been watching her for a while. He was angled forward in his seat, fingers pressed into one another.

She *had* come to him this time. *Her* choice.

'There's a man who lives at the bottom of the valley, at the back of the nursing home,' Millie said. 'The house is sort of on its own. There are others but they're all spaced out.'

She stood, crossing to the big map on the wall and pointing towards the spot she was talking about.

'About there,' she added. 'I figured you know more about this town than anyone...'

Guy joined her at the map and traced the road with his finger. 'I remember when it was all fields out that way,' he said. 'Years back. Probably fifty.'

'The guy said his name was Dean,' Millie added.

That got a nod. 'Dean Parris. Double-r. I went to school with his dad.'

Millie wasn't sure what she expected – but it wasn't such instant recognition. 'His *dad*? Dean's got to be about fifty...'

Another nod. 'People were younger when they had children back then. Dean's dad would've been about eighteen or nineteen when he had him – so you're probably right that he's around fifty.' Guy turned, lips pursed. He leaned on the corner of a desk. Millie realised he was in his element. He could talk about the town and its residents all day. 'His dad had a heart attack about twenty years ago. Dropped dead on a building site, in front of the crew.' He blew out a thoughtful breath. 'I think Dean might've been there. Maybe some sort of family business...?'

'I heard Dean's working as a handyman...?'

Guy nodded along – and then sprang into action, as if his feet had been set on fire. He almost danced to the other side of the room and then began hunting through a pile of newspapers that were stacked underneath the window. He was talking to himself, then tutting, before he stopped and turned in a circle.

'They might be in the attic...' he said, although it was unclear whether he was talking to Millie.

'What might be?' she asked.

The manic energy had died as quickly as it had arrived as Guy pressed back onto the windowsill. A chunk of wood promptly broke off, which he picked up and placed next to the glass.

'If I remember rightly, Dean's wife died in childbirth,' Guy said. 'It wasn't long after his dad died. I wrote the story and I'll have the paper somewhere.' He screwed up his lips and then added: 'That year might be in the kitchen...'

Millie almost asked why he kept newspapers in the kitchen, except it felt as if there were papers in every room. Probably stuffed into the wall as insulation, or used as impromptu tables all around the place.

'Did the child survive?'

Guy had been lost in trying to remember where the paper could be – and it apparently took him a moment to remember that he'd said Dean's wife had died giving birth. Millie needed that moment, too. Her initial visit to Dean's house suddenly had new meaning. He'd clearly been through a lot – and likely didn't want or welcome strangers showing up to his door, banging on about some old woman's fantasies.

Then Millie was back in Guy's cottage.

'I don't remember,' Guy replied. 'I can probably find out.' A moment passed and then the inevitable came: 'Any particular reason for your interest...?'

Millie thought about the question. It was a fair one – and she had come to him for answers. Except she wasn't ready to let things go. She stepped back to the chair, spun it around, and then plopped herself into it.

'I'd rather talk about how you ruined my life.'

TEN

It was Guy who broke eye contact first. Millie *needed* it to be him. He'd been watching her but shrank away and started picking at one of his fingernails.

'That's fair,' he said. 'Do you want a drink? Tea? I've got—'

'Why'd you write it?'

Guy opened his mouth but, before he could say anything, there was a rustling and then a scraping from the door. The handle popped down and up and then a shaggy gingery-brown dog trotted inside. It looked between Guy and Millie and then ambled across to her and lay on her foot.

'Barry's not much of a guard dog these days,' Guy said.

Millie bent forward and offered the back of her hand to the dog. He sniffed it and then drooped lower, as she scritched the back of his ears. His fur was frizzed and soft, and he made a gentle cat-like purr as Millie worked her fingers across his back.

'Did he open the door himself?' she asked.

'Taught himself how to do that as soon as he was tall enough.'

'What else does he do?'

'Not much nowadays. He's a rescued labradoodle, so I don't

know his exact age – but he's ten or eleven. He enjoys being in the woods but he's a bit of a grump in his old age.' A pause. 'I guess that makes two of us...'

Millie didn't reply to Guy, though she did drop down from the chair until she was sitting on the floor. Barry placed his head in her lap and nuzzled into her leg as she worked her fingers through his fur.

It was emotional blackmail. She *wanted* to be angry.

Guy waited for her to look up. 'Your dad used to be one of my best friends,' he said. 'We went to school together and spent every day of the summer holidays with each other when we were that age. There were a few of us. Born here, grew up here, never left...'

Millie's fingers caught on a matted patch in Barry's fur. He flinched momentarily but then resettled and allowed her to wriggle her finger through the hair.

'I went into newspapers,' Guy said. 'It was always what I wanted to do. Your dad wanted to be on TV – and he was. He met your mum and I was his best man. We fell out and then...' Guy snapped his fingers and slumped further back into the window frame.

'It was sudden for me, too,' Millie said.

The slippers on Guy's feet had holes in each of the toes, with the sole flapping from one. Guy's attention was fully focused on them. Anything that wasn't Millie.

She recited from memory the words he'd written. The ones that had haunted her for a year.

'"Police say their surviving daughter, Millicent Westlake, is not a suspect".'

Millie waited but there was no answer.

'You must've known that saying I *wasn't* a suspect would make everyone think I was? Especially when it happened like it did? Some kid in the cheese aisle yesterday asked if I killed

Mum and Dad. It happens at least once a week. Sometimes more than that a day.'

Guy's reaction came slowly, as if he was on a video call with a delay. He started to nod and then took a long breath. 'At the time, you were... well, you know...'

'I had an affair,' Millie replied. 'You can say it.' Even though she herself hadn't said those words for a long time. 'People have affairs all the time – it's just that mine ended up on the news.'

Barry raised his head and glanced sideways up towards Millie, as if making sure he was still safe. She rested a hand on his belly and rubbed gently, calming herself.

'Yes...' Guy replied.

'So, because of that, you decided to tell everyone that I was suspected of killing Mum and Dad?'

'I wrote the opposite!'

'No, you didn't. You knew what would happen. I was the only other person living there. You didn't have to say anything.'

Barry pushed himself up from Millie's lap. He took a couple of steps away and stretched low and long, as if there was whale music playing and he was easing into a yoga class. He took one more glance at Millie and then crossed the room until he was at Guy's feet, making it clear where his allegiance lay.

'I knew...' Guy said.

Only two words and yet they were more important to Millie than the millions that were printed on the papers around her.

'I knew what it could do,' Guy said. 'I was hurt and I suppose I couldn't understand why they did what they did.'

'Why they killed themselves?' Guy didn't react and so Millie continued. Without Barry on her lap, the malingering anger was back. 'That's what the coroner said. Suicide. A double overdose.'

There was still no reply. Millie pushed herself up until she was standing. She wanted to leave, except her legs wouldn't quite allow it. Perhaps she'd taken a small step towards the door, or perhaps it was more of a thought – but Guy cut her off.

'Every crime I've written about, I ask myself who benefits. David and Karen had no reason to kill themselves – so, when the question is asked "who benefits?", there's only one answer...'

He was looking at Millie now. Asking without asking.

There was a moment, a fleeting, minuscule, half-second in which she thought about telling him the lot... except that wasn't why she'd come to the cottage.

This time, she did take a step towards the door. Then a second. She was holding the handle when Guy spoke again.

'Why are you asking about Dean Parris?' he said.

Millie stopped, fought that urge of flight, and turned back. Barry was now in the middle of the room, giving it the big eyes. He had that look which all dogs somehow know how to pull off. Pretending they're never fed, never given any attention – and that only *you* are the answer to their puppy prayers.

And so Millie found herself telling Guy what had happened. She volunteered at the nursing home, where her friend worked – and one of the residents reckoned they saw someone pushed from Dean's roof. The drop was too high to have happened without some sort of injury. There was no blood. But there was the cracked tile sitting in Millie's kitchen that had seemingly come from the roof.

'Ingrid sometimes thinks her husband is still alive,' Millie added. 'She's not always sure what's now and what's then.'

Guy thought on that and then: 'Do you believe she saw someone pushed?'

Millie had to think about that. It didn't feel like a yes/no question. 'I don't know. Maybe. "Pushed" feels like a stretch. That would mean two people on the roof and one of them trying to shove off the other. I'm not even sure about falling – except I went to Dean's house and asked – and he was a bit funny with it. Then he was at the nursing home today. Some-

thing about offering handyman services. That can't be a coincidence, can it?'

Guy took a couple of steps across to the large map on the
wall and peered closer at it. 'Could be. If you spoke to him
about the nursing home, it might have been on his mind if he
was driving past later that day? Perhaps he saw something that
he thought needed fixing?'

As he said it, Millie wondered if that *was* what had
happened. Dean had probably not thought of the nursing home
much at all – but then she'd put the idea in his head. If he'd
been driving past, he probably *would* have paid more attention,
and then spotted a gutter hanging loose, or something similar.
The home *did* need lots of little handyman jobs doing, and
perhaps he was simply offering his services.

'Maybe...'

Nobody spoke for a while. Barry walked in a tight circle and
then lay in a ball on a rug that was almost as shaggy as he was.

'What would you like from me?' Guy asked.

'I don't know...'

'I can go through my archives and see if there's anything
about Dean Parris that could be interesting. Other than that,
I'm not sure I can really help.'

Millie caught his eye. 'Too busy chasing imaginary
panthers?'

That got a smirk, perhaps even part of a laugh. 'Three
different people have seen something...' There was another
pause and then he added: 'Can I say something you might not
want to hear?'

Millie paused for a moment, curious, though figuring it
wouldn't be anything she hadn't heard before. 'May as well.'

'If you're facing such hostility around the town, perhaps
that's why you want to believe your friend at the home?'

He had a cheek, considering much of the hostility had been
whipped up by what he'd written. His piece had been relayed

and quoted on Facebook and the like. Millie had seen the posts – *I heard the daughter did it* – which were almost all still up. All the replies were there: *You know what* else *she did, don't you? What about her poor husband? She has a son, you know?*

The incident with the boy in the supermarket wasn't the first time something similar had happened. Sometimes she wondered if she was imagining the sideways looks she'd get around town – and then something like the cheese aisle incident would happen and she'd retreat into herself.

Perhaps Guy was right?

The nursing home *was* a haven, of sorts. And maybe that was why she was so keen to believe Ingrid? Ingrid spoke to her as if she was a real person, not someone who'd been caught in more than one recent news scandal.

Millie picked up a pen and flipped a few pages on the nearest notepad until she was on a blank page. She scribbled on the paper and then dropped the pen back down.

'That's my number,' she said. 'You can call if you find something.'

ELEVEN

Millie's footsteps echoed on the hard floor of her parents' kitchen, booming around the empty house. The blinds were open but there wasn't much light spilling through from outside. The nights were drawing in, as Millie's father used to say. It would almost certainly be followed up with the number of weeks until the days started to get longer again.

She opened the fridge but there was little in there apart from two eggs she couldn't be bothered to cook, and a few slices of bread that had been in there for a while. The cupboards weren't much better. Some canned fruit that had gone out of date six years earlier, some beef sandwich paste that should probably be in the fridge, a crusty bottle of ketchup – and not much else.

It would be quite the bleak episode of *Ready, Steady, Cook*.

Millie didn't particularly want to live in this house – but it was now hers, after all. After Guy's mini rant against selling his place, she'd realised that they at least agreed on one thing. If she were to sell, what then? Despite everything, she didn't particularly want to leave Whitecliff – but where else could she afford in town, even if she did sell?

The stairs creaked as Millie headed up to her room. *Her* room. She'd moved back in after calamity part one a little over a year ago. Late-thirties, and she was sleeping in her childhood bedroom once again. That was long after her mum had thrown out all her old stuff and turned it into a guest room that was never used.

What was the alternative? The spare bedroom was full of things she hadn't got around to clearing out. She'd not been into her parents' bedroom in months. She'd only opened the door a handful of times since the forensic team had left. She certainly wasn't going to sleep in there, even if it was twice the size of her current bedroom.

There used to be a large, framed photo of her parents at the top of the stairs. Her dad in a suit after winning some TV award; her diligent, supportive mum at his side. It wasn't there any longer. The halls and the living room were now littered with irregular rectangles on the walls, where pictures had once been and the paint had faded around the edges.

Millie sat on the guest bed and felt it sink underneath. It was a cheap mattress and a squeaky frame. The bedding was a grim pink, the sort of thing that looked good in a brochure but was far too warm to sleep underneath. Style over substance. Millie usually slept on top of it – and, even though she could buy something new, there was a part of her that couldn't quite let go.

She thought about going to sleep early, or at least lying in bed and listening to the sounds of the empty house. Millie remembered Guy and the simple two-word admission that he'd known what he was doing when he'd written that she wasn't a suspect. It was all double-speak, as she'd thought. He could've left her out completely, or said that her parents were survived by their daughter, and yet he'd *chosen* not to.

Did he deserve any credit for actually admitting it nine months down the line?

It was other people who'd run with the rumours. Everyone liked a good gossip, especially in a small town like Whitecliff. When Millie had been a girl, there was a woman who lived in a rickety house near the school, who everyone said was a witch. Some kids reckoned the woman had drowned her daughter. Others that she lured unsuspecting children into her house, Hansel and Gretel-style. The boys in the year above would dare each other to jump the fence and run a lap around the house – and Millie would watch and laugh, along with everyone else.

Those were untrue rumours. It was just a normal woman – and yet Millie had gleefully gossiped herself.

Was it different now, simply because *she* was the subject of that innuendo, instead of the one spreading it?

Millie's thoughts splintered as she realised her phone was buzzing. It took a moment to remember she'd put it on the floor, next to the bed, and that it was now vibrating its way towards the wall. She crouched and reached, then sighed as she saw who was ringing.

Her ex-husband's name rarely brought good news.

'It's Alex,' he said as soon as she answered. 'Can you have Eric tomorrow?'

Millie didn't remember exactly when her former husband had abandoned all sense of niceties but it felt like a while ago. She needed a second to realise what he was asking, except he was still talking.

'...It's teacher training day at school but it wasn't on the calendar for some reason. You know what teachers are like: always on holiday.'

'I've got a dog grooming session in the afternoon,' Millie replied, 'but Eric doesn't mind being around for them.'

There was a short pause, though long enough for Millie to sense the silent sneer of *you're-still-doing-that?* from the other end.

'Great,' Alex replied, with no enthusiasm at all. 'Rach will drop him off in the morning.'

The silence hung momentarily and Millie knew he was daring her. The new girlfriend dropping off the son to the ex-wife *could* start an argument. It might have done at one time, but not now.

'That's fine,' Millie replied.

'Will you be at your parents' house?'

'I'll be at *my* house.'

That got a snort. 'Fine. Whatever. See you tomorrow.'

She waited to see if there'd be any more – except the screen was blank and Alex had gone. Short and sharp was pretty much all she expected nowadays.

The call ended so abruptly that it took a moment for her to realise she'd get to spend time with Eric. The day had a sudden purpose! Not simply a few hours of custody swapped for another – but some time with her son that she hadn't expected. Without realising, Millie found herself making a mental list of places they could go, or things to do. Should she cancel the grooming appointment? Was it supposed to rain? She'd have to check. Or, perhaps, it would be better to let him play on his Xbox and simply watch him having fun? There was joy in that, too, because it was what he wanted to do.

Sometimes, Millie fought against her own desperation to drag him out to various places he probably didn't want to go. They had so little time together as mother and son that she wanted it to count. Except, maybe, she tried *too* hard. That's what the little voice told her late at night, when there was nobody else around.

Millie realised she was smiling as she crouched to look for her charging cable. As she did, a flash of light swept across her, illuminating the room. It was like a search beam on the open sea and gone almost as quickly as it had come.

Millie crossed to the window, which overlooked the front of

the house. There were no lights now – though, as she was about to turn away, she noticed the vague outline of a vehicle parked directly outside the house, partially obscured by the bushes.

It wasn't entirely unusual... except Millie lived in an area where nobody parked on the street, especially in the evening. Everyone had driveways and garages. Cars left on the road were the sort of thing that could drag down house prices, which seemed to be more or less the only thing anyone in the area cared about. What's more, as Millie's eyes adjusted to the light, she realised that it was bigger than a car.

She headed downstairs and opened the front door. Cold air rushed inside, and Millie considered going back inside for a jacket. The outline of the vehicle was clearer now she was downstairs. Definitely not a car; probably a van.

As she stepped into the night, the driveway chilled through her thin slippers. Three more steps and the motion-sensor hummed above her, spreading light across the driveway.

The reaction was instant.

An engine growled to life and headlights flared from behind the hedge at the end of the driveway. There was a glow of something red, then white, as Millie heard the squeal of a vehicle reversing.

Millie hurried now, scuttling across the freezing stones, and reaching the end of the drive just as the van finished reversing in a semicircle. Its large hooked tow bar protruded notably from the back. It was under the gloomy orange street light now, and there was a moment in which time froze.

Millie spotted Dean's face in the reflection of the van's wing mirror at the same moment as he saw her. It lasted a second, not even that, and then the van surged forward and roared its way down the road.

She shivered, and yet stood and watched until he was out of sight. Even from the window upstairs, she'd somehow known that she would find Dean outside her house.

Now he'd gone, she still felt watched.

Millie turned in a half-circle until she was facing the other way. It was a long, largely straight, road that eventually ended in a dead end. One of the reasons her parents had chosen the area was that there was no through traffic. There was privacy and peace in this part of Whitecliff.

And yet...

There was something in the road, barely visible through the descending mist. Something dark, something sleek and low to the ground. Some sort of dog, or...

Millie shivered again as it shifted slightly – and, suddenly, she *really* felt watched. She couldn't see eyes, she could barely make out the shape properly, and yet she knew it was watching her.

She blinked and then, with a blur of movement, the black fuzz darted sideways, into the mist, and was swallowed whole by the night.

TWELVE

Millie opened the front door before Eric had the chance to ring the bell. She'd been watching from the downstairs window and he jumped backwards as the door swung open. He was only seven and sometimes still had that wonder in his eyes when something unexpected happened.

He reeled back a little and looked up to his mum. 'How'd you know I was here?' he asked.

'Heard you coming with those big feet of yours.'

Eric eyed her with suspicion, though didn't question it.

Millie grinned at him and held the door wider. He ducked past her, before bounding down the hall. He was still in the phase of running everywhere, which often led to things mysteriously tumbling off tables and counters when he was near. Nothing to do with him, of course – unless she specifically saw something fall.

Millie waited on the doorstep as Rachel slipped from the driver's seat of her sparkly new Corsa. She was in her work suit, ready for the office – even though Millie had never been quite clear what she did. Alex said it was 'something in accounts' –

but, by that sort of stretch, a professional thief did 'something in relocation'.

They'd known each other since school. That was the problem with Whitecliff. Everyone went to the same schools, attended the same clubs, and got jobs in the same places. Millie and Rachel had never been friends, not really. Not enemies, either. Just sort of... acquaintances. Part of the same group, almost through the accident of age.

While the divorce was rumbling on, Millie's solicitor had told her to be polite to Alex and Rachel at all times, else it could end up being used against her with things like custody hearings. It wasn't only that. With doorcams, dashcams, and everyone having a phone, nothing was ever really private. Millie knew that as well as anyone – and having some sort of public argument would never look good for her.

And so, around Rachel, Millie became a version of herself who acted like she was going for tea at the palace. She forced the politeness into her voice, until it sounded like someone else.

'Do you want me to drop Eric back later, or is Alex coming for him?' she asked.

'Don't know,' Rachel called back. She had her tea-at-the-palace voice – which Millie felt sure was largely there to wind her up. 'I can ask Al to text you...?'

Al.

Who called him 'Al'? It was *Alex*. It had always been Alex. When he'd exchanged vows with Millie, he'd called her Millicent and she'd called him Alexander. Both names sounded ridiculous. They were Alex and Millie – and he definitely wasn't 'Al'.

'That'd be good,' Millie replied, wondering why this hadn't been sorted out before. Wondering why she couldn't ask *Alex* herself.

'He's had breakfast,' Rachel said. 'Just in case he tries it on.'

Millie put on one of her best fake smiles. She was at the

palace and someone had offered her a mince pie, even though she hated mince pies. What even was mince? Nobody seemed to know. And why was it called mince? There was beef mince, lamb mince, and then some sort of weird fruit thing that was called mincemeat, even though there was no meat. But, if she was ever at the palace, and *if* anyone ever offered her a mince pie, she would smile politely and say 'yes please', because she assumed that was what people at the palace did.

'No worries,' Millie said.

The two women smiled their poisonously polite smiles at each other, neither of them meaning it.

'I might as well message *Alex*,' Millie replied. 'Find out if he's coming over, or...?'

Rachel shrugged. 'Suit yourself. I'll see you around.'

She got back into her car – even though there'd been no particular reason to get out. Millie watched and waved her off, waiting until she was out of sight before finally letting her face fall.

The massive cow.

There was a fluttering of curtain from over the road, because of course there was. Millie gave whoever was there a wave, too – although this was far more sarcastic and with a muttered insult under her breath. It was probably paranoia but she thought there was likely a neighbourhood WhatsApp group that didn't include her. They'd fire messages back and forth, reporting sightings of Millie and speculating on whether she'd killed her parents.

If it wasn't paranoia, then it was some sort of narcissistic disorder. Millie didn't know what would be worse.

The wave became a V and then Millie turned back to her own house. It might have been annoying to see Rachel – but at least she'd get to spend a day with her son.

· · ·

By the time Millie got into her living room, Eric had already unpacked his Xbox from a rucksack. It was on the floor and he was carefully unbundling a spool of cables. As he was separating everything out, he looked up, realising he was being watched.

'Can I use the big TV?' he asked.

'Looks like you've already given yourself permission...'

He smirked and it was impossible for Millie not to return it. Her son had Alex's smile. He had a lot of Alex about him: the same dark eyebrows, the high cheekbones, even the way he stood tall while somehow making it look like he was slouching at the same time. Millie never used to bother that he was so much like his father and so little like his mother.

There was a lot of things that never used to bother her...

'Is it OK?' Eric asked again.

'Fine – but not all day. I want you to rest your eyes.'

That got a *roll* of the eyes she wanted resting – and then Eric was passing her cables and asking her to plug them into the back of the television. Millie did as requested – and then got out the way as her son finished setting things up so that he could play his game.

Millie sat in the armchair and watched. She wanted to ask questions about school, or what they should do together the next time it was her weekend for custody. But there was pleasure in this, too. She spent so little time with Eric that simply watching him go about his normal day was enough. Besides, it was important that he *wanted* to spend time at hers, even if it was playing games. If she forced him to stop and have some sort of conversation he didn't want, it'd only end up being more ammunition for Alex along the line.

Eric loaded his game and clipped on the headset. He pressed a few buttons and then started speaking. For a second, Millie thought it was to her – but then she realised his friends were already online. From what Millie could tell, they were building some sort of shelter together.

That little voice told Millie that she should have fought harder for her son when custody was decided. She wanted to tell everyone what she'd discovered about Alex, why she'd had the affair... except there was no proof. It would be her word against his – and her reputation had already been ripped apart.

That was before what happened to her parents. What happened with them had only made things worse.

Because there was no evidence, Millie had kept quiet and let the custody continue almost without a battle. She accepted only having Eric every other weekend. Her solicitor had said it would end up looking better in the long term. Things could be changed at a later date if Millie proved she was a competent, non-combative, parent. If Eric wanted to spend time at hers. It was a marathon, not a sprint, she'd said.

To Millie, it didn't feel like either a marathon or a sprint. On the one side there was Alex, the lawyer – and his girlfriend, Rachel, who 'works in accounts'. Then there was Millie, the dog groomer who'd given up her previous career and who'd had the affair that had broken up her marriage. The affair she hadn't realised was public. Millie, who large groups of people seemed to believe had bumped off her parents.

As Millie watched Eric play, she realised the structure he and his friends were building was a small part of something much larger they'd already created.

'What's it going to be?' she asked.

The reply wasn't instant as it took Eric a moment to realise the voice had come from somewhere other than his headset. He tapped something on the earphone and then turned to her. 'A stadium,' he said.

Now that he'd said it, Millie realised that the giant wedge at which she'd been looking was some sort of stand. She wondered how many hours it had taken to build but didn't ask.

She didn't ask much, instead she watched Eric play. Occasionally, she would slip in a question about what he was doing, or how something worked. He took the time to answer, as if she was the child and he was the adult.

Millie felt so old sometimes. It came to every generation, she supposed.

Time passed and then Eric stopped and said he was going to get a drink. Millie had got up early that morning and hurried to the twenty-four-hour Tesco to stock up on things her son might want. The day before his visits were more or less the only time Millie bothered to go food shopping for anything more than cheese.

She told him there were cans of Coke and some Penguin bars in the fridge. She expected him to return with one of each, perhaps even two of the Penguins if he was being cheeky, but, instead, he arrived back in the living room with a notepad page in his hand.

'What's this?' he asked.

In the rush of everything from the night before, trying to sleep, and then getting up to go shopping, Millie had forgotten what she'd left on top of the stove.

Eric looked at the doodle and then turned the page for Millie to see.

'It's a cat,' she replied... which wasn't strictly speaking a lie.

Eric turned the page back towards him and pulled a face. 'It doesn't *look* like a cat.'

'That's because I'm not very good at drawing.'

'Why did you draw a *black* cat?'

'Because I wanted to.'

He lowered the page. 'I thought you said you were a dog person.'

'I am – but people are allowed to like cats *and* dogs.'

Eric seemed to think on that for a moment, as if the idea had never occurred to him. 'Dad's a cat person,' he said.

'Is he?'

'I asked why you didn't live together any more and he said it's because he's a cat person and you're a dog person. He said cat people and dog people don't get on.'

Millie struggled for a moment, trying to think how to reply. Had Alex offered that as a metaphor which had gone over Eric's head? Did he literally mean he preferred cats?

At least he hadn't told Eric the full truth of why they were no longer together. Or *his* truth.

'It's a bit more complicated than that,' Millie said.

'Dad and Rachel are getting a cat,' Eric replied.

'Are they? Your dad hasn't said.'

It wasn't a particular surprise. Quite often, Millie would find out things from a good ol' fashioned social media stalk. Rachel would put up some photo of her with the cat, hashtag blessed, and then all her stupid friends would click the stupid heart button, and make their stupid comments, with all their stupid emojis.

Millie blinked. Breathed. She had to make the most of her time with her son.

Eric looked at the picture again and then returned to the kitchen with it.

Millie wasn't quite sure why she'd sketched it, let alone why she'd kept it. As she'd tried to sleep last night, she'd told herself that what she'd seen in the road was simply a neighbour's cat. The angle and the mist had made it seem much bigger than it was. There obviously wasn't a panther loose in Whitecliff and, even if there was, she was the last person who should be putting her name to such claims.

She'd also told herself the lights through her window and the van outside was something innocent and normal.

When Eric reappeared, he had a can of Coke in one hand and a pair of Penguins in the other. He gave that little smirk he always did when wondering if he'd be challenged. Then he sat back with his controller and headset.

'I've got an appointment in about an hour,' Millie said. 'Someone's bringing over their dog for a haircut. I was wondering if you wanted to help...?'

One of the chocolate bars was hanging from Eric's mouth as he chewed, while using both hands on the controller. He mumbled something like 'huh?' while not turning around.

'You don't have to,' she added.

The second half of the bar had disappeared into Eric's mouth and he chomped away. 'Maybe,' he managed.

The 'maybe' turned out to be a more predictable 'no' once the time arrived. The woman was in a rush and said she'd be back in a couple of hours. Once she'd gone, Millie led the poodle along the hall, through the kitchen, and out to the shed in the back that she'd converted into a dog grooming station. She spent the next couple of hours bathing, shampooing, combing and clipping the dog, while occasionally checking in on her son, who had barely moved. It was soothing, almost meditation, on the days when dogs behaved and didn't mind getting wet.

Guilt clawed at her, that she should've cancelled the appointment and spent the day doing something with her son. That she was a bad mother for letting him play his games. Except, all she had was her relationship with him. If that somehow broke and he ended up getting on better with Rachel than her, what would she have left? Eric was doing the thing he wanted and, if he was happy, that meant he was happy *with her*.

The dog owner turned up when she said she would – and was delighted at Millie's work. Millie handed across a checklist of everything she'd done, which included the complimentary agility training, and then the owner said she'd transfer the money as soon as she got home. She had turned to go when Millie asked if she'd leave a review. It felt dirty to ask such a thing – and the woman seemed momentarily confused, before saying she would.

Anything that would help increase Millie's 1.75 rating. It was a wonder she got any business. The genuine fours and fives had been drowned out by the ocean of invented ones from people who'd seen the headlines and Facebook posts and made their minds up.

As she closed the door, Millie found herself checking her page, even though she knew it was too soon for a new review. Even though the ones that said she'd killed someone's dog, or hit someone's dog, or lost someone's dog, all remained.

She headed into the living room, where Eric was still playing, and told him he'd have to take a break soon. She'd learned that, when it came to computer games, breaks could never simply be taken. There had to be some sort of fifteen- or twenty-minute cool-down period until Eric was at a good place to save.

Or so he said.

Millie let him continue doing what he was doing as she doomscrolled through her reviews. She'd told Jack more than once that she no longer looked, except she wasn't sure she would ever stop. She didn't know why – but she certainly didn't want anyone's opinion about what it might all mean.

She'd flick between her own reviews and ones that people left for the town's various attractions. Something about those one-stars made her feel better about her own.

Whitecliff Pier

It's a bridge that ends in the sea, so you have to turn around and walk back to the start. There's no Wi-Fi at the end and the water is too loud. Waste of an hour.

One star

It was as Millie scrolled through the reviews of Whitecliff's beach that she realised she was being watched. The television was still on but Eric was no longer playing his game and had turned to her. There was a smudge of chocolate above his top lip and a curious, hard-to-read expression on his face. As if he was confused by something.

'What's going on?' Millie asked.

He gulped, summoning up the courage in the way he always had when he wanted to ask something. He'd been less confident when he was younger, always hesitant to ask in case he was told 'no'. He'd been getting better but there was a nervousness that Millie hadn't seen in a while.

'I, um...'

'You can say.'

Eric bit his bottom lip and then looked away, talking without looking at her. 'What's a whore?'

THIRTEEN

Millie was frozen momentarily. Eric had picked up the game controller but wasn't doing anything with it. He wasn't even looking at the television, instead focusing on the floor.

She *thought* she'd heard correctly and didn't particularly want her son to repeat it, yet Millie found herself asking what he'd said.

Eric still didn't turn. 'Do you know what a whore is?' he repeated. There was innocence in his tone.

'Where did you learn that word?' Millie asked.

'Adil at school said you were a whore. Then Ben said his dad reckons you're a slapper.'

Millie couldn't move. She was blinking rapidly, gripping the armrest, trying to fight the furious instinct that was bubbling.

'Those are bad words,' she said. She was trying to be calm but was unable to stop the quiver in her voice. 'You shouldn't call women or girls those things.'

Eric turned now, honing in on Millie, just as she felt unable to look at him. She was drawn into the stare. 'But what does it *mean?*' he asked.

Millie could feel herself starting to panic. There was a pain in her chest and her heart was thumping so loudly, she was surprised Eric couldn't hear it.

How could something like this be explained to a seven-year-old? There was no parenting manual for this sort of thing, not that she knew of.

She half-expected swear words and the like. That was a child testing boundaries. Eric had gone through a stage when he was about four of saying the word 'willy' all the time. He found it hilarious and would somehow keep himself amused for an hour at a time. It was *less* funny when he said it to old women in the supermarket.

This was something different, though. Something much darker.

'It doesn't really mean anything,' Millie said. 'They're bad words that men sometimes call women when they're trying to be horrible to them.'

Eric continued staring for a moment and then nodded, presumably – and hopefully – satisfied.

Millie wanted to ask about context – but knew she couldn't. Had Adil said anything else? Or that Ben kid? Or that Ben kid's stupid dad? It was always going to be difficult to explain to Eric what had happened because of his age. She and Alex had gone for the old 'Mummy and Daddy aren't getting on at the moment', and that had held for the time being.

But there would be questions one day.

A little over a year ago, Millie had an affair with a married Member of Parliament that had been exposed by a Sunday newspaper and its website. Her face had been shown in photographs – and the first she knew of it was when her phone had exploded a little after ten o'clock on a Saturday night. She'd been at home with Alex; Eric was upstairs in bed. In the hours after, she was thrown out by her husband and, with nowhere obvious to go, Millie had ended up back with her parents.

Millie's mother didn't talk to her for more than a week after she moved back. Her father would never look at her directly.

That was two months before *they* died.

Within hours of the story about the affair being *everywhere*, Millie had watched a video on her phone of a live news feed. The man with whom she'd been having what she believed to be a loving relationship, stood outside his home. He called everything an 'enormous mistake'. A 'massive lapse of judgement'. The 'biggest error of my life'.

And that was that. Millie had never heard another word from him. He'd gone back to his life with few, if any, consequences.

The affair had been her choice, of course – even if there were deeper, darker reasons that she'd never explained to anyone. She'd never tried to pretend it was anything other than her decision. She had picked the man – the affair – over her son, knowing what could happen.

And now the MP was back with his wife, keeping his head down, pretending none of it had happened. Meanwhile, Millie was trying to navigate explaining to her seven-year-old son what a 'whore' was.

Millie blinked back into the room, where Eric had part-turned away. The time would come soon when his questions would get harder to answer – and she'd find her choices harder to justify.

It wasn't as if she could tell him the truth about his dad…

Millie nodded towards the television. 'Is there anything I can play with you?' she asked.

His features creased with confusion. 'What d'you mean?'

'Any games for two of us…?'

He laughed, thinking she was joking. 'You don't play games.'

'I did a long time ago. Me and my friends used to play

Mario Kart. We'd sit in one of our bedrooms and race each other.'

Eric snorted, though not unkindly. 'Why were you in the same room?'

'Because we didn't have the internet like you do now. If you wanted to play together, you had to *be* together.'

Eric was wearing the same expression of bafflement he did when he was doing his spelling homework. As if she was trying to explain to him the concept of typewriters or black and white television. His attention had slipped anyway, as he pointed to the wall behind Millie.

'What was there?' he asked.

Millie turned to look at the rectangle that was a little brighter than the paint around it.

'It was a photo of Nana and Granddad,' Millie said.

'Where did it go?'

'I took it down after they died.'

'Why?'

It was another thing Millie couldn't fully explain to her son.

'I found it hard to look at them,' Millie said – which was at least one truth.

The creased look on her son's face made it seem as if he was going to follow up one 'why?' with another – but he didn't. By the time Millie's parents had died, she had already separated from Alex – and their access to their grandson was more limited than hers.

Eric glanced around the room, taking in the gaps where the other photos had once been. Lots of Millie's parents had been there. None of her. The only ones remaining were the couple of him, by himself. Those posed school photos that cost the same as a used car. Millie would put up more of him if everything she had wasn't on her phone.

'Where are they?' he asked.

'Some are in the attic,' Millie said. *Some are at the tip*, she didn't.

Eric pushed himself up into his chair and looked towards the window, staring into the distance.

It had been a long few months for the mother–son relationship. Lots of questions and nowhere near enough answers. She'd seen the distant look from Eric too much in the past year or so. The look that meant he had something to say, without knowing how to put it.

'Adil said you killed Nana and Granddad,' Eric added. 'He said you'd kill me.'

Millie felt a trickling chill creep through her. 'Look at me,' she said.

Eric twisted in his seat until he was watching her once more.

'I'd never hurt you,' Millie said. 'Those are really bad things to say to people.'

'Did you kill Nana and Granddad?'

Millie was unable to move, unable to stop staring at her son. What child should ever ask such a thing of their parent? She wondered how many other people thought this of her. It was one thing for strangers to believe something but Eric was *her son*.

'Do you think I did?' she asked.

The reply arrived with merciful speed: 'No.'

'Why do you think that?'

'Because you wouldn't do that.'

Millie nodded. 'Exactly.'

She wondered if there was more to come. Thought about whether she should contact the school and report this Adil kid. If that would make it worse? She wasn't sure what to do – and bringing it up with her ex-husband didn't seem like an option, either. She figured the more she spoke about things, the more other people would.

'Come here.'

Millie beckoned Eric across and he came, slipping onto her lap and falling into her. She cradled his head, as she had seven years before when he'd been born. His heart was tip-tapping gently through his T-shirt. If it was down to her, she'd have stayed like that until there was nothing but pins and needles in her arms and legs.

It was Eric who moved first, rustling his head away from her shoulder. 'Is that your phone?' he asked.

Millie hadn't noticed the vibration but, as soon as Eric had said, she realised there was something buzzing around her leg. She reached for her phone, which had jammed itself between her and the armrest. She glanced at the screen before pushing it back.

'It might be Dad,' Eric said.

'It's not his number.'

'Maybe he's calling from work?'

Millie wanted to ignore it – but Eric had already wriggled back onto the carpet.

The number was an 01 landline, the sort that Millie hadn't seen call her mobile for years. She pressed the button to answer and held it to her ear, expecting some sort of marketing call.

It wasn't that.

'Is that Millie?' came a man's voice.

'Who's calling?'

'It's Guy. I've got something for you about Dean Parris.'

FOURTEEN

Millie told Guy to hang on. She held her hand across the bottom of the phone, even though she wasn't sure if it actually blocked her voice.

'I've got to take this,' she said, talking to Eric.

'Is it Dad?'

'No,' Millie replied. She said she'd be back and then headed through to the kitchen and closed the door behind her.

When she lifted the phone back to her ear, she could hear Guy's steady breathing, like an old-school dirty phone call.

'I'm back,' she said.

Guy didn't mess around. 'I've found the paper with the story about Dean's dad's death,' he said.

'Oh...' Millie couldn't think of anything better to say. With having Eric for the morning, and then everything from the past few minutes, thoughts of Guy, Ingrid and the girl on the roof had slipped her mind.

'There are two pieces and I wrote both of them,' Guy added.

'*Two* pieces?'

'It wasn't a year between Dean's father dying and his wife –

it was only three weeks. There was a hold-up with his dad's autopsy because of the sudden death. They'd not even had the funeral when Dean's wife went into early labour and passed away.'

Millie found herself sighing under her breath. It was *awful*. Inconceivable. She glanced towards the living room, where she could hear Eric rattling around with something.

Then she realised what Guy had said.

'Do you know what happened?'

'Not exactly. Some sort of complication with childbirth. I've been trying to find a follow-up article but I either never wrote it, or there were no details.' He paused. 'No reason for the family to give us the details, I suppose.'

By 'us', she supposed he meant the newspaper for which he used to work.

'There's a daughter,' Guy said. 'The wife died at the hospital – but she gave birth to a girl they named Beth. There's a quote through the hospital where Dean says they'd already agreed on the name.'

'Beth...' Millie rolled the name around her lips. 'How long ago was that?' she asked.

'Twenty years, give a few months.'

Millie puffed out a breath. She'd have been a teenager, seventeen or eighteen, probably bumming around college and wondering what she'd do when it was over. Her dad would have been at the peak of his fame, on the six o'clock local news. He'd have likely reported on the tragedies surrounding Dean himself.

'Do you want me to keep looking?' Guy asked.

Millie had been daydreaming and wasn't ready for the question. 'I don't know,' she replied, while looking at her doodle of the panther on the table. At the doodle of the *regular, domestic* cat that happened to be black. 'Any more sightings?' she added, quickly.

There was a glimmer of amusement in Guy's tone as he

replied. She wondered what he found funny but then realised it was more that he'd cracked her into asking. 'Nothing reported to me,' he said. 'But I've got an interview with an expert on big cats in a couple of hours. He's coming in on the train and we're going for tea.' He waited a beat. 'Come along if you fancy it...?'

Millie stuttered a reply, before settling on: 'Why would I?'

She could almost hear the shrug. 'You seem inquisitive and bright,' he replied. 'Interested in finding things out...'

Millie didn't know how to reply. She wasn't used to compliments, if it *was* a compliment. It was hard to know. Apart from Jack, she wasn't sure the last time anyone had taken a particular interest in her. Guy had spoken like some sort of teacher handing back a piece of work that had an 'A' etched into the corner.

As if anticipating the awkwardness, Guy continued: 'The offer's there if you change your mind. We'll be at the Finch Tearooms at four. Tea and scones on me, if you can make it.'

'I've got my son today.'

Millie wasn't sure why she'd told him that, other than that she didn't want him to think she'd stood him up. Even though she had every right to stand him up – and no reason at all to end up on a dumb Loch Ness Monster trek.

'Not a problem,' Guy replied cheerily. 'You know where I am if anything changes.'

Millie suddenly wanted to reply, to say that listening to an expert talk about whether panthers really could exist on the outskirts of Whitecliff sounded, well, interesting. Perhaps even fun.

And that wasn't even to mention the scones.

Except, by the time she'd thought of any of that, Guy had gone.

FIFTEEN

Millie had barely finished the phone call when the doorbell sounded. Even from the other end of the hall, she knew who was there, based on their silhouettes. She'd often mocked Jack and Rishi in the past because of the way they leaned towards one another when they stood. They were like Ant and Dec if they each had one leg shorter than the other.

She opened the door and her friends gasped breaths of cool air into the house before stepping inside. Rishi was wrapped in an array of scarves, as if he'd got caught up in someone's washing line. Jack was in a coat so big, he could take part in a zorbing race without the giant ball.

'We're both on half-days,' Jack declared, 'so we've come to take you out for the afternoon. We were thinking cocktails and cake in town – then an Uber home.'

'Or we can just stay out,' Rishi added. 'It is Friday, after all.'

Millie couldn't remember the last time she'd had a night out, let alone on a Friday. She had vague memories of everybody suddenly looking really young in Whitecliff's pubs and clubs. One minute those places were full of familiar faces with whom she used to go to school, the next she was one of those old people she used to laugh at.

'I've got Eric,' she said, nodding towards the other room.

Jack and Rishi exchanged an excited look.

'Even better,' Jack replied.

It wasn't only them who was delighted. As soon as they entered the living room, Eric was on his feet with a cry of 'Uncle Jack!'

Before Millie could say anything, Jack had lifted her son off his feet and spun him in a circle. A moment later it was Rishi's turn – and then Eric and Rishi were off to the garden for an impromptu game of something that looked like tag. Rishi's scarves had been abandoned on the kitchen table and Millie was leaning on the kitchen counter, watching the back garden chase.

'Rish enjoys this sort of thing more than the kids,' Jack said, as he slotted in at Millie's side. He momentarily wrapped an arm around her waist, gave her a gentle squeeze, and then slipped away. 'You should see him with his own nieces and nephews. He does no exercise all week and then does a half-marathon charging around after them. They never get tired. I swear the parents are slipping them amphetamines.'

Millie couldn't tell if Rishi was trying to get caught but he'd managed to get himself cornered. He was in a spot close to where she and Guy had found the dimpled triangle in the earth. Eric tagged Rishi and then turned and ran at full pelt in the opposite direction.

'He's talking about adoption again,' Jack said solemnly. He took another step away and then began folding Rishi's scarves into neat piles.

'You don't sound too excited,' Millie replied.

Jack didn't answer that. He continued folding until all the scarves were tidied on top of one another.

'Your mate was at the home again today,' he said.

'My mate?'

'Mick said you knew that contractor guy who came over yesterday. Dean. He was back today.'

Millie turned from the window, to where Jack was now hunting through the cupboards.

'What was he doing?' Millie asked.

'Not sure. I forgot my coat and went back to get it. Someone said he'd been checking the window seals in all the rooms, making sure nothing was leaking.' He stopped talking as he found the chocolate digestives Millie had bought earlier that morning. 'Can I open these?' he asked, as he removed the packet from the cupboard.

'Fine.'

Jack took a knife from the rack and sliced close to the top. Crumbs scattered across the counter and he started picking them up bit by bit, feeding them into his mouth.

'Even Eric doesn't do that,' Millie said.

'I'd put that down to questionable parenting.' Jack grinned as finished the crumbs and removed a full biscuit. 'I prefer dark chocolate, for future reference,' he said.

'I didn't buy them for you.'

Jack settled at the table with what was now his packet of biscuits. He started to lick the chocolate from the top, like some sort of demented cat.

'Was he in Ingrid's room?' Millie asked.

'Who?'

'Dean. The handyman.'

'I think he was in every room,' Jack replied. 'How do you know him?'

'I don't. Not really. He owns the house where Ingrid says she saw someone pushed off the roof.'

Jack stopped whatever obscene act he was performing on the biscuit. 'Oh...' He waited a moment, the soggy digestive hovering a little away from his mouth. 'Did you ask him about it...?'

'Yes – and then he turned up at the home the next two days in a row.'

Jack lowered the biscuit and stared at her. Millie knew they were thinking the same thing.

'There's a missing tile on his roof,' Millie added. 'Just below the skylight.'

She opened the cupboard above the hood of the cooker, the one she needed to stretch on tiptoes to reach. Millie removed the tile and placed it on the counter.

'*That* tile. I picked it up off the floor at the back of his house.'

Jack looked at the tile, then Millie, then his biscuit; which he bit in half. He chomped as he thought.

'This is too much to take in without a cup of tea,' he said.

'Kettle's there,' Millie replied, nodding towards it.

Jack pouted his bottom lip, so Millie rolled her eyes and filled it, before flipping it on.

'What's this?' she asked, nodding at the biscuits. 'Post-lunch? Pre-tea?'

'Afternoon snack,' he replied. Jack finished his biscuit and then added: 'That roof looked really high.'

'It is.'

'No one fell off that roof,' he said. 'They'd have broken their legs. Broken their back, or whatever.'

Millie couldn't dispute that, even though she had vague memories of reading a story a few years. Someone had fallen from a plane and their parachute hadn't opened. She couldn't remember how but that person had got out alive, so stranger things had happened.

Something still didn't sit right, though. It was hard to believe someone had leapt, or been pushed, from the roof and been fine, much less disappeared.

'He parked outside the house last night,' Millie said, nodding towards the front.

Jack had reached for another biscuit but stopped midway. 'The handyman?'

'Dean. He parked his van behind the bushes but drove off when I went out.'

Jack sat up straighter. He'd seemed partially sceptical about everything until now. 'Are you sure?'

Millie faltered as she questioned herself. It didn't *sound* like something that was plausible... and it had been dark. 'Not really,' she replied. 'I saw him in his mirror as he drove off.' Another pause and then: 'I think it was him.'

It sounded like she was trying to convince herself, probably because she was. In the hours since she'd seen the van, it felt less like it had been anything out of the ordinary.

'Mill, that's not good if it was him,' Jack said. 'How'd he know where you live?'

'It's easy enough to find out. He knew *who* I was – and that's good enough.'

Jack put the digestive on the table and pressed back in his chair. 'You can't—'

He didn't get a chance to finish because the back door burst open and Eric flew inside. He was cherry-faced and breathless as he charged to the opposite side of the table and stood behind Jack. Rishi was a few paces behind. He closed the back door and then stood on the opposite side of the table.

'He's It!' Eric shouted, as if warning everyone there was a shark in the water.

Rishi feigned a step to the left and, as Eric moved in the other direction, he darted back right and then tapped Eric on the shoulder.

'Boom! Who's It now!'

Eric's face fell but then he looked up to his mum.

'Doesn't count,' Millie said. 'No tags inside. Standard rules. Been played like that for eight hundred years.'

A grin poured onto Eric's face. 'I win!'

Rishi faked annoyance, slumping into the seat opposite Jack, giving a large, dejected sigh, and reaching for a digestive.

'You better never go outside again,' he said. 'because I'll be there when you least expect – and then you'll be It. And no tag-backs.'

Eric slipped onto a third chair and also took a biscuit. He gasped for breath and then took a bite.

Millie made eye contact with Jack but it wasn't the time to speak. Instead, she reached the tile back up to the cupboard and then, as the kettle finished boiling, she hunted around the kitchen for mugs and teabags. The next time she looked back to the table, she realised Jack was watching her.

'*Be careful,*' he mouthed, silently.

It was only as he spoke that Millie found herself stopping to wonder if, maybe, there really *was* something about Dean that should worry her.

SIXTEEN

Eric dashed into the house that his parents had once shared. Alex stood in the doorway, holding it open, and letting their son dart underneath his arm.

'How was he?' Alex asked, when it was only him and Millie on the doorstep.

'Good. He played his games for a bit, then did some of his homework. Jack and Rish came over in the afternoon.'

It was a stretch to say Eric had done *some* of his homework. He'd first claimed he didn't have any, then shown Millie the maths book in which he was supposed to be working. She still thought it was ridiculous that kids so young were meant to take their work home with them.

Either way, it wasn't that which made Alex's nose wrinkle. He'd never been a fan of Jack, while also never admitting it. Millie had wondered for a long time if it was because he didn't like her being good friends with another man. He could definitely be a bit old-fashioned with things like that, something that came from his parents. When they started going out, he'd insist on paying for things and opening doors for her. Not every tradition remained through the course of their relationship...

'We're off to Center Parcs this weekend,' Alex said casually. 'Going first thing tomorrow and staying one night. Eric doesn't know yet.'

Millie was speechless for a moment. A couple of years before, when she and Alex were still together, she'd suggested going to Center Parcs for the weekend but Alex had called it 'a bit tacky'. He'd made her feel silly for even suggesting it.

He stood with a straight face, either not remembering that – or, more likely, challenging her to bring it up.

She bit her lip, literally, and realised she was bobbing anxiously on the spot. 'Eric will love that,' she said. 'I always said it would be good for him. I hope you have a great time.'

'I guess I'll see you around.'

Alex had taken a step back into the house, with one hand on the door. She'd not taken the bait, so there was little left to say. They both hovered for a moment, as they always seemed to do. Things never felt finished between them. It was Millie who eventually forced herself to turn and head to the car.

On the way back home, Millie decided on a short detour. There were many ways to get from one side of Whitecliff to the other but, instead of heading in a straight line, she took the scenic route. It wasn't long before she was on the coastal road, with the wind buffeting her car towards the centre line.

Millie slowed as she drove past the entrance to Dean's road. There was no one behind, so she stopped, staring along the length of the street, before doubling around until she was on the parallel street. She was in the same place where she'd entered the alley that led to the back of his house. This time, she had a different plan.

First she checked the glovebox for the reading glasses she needed if she was tired. She then dug into the far reaches of her car boot until she'd found the bobble hat that had been stored the previous winter in case she broke down. She put both on and then walked along the road until she was at the house diagonally opposite Dean's.

A For Sale board had been hammered into the lawn at the front, along with a phone number for an estate agent in town. Millie had spotted it the previous time she'd been – although not paid it too much attention.

She headed along the path and knocked on the door.

It took a minute or so, among a series of 'hang on' calls from the inside – but then a woman appeared at the door. She was leaning on the wall, clutching a potato in one hand.

'Can I help you?' she asked.

Millie pointed back towards the For Sale board. 'My brother's looking for a place,' she lied. 'He saw pictures on the website but didn't know much about the area. I told him I'd drop by and see what it was like...'

The woman's demeanour changed in an instant. She stood taller and straightened her top, before realising she was clutching the potato. She held it up, as if she'd noticed she'd grown a sixth finger. 'I was just starting tea,' she said.

'What are you having?' Millie asked, offering her best friendly grin.

'Mash and peas.' The woman answered instantly and then softened slightly. 'Sorry, you caught me unawares. I don't get many visitors. The area's nice and quiet. If that's what your brother's after, he'd love it round here...'

She was fishing for details of the mythical brother but Millie let it sit as she made a point to turn and look around the street.

'There's no main road through,' the woman continued. 'We've got an old people's home at the top of the hill, then a church over there.'

When Millie turned back, the woman was pointing along the street, towards where she'd parked.

'What are the neighbours like?' Millie asked.

'No trouble. I think the lady at the far end has a couple of kids. I don't know if your brother does...?'

Millie twisted again, staring across the street towards Dean's house. 'Who lives there?' she asked.

The woman moved forward, onto the doorstep, and followed Millie's gaze. 'Bloke called Dean,' she said. 'He's a handyman and helped with my gutters last Feb when the wind took it down.' She pointed up. 'He redid the whole lot, and the pointing, so all that's up to standard. Brand new, in fact.'

Millie thought for a moment, wondering how best to phrase things. 'That sounds like a useful neighbour to have,' she replied. 'My neighbour's a plumber – but he's got a noisy dog. This big thing which barks at anything that goes past. He's got a teenager who always has mates over, too. They chuck their cigarettes into my garden all the time.'

The woman looked horrified.

'I think they smoke marijuana,' Millie added.

The homeowner's face went from horror to disgust. 'There's nothing like that here,' she said quickly, trying to disguise her expression. 'He lives by himself now but he's got a grown-up daughter. She used to babysit for my boys back in the day. Lovely girl. I was the first person she told after she passed her driving test. She got home all excited but her dad was out, so she came knocking on my door. Clever, too. I waved her off on the day she went to university.'

Millie almost repeated the name 'Beth' but stopped herself just in time.

'That sounds a lot better than the guy next to me,' Millie said. 'My brother wants somewhere nice and quiet, so I'll tell him what you said.'

The woman was still holding the potato, which she used to point across the road in the other direction. 'You'll never get any trouble round here, love. I've been here twenty-five years and there's never any problems. The land out the back of mine is protected green-belt land, so nothing else can be built. If your brother's interested, he won't find anywhere better.'

Millie took a step away, feeling a small twinge of guilt that her non-existent brother wouldn't be buying the house. 'I'll make sure I tell him,' she said.

She was at the end of the path when there was a growl of an engine, followed by a rustle of gravel. She waited by the For Sale sign, attempting to hide behind it as a scruffy white van shot around the corner. There was a grinding of brakes and a low squeal as it turned onto the plot of land at the side of Dean's house. Moments later, the driver's door clanked open, and Dean hopped down, tossing the keys from one hand to the other.

He headed directly to his front door, rammed the key into the lock, and then disappeared inside.

Millie stepped away from the sign, into the open. The van was on the other side of the street, with a crust of mud and dirt kicked up onto the lower half of the paintwork. She could barely read the number plate from this distance – but that didn't matter. She now knew one thing for sure. The large, hooked tow bar was as prominent as it had been the night it was parked outside her house.

SEVENTEEN

Millie was sitting at her kitchen table as she scrolled through Guy's Whitecliff News website. The chocolate biscuits had been left out and it felt a shame to have them go to waste. She nibbled on one as she scrolled up and down the page, looking for something about the panther.

Alleged panther.

Guy hadn't written a single story about it, despite the sighting he'd mentioned. Millie had been hoping to read something from the expert he'd said he was meeting – but the most recent story was from the day before. Something about cuts being made to the lifeboat service.

Despite her father's job – or, perhaps, because of it – she'd never had much of an interest in local news. Except there was something about the way Guy had discovered those details about Dean that couldn't help but intrigue her. It was a story from twenty years ago, something which wouldn't have been digitised. Yet his wreck of a cottage was a library that nobody else would understand or have access to. It felt... *important* in a way Millie couldn't quite figure out. She didn't want to like him, and yet...

She clicked onto the next story, something about an increase in fly-tipping around Whitecliff. Someone at the council reckoned it cost 'six figures' to clean up the annual mess, while there was a woman pointing at a sofa that had been left in her front garden. Towards the bottom, there were historical quotes from a different councillor, made years before, that Millie assumed must have been dug out by Guy from his own records.

Millie closed the browser and picked up another digestive. Half the packet was gone – which was precisely why she didn't allow herself to have things like this in the house.

There was something else about Guy that was bothering her. He said he'd been her dad's friend, his *best man*, and yet she didn't remember a time when he was part of their family life. Wouldn't she know someone that close to the family? She thought he'd said something about them falling out. Yet another thing she hadn't followed up.

Millie wondered what had happened between Guy and her father. Or, perhaps, between Guy and her mother.

Did she want to know?

Her family had enough secrets.

Millie navigated away from Guy's website but found herself looking at her own reviews once more. There was a new five-star at the top, from the woman with the poodle. With that, her overall average was up to two. If she could actually get some of the fake ones removed, things might start to turn around.

It had been a decent day overall. Time with Eric, time with Jack and Rishi, a five-star review, a nice comment from Guy, of all people.

Lots of good things.

That's when Jack's text came through.

Come in tomoz if u can. Something weird going on

Millie replied instantly with 'What's happening?' but there was no reply. She tried calling but there was no answer.

It took forty minutes for Jack to get back to her.

Can't talk. Busy

Millie had barely got through the double doors at the front of the home the next morning when Jack spotted her. He was pushing a trolley filled with dirty bowls and plates along the corridor but skidded to a halt outside the manager's office. He stage-whispered a 'wait there', before disappearing out of sight with the trolley. When he returned a couple of minutes later, he was drying his hands on the back of his pants.

'This way,' he said.

Millie followed wordlessly as he led her through the corridors into the residents' wing. They went past Ingrid's door, around a corner, and then stopped next to a fire exit. Jack pushed himself onto tiptoes to peer over her shoulder along the hall and then dropped back down.

'What's going on?' Millie asked.

'Shush.'

Jack knocked twice on the nearest door, next to the fire exit. The name 'Keith' was printed underneath the number '41'.

There was a rattle of a lock and then the door swung open. The man on the other side was one of the younger-looking residents, although Millie guessed he was still in his eighties. He stood taller than many of the others, with a leaner physique. He was in short sleeves, although the skin on his arms was loose, as if he'd recently lost weight.

'This is Keith,' Jack said, as he ushered Millie into the strange man's room.

The three of them ended up in what was close to a carbon

copy of Ingrid's room. There was the dresser and the television, the bed, a small bathroom in the corner, and then the large floor-to-ceiling patio doors that looked out over the valley.

Jack perched himself on the edge of the dresser as Keith moved across to the windows.

'I got called in last night,' Jack said. 'Had to do a couple of hours because Tina had a stomach bug.' He nodded at Keith. 'Tell her what you told me.'

Keith folded his arms defensively and turned between Millie and the window. Even though Millie had been volunteering for months, she didn't recognise Keith and wondered if he was new. They'd certainly never spoken.

'There was a girl,' Keith said. He sounded hesitant, though it didn't feel like nerves. More because he and Millie didn't know each other. 'I saw her the other night, down there.'

He unhooked an arm and flapped it towards the window and the valley beyond. He shot a glance towards Jack, as if wanting to know why he had to repeat this.

'What about her?' Millie asked. She knew what was coming.

Keith shrugged, as if it was the most normal thing in the world. 'She jumped off that roof,' he said.

EIGHTEEN

Millie stared at Keith, wondering whether it would turn out he was talking about a movie that had been on, something like that.

Except he wasn't.

'Down there,' Keith added, pointing towards Dean's house in the distance. 'She was all in white. I looked over and she was on the roof and then – bang! – she jumped off. Disappeared behind the hedge.'

Millie felt Jack watching her and there was an energy in the room.

'If it was night,' Millie asked, 'how did you see her?'

Keith hmmed to himself for a moment. 'My eyes still work.'

'I didn't mean that. I just meant—'

'I know what you meant.' His reply was snapped and sharp. Millie wondered if the conversation might be over but Keith shook his head a fraction and continued. 'I guess it was the moon, or something. It was bright out there. You could see all the way across the bay.'

That's what Ingrid had said.

Millie pressed back onto the other end of the dresser from

Jack. The angle of the wood dug into her backside as she thought things through.

'Do you know Ingrid?' she asked.

'From down the hall? I know *of* her.'

'Have you talked to her recently?'

A shake of the head. 'I don't think we've ever spoken.' He laughed to himself and there was a definite edge. 'Just because we live here, doesn't mean we all know each other.'

Millie felt chastened. It wasn't what she'd meant but he had a point. It did mean Keith and Ingrid hadn't swapped notes.

'Why are you bothered?' Keith said. He looked to Jack and it was unclear who he was asking.

Millie felt Jack staring sideways towards her. Somehow, this had become *her* mystery.

'Ingrid saw the same thing,' Millie replied. 'She told me the other day and I was trying to find out if it actually happened.'

'Oh, it happened,' Keith said. 'It was really quick but it happened. One minute she was up there, white dress, dark hair, then she was gone. I didn't know if I should tell someone but it was already dark and I thought...' He tailed off, then added: 'I don't know what I thought.'

Ingrid had specifically said blonde hair, while Keith said dark. Ingrid said pushed, Keith said jumped. Perhaps the angle meant they could both be right?

'Did you notice anything about how old she was?' Millie asked.

That got a dismissive shrug. 'I don't know. She was too far away.'

'But was it a *girl*, or a woman?'

Keith had unfolded his arms but re-crossed them tightly. It was the sort of question that implied criticism, even though Millie hadn't meant it as harshly as it came out. A girl and a woman were different, after all.

'Look, I only told yer mate because we were talking about

the view. I didn't know I'd get the whole third degree about it. I don't even know who you are...'

He took a step towards the door and the moment was lost.

Millie found herself apologising as she and Jack were ushered into the corridor. The door closed with a clunk behind them, leaving Millie blinking into the gloom of the hall.

Before she could say anything, Jack had set off, leading her back through the web of corridors, past reception, through the staff area, and then out into the smoking area. He immediately began fishing through his pockets until he found his vape pen.

'We can add Keith to the list of people you've made good first impressions on...' he said, although there was a twinkle in his eye.

'I didn't mean—'

'Don't worry about it. Keith's an old grouch. I asked him if wanted dessert the other week and he started giving me a lecture about growing up in the dockyards. Something about bread pudding. I wasn't really listening. Some of them round here just want to be left alone.'

That hadn't been Millie's experience of volunteering – but the whole purpose of her coming in was to mingle with people who wanted to be mingled with. That was probably why she didn't recognise Keith.

'Did he tell you anything else last night?' Millie asked.

'Not really. He said that handyman guy had been round earlier in the day. Something about the window seals but I didn't want to push him on it.'

Jack inhaled on his device, waited a moment, and then blew out a guff of something fruity.

'You won't be able to do that if you're going to adopt,' Millie said.

Jack eyed his e-cigarette and then took another puff. 'Rish is always going on about me giving up.'

Millie knew that would be that. It wouldn't be that week,

and probably not that month. But, at some point in the next six months, Jack would go nicotine free. Rishi always got his way with things like this.

Jack used to work at a travel agent, even though he hated the work and, more than anything, his boss. Because the money was decent, the hours were good, and he got air miles as one of the perks, he'd have continued doing the job, regardless of how miserable he ended up. It was Rishi who'd persuaded him to give it up. Millie knew Jack would be giving up vaping in the same way Jack knew it. The only question was when.

'I thought Ingrid was imagining it,' Jack said quietly. 'I know I told you to go with the things she says so she doesn't get upset about the timelines. But I thought you were mad to *actually* go along with it.'

He paused for another suck on the vape pen.

'I can't believe you went down there and asked the home-owner about it.'

Millie didn't know how to reply. It didn't sound like a compliment, though it also didn't seem like a criticism. 'What if someone *did* fall? Where is she? *Who* is she? Why wasn't she injured?' A pause. 'Aren't you interested?'

Jack stared into the distance, perhaps thinking about it.

'You told me to be careful,' Millie added.

That got a nod. 'People know who you are, Mill. Half this lot already have it in for you – and now you're poking your nose into people's business.'

By 'half this lot', she assumed he meant the town in general. It was hard to argue. Except that, much of the time, true or not, it felt like a lot *more* than half the town.

'Do you think we should call the police?' Jack asked.

'What would we tell them?'

'That two people here saw someone fall off a roof – and that the guy who owns the house is stalking you.'

'He's not stalking me.'

'You said he was parked outside your house. Not only that, you must have told him you worked here – and then he turned up here the next two days. And those are the times you've noticed him. He could be parked across the street now. He might have been outside your house when Rish and Eric were in the garden yesterday.'

Millie shivered at hearing Eric's name connected to it all.

'Why?' she said. 'What would he get from any of that?'

'I don't know, Mill. That's why I reckon we should call the police.'

'But all we have are two people in their eighties who think they saw something – and they contradict each other. One says dark hair, one blonde. One says pushed, one jumped. Then I *might* have seen a van outside my house. None of it feels real – and what would the police do anyway?'

Jack didn't have an answer to that.

'Calling the police' was often suggested by people who'd had little to no interaction with them. Or those who watched cop shows on TV and thought it was real. Some thought of the police as magicians who'd solve all their problems, rather than human beings with their own issues.

Millie had learned that a lot could be figured out about a person by how fast they leapt towards calling the police as a solution. There were people from certain communities, with different upbringings, for whom the authorities were a sign of corruption, danger, or incompetence. Calling the police wouldn't even occur to them, let alone as a first resort.

Millie had been brought up differently to that. Her parents, her dad in particular, was part of the establishment. She'd grown up being told to call the police, to put her faith in the system, if she needed it. But that was the system that had splashed her photo on the front page and then left her with no choice but to give up custody of her son.

She didn't deny she was to blame for much of what had

happened to her – but the people with power hadn't done anything other than make it worse. If the past year had taught her anything, it was that she could only rely on herself.

Millie had never explained that to anybody. Perhaps Jack sensed it, or maybe he had picked up on a lot more about her than she realised. When he next spoke, it was as if he understood everything.

'Call me if you need something,' he said. 'I'll put you on my safe callers list, so if my phone rings at three in the morning, you'll get through.'

Millie touched his arm, gulped away the lump in her throat. There hadn't been many who'd been there for her after everything. No one, really.

She took her hand away and stood for a second. 'Is this because you want *me* to put *you* on *my* safe list, so my phone will go off if you need picking up from town at three in the morning.'

He laughed. 'That'll be a bonus – although I've not seen three in the morning in ages.'

Millie wished she could say the same. She woke between three and four with such regularity that it was as if she was setting a silent alarm. She'd lie in bed, staring at the ceiling, counting the number of hours' sleep she'd get if she were to fall asleep within five minutes. She'd give it a couple of hours and then get up.

Before they could say anything else, the door clicked open and one of the staff who worked in the kitchen appeared. He removed his hairnet, which unleashed a flood of sweat that poured across his brow and onto the collar of his uniform. He reached into a side pocket and pulled out a packet of cigarettes, before offering one to Jack.

Millie had to hold back the smile as Jack made eye contact with the newcomer, flicked his eyes in Millie's direction and said with a ridiculous amount of clarity that he Did Not Smoke.

The chef frowned momentarily, then glanced towards Millie, got what was going on, and lit one for himself.

'Did you hear about Gloria's mum and dad?' he asked, talking to Jack.

'Gloria from reception? What about them?'

'Someone tried breaking into their house last night. Her dad woke up and heard someone coming up the stairs. Gloria moved out ages ago, so it's only him and her mum who live there. He was on the landing and then he and this burglar guy came face to face on the top step.'

Jack had been staring into the distance – but was now looking at the cook. 'What happened then?'

'Her dad managed to chase the bloke out of the house. He called the police but it took them over three hours to get there. Gloria reckons he was sitting in the kitchen with a cricket bat until half-six.'

Jack let out a long, low breath. 'Where do they live?'

'One of those old houses near the docks, at the back of the Nando's.'

Jack straightened and clasped a hand on the cook's wrist. 'Are you joking?'

'That's where Gloria said.'

'That's where I live! I'm in one of the new flats where that factory used to be.'

The cook's cigarette was halfway to his mouth but paused in mid-air. 'Oh,' he said. 'What's that? A five-minute walk?'

Jack didn't answer, though Millie knew it was. The house in which Gloria's parents must live was one of a few older ones that had survived being knocked down.

'What happened when the police got there?' Jack asked.

'Gloria says they got that fingerprint powder everywhere and her mum had a right fit about having to hoover it up. The guy got away – and they're not expecting to hear much more about it. Even though they were face to face on the stairs, the burglar was wearing a balaclava, so her dad didn't get a proper look.'

'Did the burglar take anything?' Jack asked.

'Gloria doesn't think so. The TV's still there – and her dad went through all his records to check if anything had gone. Gloria was taking the piss, saying he couldn't give away his Shakin' Stevens stuff, let alone have it nicked, but I don't think her mum saw the funny side. She said all her mum's jewellery is still safe, so he never got that far.'

Millie nudged Jack with her elbow. 'At least you know where to look next time...'

She expected a laugh but got nothing except a suspicious sideways look from the cook and a *not now* roll of the eyes from Jack.

The cook puffed on his cigarette, shot her a suspicious sideways glance, and then looked back to Jack. 'They only moved in a few months ago,' he said. 'Gloria reckons her mum already wants to put the place up for sale again. She doesn't feel safe sleeping there any more, so her dad's there now, trying to install a burglar alarm.'

'I'll have to tell Rish,' Jack said.

'So he knows where to look next time...?' the cook replied.

Jack laughed far too loudly as Millie stewed silently about the stolen joke.

'I've got to get back,' the cook said. He stubbed out his cigarette in the slot and then stretched out his hairnet before putting it back on his head. He was already at the door when he stopped and turned back towards them. 'I've been meaning to ask,' he said, nodding at Millie. 'Are you David Westlake's girl?'

Millie felt momentarily stunned by the mention of her father's name. 'Yes,' she replied.

'I used to watch him on the telly. My dad always had the news on. He'd watch it all evening. Six o'clock on BBC, then switch over for the local news on ITV. He'd do Sky News, then the *News at Ten*, then *Newsnight* or *Question Time*, then bed.'

Millie nodded along, as if five hours of news every night was perfectly normal.

'Shame what happened to him,' the cook added. 'And what they did to you.'

Millie was temporarily speechless. In the year since her life had fallen apart, she didn't need many fingers to count the number of people who'd offered sympathy. She certainly wouldn't need any thumbs.

'Oh...' she found herself saying.

'I never voted for him,' the cook added. 'Peter Lewis, MP, huh? Always thought there was something not right about him. He has that sort of face. The type of bloke who goes around punching cats.'

It was a lot to take in. Peter Lewis, Member of Parliament, had always been simply 'Peter' to Millie.

'I don't think he's ever punched a cat,' Millie found herself replying.

The cook shrugged. 'Aye, well I wouldn't put it past him – and that's the point. Never trust a cat-puncher, my nan used to say.'

Millie doubted anyone's grandmother had a saying about such a thing – but she was grateful for the support regardless.

The man jabbed a thumb towards the door. 'Anyway, gotta get back – but if you ever want anything from the kitchen, come on by.'

'What about me?' Jack asked, probably feigning the hurt in his tone.

'You can get free food when you pay me back for the forty-four ciggies you owe.'

The cook gave Millie a wink and then disappeared inside. There was a momentary guff of warmth from inside – and then only the cold.

'Don't tell Rish,' Jack said. 'I told him I gave up six months ago.' He held up his vape pen. 'This is supposed to be a compromise.'

Millie left him a moment and then: 'I think I might call the police,' she said.

'But you—'

'To report a joke theft – and a betrayal from a friend.'

Jack grinned. 'It was funnier when he said it.'

'You just fancy that whole hairnet-sweatbox thing.'

Jack shrugged and had another puff on his vape device. 'People are going to lose it,' he said. 'Facebook will be full of nutters later, wanting the riot squad brought in.'

It took Millie a moment to realise what he was talking about. When she figured it out, she knew he was right. Whitecliff was the sort of town where burglaries didn't happen, especially in the winter when the only people around were locals. Crime rates went up along with the temperatures. Tourists came in for the summer, and by sheer numbers alone, the arrests for drunken behaviour, public nudity, assaults, thefts, and everything else rose.

Even with that, Millie would've needed even fewer fingers to count the number of burglaries than she did to count the amount of sympathy she'd had from people.

Nothing happened around Whitecliff in December. The council had even stopped bothering with Christmas lights because someone from *Emmerdale* had been hired to turn them on. He called the town a 'dump' on the microphone as a poorly thought-out joke.

This attempted burglary, especially close to the bay itself, was going to bring out the usual lot calling for police on every corner and capital punishment for anyone who wore a baseball cap the wrong way around.

Jack was watching her again and she knew what he was thinking. The last time a news story had raced around the town had been when Millie's parents had died. Two months before that, it was when she'd been caught having the affair with the town's MP. A failed burglary wasn't going to eclipse any of those – but people would want to talk about it.

Millie caught his eye and Jack tilted his head a fraction, not needing to say anything more. They'd never talked to any degree about the death of her parents, about what happened. If Jack had asked, perhaps they wouldn't still be friends? He'd only asked how she was – which is also what he'd done after Alex had thrown her out. He said there was room in the flat but Millie didn't want to be the third person in a one-bedroom apartment. There had never been any judgement, let alone awkward questions. All he did was ask how she was.

'What are you doing this afternoon?' he asked now.

'Not much,' Millie replied. 'Eric's with his dad this weekend. They're off to Center Parcs.'

'But what are *you* up to?'

Millie let out a breath and part turned to gaze down towards Dean's house at the bottom of the valley. Beyond that, the tide was in and the bluey-brown ocean was hammering into the cliffs.

'Enemy of my enemy stuff,' she said.

That got a quizzical, amused look. 'Are you defecting to China?'

'Something like that.'

NINETEEN

There was no answer when Millie rang the doorbell at Guy's house. She walked around the front of the cottage, checking the windows, but there was nobody in the study where she'd seen him before. It took her a moment to realise the next room was the kitchen, largely because the cooker had mounds of newspapers piled on top, as did every other surface. She wouldn't have been surprised if she were to open the ancient fridge and find mounds of papers in there, too.

Millie ambled back to the front, figuring she probably should have called his landline to see if he was in... except that might have meant admitting she *wanted* to see him, rather than 'being in the area'.

Realistically, nobody could ever accidentally be in the area where Guy lived. His cottage was isolated on the cliff top, far above the town, on the opposite side from where Dean lived. There was a single road that wound its way out of Whitecliff, past Guy's place. It continued until it reached the old power plant a few miles along the road.

There was misty rain in the air and Millie could feel it soaking through her shoes as she headed along the path back to her car. The gate was squishy between her fingers, like squeezing an overripe peach, as the wood smushed and warped.

She was inside her car when headlights flared over the ridge, burning through the foggy haze. The grinding chug of the engine was enough for Millie to know who was driving, as Guy's Volvo turned from silhouette to definable vehicle.

There was a crunch of the handbrake as he stopped, got out, and rounded the vehicle to open the passenger door and let Barry jump down. The dog shook himself and then trotted across to where Millie was again waiting by the gate.

'Lovely day for it,' Guy said, as if he'd expected her. He was in the same ancient, patchy, wax jacket he'd been wearing when he'd shown up on Millie's doorstep.

Millie crouched and ran her fingers through Barry's fur as Guy held the gate open. They didn't speak as Millie headed along the path for the second time in as many minutes, up towards the front door. Guy searched through a series of pockets, muttering under his breath, before finding a key inside his jacket. The distorted wood of the door stuck in the frame and Guy kicked it low down, before barging it with his elbow to get them inside.

'Keep meaning to get that fixed,' he said, mainly to himself, as they bundled inside.

Once his jacket was off, and Barry had shaken again, Guy led them along the hall, around the wobbling piles of newspapers, and into the kitchen. He picked up a stack of papers and put them on the floor. He filled an old-fashioned whistle kettle, filled it and put it on the hob, which he lit with a match.

He nodded towards the log fire in the corner. 'I can set that going if you're cold?'

'I don't know how long I'll be here.'

That seemed enough of an invitation for Guy, who hefted a pair of logs into the fireplace and then lit that too.

Millie had never been in a house with an actual, working,

fireplace. It felt like the sort of thing that only existed in Christmas movies where everyone ended up happy ever after. Or horror movies in the woods, where there wasn't much 'ever after' for anyone.

Guy moved around more newspapers, freeing up a spot at the table, where Millie sat, warming her hands in front of the flames. She couldn't help but feel that, with all the papers – and the open fire – an accident was waiting to happen.

'I wasn't sure you'd be back,' Guy said. He was standing on the other side of Millie. At some point, he'd taken off his shoes off and was now offering his sock-covered feet towards the flames.

'A second person at the nursing home saw someone fall from Dean's roof,' Millie said.

There was a moment of silence and then a gentle *hmm*. 'That's a second source,' Guy said.

'What does that mean?'

'In the old days, we'd only publish a story if we had two sources to corroborate each other. Not like that now. Anybody can publish anything, then people copy stories from one place to the next. One mistake gets duplicated over and over. Then it's said so often that everyone assumes it's true.'

It felt as if he might start on a rant about the state of the modern world – but he didn't.

'Did the two people at the home talk to each other?' he asked.

'They said not – but I can't say for sure. I don't think so.'

Barry was laid on his side in front of the fire, his eyes closed, belly exposed. Millie crouched and rubbed it gently for him as he started to purr as if he was a cat. Behind them, the kettle was whistling, so Guy hopped up and started fiddling out of sight. He asked about milk and sugar – and Millie didn't have the heart to tell him that she didn't really drink tea. She said she didn't mind and, when she sipped from the chipped mug he handed her, the amount of sugar made her teeth ache.

Millie put down the mug on the table, as she noticed the two *Whitecliff Journals* that had been left on the surface. The pages were crispy, with a date from twenty years before, and 'Tragedy On The Prom' in big letters on the front. She scanned the story and then turned inside, reading about how Dean's father had collapsed while working on a renovation project at the promenade. The ambulance had been there within six minutes – but he was already dead from a cardiac arrest.

Millie read the article twice and then put it back on the table. The final line had sprung out to her.

'He was survived by *two* sons?' she said.

Guy was back in his seat, feet stretched towards the fire. He nodded.

'Who's Liam Parris?' Millie added.

'Dean's *younger* brother but I don't think I can help more than that,' Guy replied. 'The name doesn't ring a bell.'

Millie took out her phone in an attempt to search for the name – but hadn't finished typing when she realised she had no signal.

'There's no masts up here,' Guy said. He delved into his pockets for a mobile phone that she didn't know he owned. It was a Blackberry with a tippy-tappy keyboard, the sort of thing that was all the rage for about two years more than a decade before. 'Company got me this,' he said. 'Reckoned we could write stories on our phones – which obviously never happened.'

He held it up higher, which reminded Millie of when she'd spotted Dean for the first time outside his house, phone in the air.

'You can get a connection sometimes, depending on which way the wind's blowing. There's never any pattern to it.' Guy nodded towards the rest of the house. 'The *Journal* paid for a cable to go in years ago – so I've got an internet connection –

but you'd have to use the computer. I never quite figured out Wi-Fi.'

Millie wasn't entirely surprised.

'Did you look up Liam Parris?' she asked.

A nod. 'No one came up who was directly connected to Whitecliff.'

The fire was crackling, making the hairs on Millie's arms tingle. From nowhere, she had a vague memory of being in a country pub sometime when she was a girl. There'd been a fire then, too. A Sunday roast with her parents, maybe? The thought twirled and danced in the fire and then crackled away.

'Why did they make you redundant?' she asked.

It was hard to know why she was suddenly interested, why the bitterness she felt so recently had disintegrated. Either way, Guy answered. 'Age, mainly. Back in the day, when the *Journal* was in its pomp, we had four reporters covering the town.'

Millie scoffed, without meaning to. 'Was there *really* enough news for that many of you? What did you do all day?'

'You'd be surprised, especially in the summer. The thing with decent reporters is that everyone's always working on something. If you send out four of us with blank notebooks, all four will come back with at least a story each. Send out eight and you'd get eight. There are always stories to tell.'

He tailed off momentarily and sipped his tea.

'Four became three, became two, became me.' The bitterness was back in his voice. 'All it means,' he added, 'is that people end up not having their stories told. The *Journal*'s still around – but it's put together by a team forty miles away. There's one poor girl who has to drive around fifteen towns and villages – and she's the only outside reporter. Those in the office copy and paste stuff from the council, or the police, or the Highways Agency. It's not *real* news. It's not telling people's stories...'

Millie let him stew for a moment as he sipped his tea again.

There was a rattle from somewhere deeper in the house, as if a wall was about to give into the elements and finally cave.

Guy didn't flinch.

'Is that why you started your site?' Millie asked.

A nod. 'They paid me off, so I got someone to design it. What else was I going to do? I basically carried on doing what I'd always been doing. I still know all the same people.' He nodded towards the phone on the wall. 'That number's not changed since they added a one to it in the eighties.'

Millie's only surprise was that it wasn't one of the *really* old phones with the rotary dial.

'I read your piece about fly-tipping,' she said, with something close to a laugh. 'I didn't think I'd ever reach the point in my life where I sat down and read hundreds of words about that sort of thing.'

Barry shuffled from his spot on the floor, edging towards Millie and rolling onto his back so she could rub his belly.

'On the paper, we got more letters about bin collections than anything else,' Guy said. 'People are *obsessed* with bins. When they swapped out everyone's old bins for the big wheelie ones, it was as close to a riot as this town ever got.'

Millie didn't know how to respond to that. Perhaps the test of a person's age was the moment they started caring about bins. Young people weren't arsed. Old people would burn down the town hall if a cleaning crew accidentally forgot to empty theirs.

'Did you hear about the attempted burglary?' Millie asked.

'The *Journal* will cover that. If it involves the police, or the other emergency services, I tend to leave it unless someone from the family specifically comes to me. I'm more interested in the stories not usually covered.'

'Like an imaginary panther?'

Millie grinned, though she hadn't really meant to, and Guy returned it. She sipped the tea and felt her teeth groaning again under the weight of the sweetness. He must have whacked at least four sugars into the small cup.

They sat in quiet for a minute or so, the only sounds the crackle of the fire and the creaking of the old house. Millie had another sip of her tea and then gave Barry a longer belly rub. There was something, well... *comforting* about it all. This man, who she'd thought of as an enemy, was some harmless old bloke with a shaggy dog and a borderline hoarding disorder. He'd once been her father's best friend.

And he *had* written that she wasn't involved. People had interpreted it their own way – because that's what people did. That wasn't entirely his fault.

Even though he'd known what the impact would be.

'I did look on your behalf,' Guy said. Millie almost jumped as it had been so quiet.

'Look for what?'

Guy motioned towards the room around them. 'My archives need a sort – but I went through as many papers as I could, looking for something more about Dean Parris. Or his brother.' He paused and then added: 'It seemed like you wanted to know.'

'Oh...'

It had somehow bypassed Millie quite how big a job it was to go through the papers littered around Guy's house. She'd only seen two rooms and the hallway, but she suspected the clutter was indicative of the rest.

'Two people saw someone fall then...?'

Guy's half-question looped Millie back to the reason she was there in the first place. It wasn't the sweet tea, or to rub Barry's belly. It wasn't even to gulp away the yawns brought on by the cosiness of the fire.

'Maybe they didn't talk,' Guy added. 'Did they get more details the same than different...?'

Millie nodded along. 'Almost identical.'

Guy scooped down from his chair and grabbed a metal prong, that he jabbed into the fire. The flames flared and roared as Millie felt the heat prickling harder.

When Guy moved away from the fire, he picked up one of the many notebooks that were lying around the kitchen and flipped through the pages. He took a pen from the draining board and drew a squiggle to get the ink moving, before writing something to himself.

That was all it took for Millie to realise that whatever was going on wasn't only on her any longer. What's more, there was a gratefulness that part of the burden had been lifted.

This was why she'd returned to his cottage.

'I once reported on a case where two cashiers were robbed at knifepoint,' Guy said. 'Happened during the summer years ago. One of them said the man had blue eyes, the other insisted they were brown. When the police caught the guy, his eyes were green. They'd both got a small thing wrong – but the big things were right. They knew he was a man, they picked up his accent, his jacket type and colour. They both noticed there was a hole in the back pocket of his jeans and that there was a tattoo on his knuckles.' Guy noted something on his pad. 'I suppose what I'm saying is that if two people independently think they saw a girl fall from a roof, I'd lean heavily towards them being right, even if the little things might be wrong...'

Millie had to turn away from Guy. She stared through the grimy window, out towards the bleakness of the weather, with the silver skies and the sideways slashes of rain. After everything from the past year, she couldn't quite describe what it meant to have someone actually listen to her. The fact she was relaying someone else's story didn't matter.

When she turned back, Guy was noting something more in his book. His pen made short, sharp scritchings and each line seemed to end with a flourish.

'What do we do now?' she asked. 'Dean lives alone and says

nobody fell. I asked a neighbour and they said Beth is grown up and is off at university. She said she'd waved her off when she went.'

A small smile crept across Guy's face. 'You asked a neighbour?'

'I couldn't think of another way to find out. I was careful. I—'

'This is why I invited you to meet my expert the other day. I *knew* you were a natural at this.'

Millie was confused: 'Natural at what?'

Guy held out his hands, indicating the house. 'Telling other people's stories. That's what proper reporting is. Everything got confused with the rush to find out what celebrities are up to but that's a different job. An easier job.'

Millie wanted to protest but didn't know what to say.

Police say their surviving daughter, Millicent Westlake, is not a suspect

Was that telling other people's stories?

Millie patted Barry's belly. When she looked up, a picture frame by the door caught her eye. She stood, rounding the table and heading off towards the doorway. She leaned in and peered at the faded photo behind the crusty glass of a frame. There was a man in a chocolate brown suit, with wide flares, standing next to a woman in a short, white minidress.

'Is that you?' Millie asked, turning between the photo and Guy.

'I can't fit in that dress now, if that's what you're asking.'

Millie laughed and it came naturally, without being forced. Like when she was with Jack and they were winding each other up.

'That's me and Carol,' Guy said. 'My wife...'

He trailed away, which gave Millie an answer she'd suspected. That unloved bowl of potpourri in Guy's study didn't seem the sort of thing he'd have bought himself.

She looked at the photo again, rubbing away a smudge of oily grease to get a better look. The man in the suit was clearly Guy now she could see properly. He had more hair when it had been taken, darker hair, too – but that knowing grin was the same.

'She had cancer,' Guy said suddenly. 'Died the day after they made me redundant. We didn't know she had it. She'd been complaining of headaches for a while but she said they were getting better. Afterwards, they said it was a tumour pressing on her brain. We went to bed that night and she never woke up.'

Millie's mouth was open but the words never came.

'It's OK,' Guy added quickly. 'I think it's the nicest way to go. Peaceful and painless, not knowing it's coming. If I got to choose, I think that would be the way.'

Millie still couldn't speak, though she also couldn't look at the photograph any longer. She stepped away, rounding the table once more and slotting back in next to Barry. She nuzzled her fingers under his chin and let him rub closer to her. His eyes didn't open the entire time.

Perhaps *that* was the sign of whether a person was old. It was nothing to do with bins, it was when a person started to worry about the circumstances of their own passing.

'Why weren't you ever around?' Millie asked.

Guy had been staring at the floor, lost in his own thoughts. Millie's question made him jolt as if he'd accidentally picked up something hot. 'How d'you mean?'

'You said you were Dad's best man and that you grew up together – but I never saw you. You were never at the house, never at birthday parties, or their anniversaries. If you were his best man, what happened?'

That got a sigh and, perhaps for the first time since he'd appeared on her doorstep, Guy *looked* like an old man. The lines around his eyes were deeper, the small blotches on his hands darker.

'Years ago, he wanted me to write a story for him,' Guy said. 'When I didn't, things were never the same. We weren't enemies. We still spoke when we ended up together at meetings, or events – but it was always professional after that.'

Millie finished her tea all in one. The liquid was warm enough to make her tongue tingle and the rest of her mouth squeaked from the sugar.

She almost didn't ask the follow-up – but then she did. 'What was the story...?'

Guy angled away, facing the fire. The dancing flames sent twinkling orange shapes flickering across his darkening features. 'I don't think that's really—'

'You can tell me. He's gone and he's not coming back.'

Millie watched Guy wince at that. It had sounded harsh but she'd meant it to.

Guy waited a moment and then started to nod.

'Your dad's boss at the TV station was having an affair with the weather girl,' he said. 'We'd met for a pint one night, which we did semi-regularly. Your dad told me that really matter-of-factly. Then he said I should write about it.'

Millie felt chills, despite the heat. It's what had happened to her, with a different man, years later.

'Why?' she asked.

'Because your dad wanted his boss's job. If his boss was pushed out because of the affair, he was next in line.'

Millie stared at the fire for a long time. She watched the orangey-black crackles around the base of a log. Watched the spitting embers. Felt her own fire swell.

When she next spoke, her words were broken. 'But you didn't write it?'

'No.'

'Why not?'

'Because it wasn't news, it was two adults doing consensual things. It would've been different if either of them had been on TV talking about their strong relationships, or family values, or condemning others for their infidelity. But it was none of that. They weren't hypocrites, they were two people in a relationship – and that's not news.'

Millie gulped. She'd waited a year for someone, *anyone*, to say something similar to her. Yes, she'd had an affair – but it wasn't quite that straightforward.

Guy suddenly sat straighter, purpose renewed. 'To answer how we find out what happened with that girl falling, we ask questions of our own.'

Millie needed a moment to realise that he was back to talking about the girl Ingrid had seen. 'But who do we ask?'

'That's our first job,' Guy replied. 'We find out if Dean has been single these past twenty years since his wife died. Have there been girlfriends? Fiancées? Boyfriends? Which university is his daughter at? Was she back visiting? We check the permits office and see if he applied for any sort of renovation permission on the attic. That could explain someone being on the roof. We ask as many questions as we can. If two people independently saw someone fall from his roof, and he says nobody did, then somebody's wrong, or somebody's lying. And who has more reason to lie? It's not a couple of residents in a nursing home.'

Guy stood and Barry also jumped to his feet. It was as if a rallying cry had been shouted and Millie felt something swelling in herself, too. She stood, mainly because everybody else was.

'What do we do first?' she asked.

'I'll keep checking the archives here,' Guy said. 'See if I can find anything from previous years about Dean, his brother, or his daughter. If it's all right with you, you should get onto Facebook, Google, and all that other stuff. You'll do that better than me.'

'Dean doesn't seem the Facebook type...'

'I agree – but perhaps someone from town put up a post about how they were going to the cinema with him? Or that they were off playing golf? That sort of thing. Maybe someone was asking for a handyman and someone recommended him? Or recommended *against* him? I'm sure there are hundreds of other things you can think of. Just because *he* might not be on something like Facebook, doesn't mean other people aren't mentioning him on there.'

Millie knew he hadn't meant to – but Guy had perfectly summed up her online experience from the past year. She was going to have to reactivate her Facebook account, even if only in a passive way. She'd also look to see if his business was pulling in reviews.

Millie began hunting around for her bag and her keys. For the first time in what felt like a long time, a *really* long time, she was energised.

'I'll let you know if I find something,' Millie said.

'I'll do the same.'

She was almost in the hall when Millie remembered the other thing she should tell Guy about. There was the shape in the road at the front of her house, a moment after she'd seen Dean drive off in his van. The dark, long, sleek cat-like creature. She waited for a moment, thinking about how best to phrase it. In the meantime, Guy was already rooting through a pile of newspapers as Barry hovered around his feet.

Guy looked up and realised he was being watched. He smiled, kindly, and she could see the energy in him, too.

'Anything else?' he asked.

Millie considered it – but she wasn't quite ready to trust him yet. Or, more to the point, she wasn't ready to let herself admit what she'd seen in the road a few nights before.

'No,' she replied.

TWENTY

Millie sat at her kitchen table with her laptop open. It was something which, in no other circumstance, would she have described as exciting.

Except it *was* exciting.

She would feel anticipation and enjoyment whenever it was her weekend to have Eric – but it wasn't the same. There was always that knowing twinge in the back of her mind, reminding her that the clock would be ticking until the time she had to give him back. Every time Eric laughed, every time he reached for her hand, or clung onto her, she'd have a wondrous few seconds before reminding herself that it wouldn't be long until he'd be leaving to head back to his dad's.

This was different.

Trying to find out what happened on the night Ingrid and Keith saw a woman pushed, jumped or fall from Dean's roof was offering Millie purpose she hadn't felt for a while.

But it was a struggle to find very much.

Google Maps had 'Dean The Handyman' listed as a business at his home address – but there wasn't much more offered than his mobile phone number. There was no website and no

extra photos. The nine reviews were all four- or five-stars, with
few details, other than that he'd done a good job fixing someone's fence. Then there was more good work helping someone
into their house after they'd locked themselves out.

It was all very normal, especially for a place like Whitecliff,
where word-of-mouth still trumped the internet. Where, for
much of the town, a mate of a mate was far more likely to fix a
leaking tap than someone who had a 4.9 rating on Google.

Millie reactivated her Facebook account, turned all the
privacy settings up as high as she could, ignored the notifica-
tions, and then went looking for Dean.

She had been right about one thing: Dean Parris was *not* a
Facebook sort of guy. Or, if he was, his profile was hidden or in
a different name. She couldn't find him in any of the other
obvious places online, either.

Guy's idea about a cinema trip or golfing was harder to
follow up than she'd thought. She checked the various social
media pages of the local cinema, plus the three golf courses in
the vicinity. She then scrolled through the pages of questions,
photos, and not-so-humble brags that people had posted.

No sign of Dean.

Without knowing what he was into, it was hard to know
what else to try.

Millie moved on, searching for 'Beth Parris', figuring a
young woman of twenty was more likely to have an online presence. Narrowing the results to Whitecliff threw up a *Journal*
story from twelve years before, when Beth had been eight, and
had won a competition to guess the number of pieces in a Lego
sculpture.

There was no byline, though Millie wondered if it had
been written by Guy. There was a photo of a man in an ill-
fitting suit, standing next to Beth. It had been taken in the
summer and she was in a vest and shorts, all elbows and
knees, with braces on her teeth. Beth was skinny and gangly

in only the way children could be. She was holding an enve-
lope and the article said she'd won a £50 voucher to spend at
the toy store in town. With great imagination, it was called
Whitecliff Toys. When Millie was Beth's age from the photograph, the shop had been her idea of heaven. It had been in
the same spot a little along from the pier for at least forty
years.

When Millie had been younger, it felt normal that everything was named after the town. Whenever she walked to
school, she'd pass shops like Whitecliff Hardware, Whitecliff
Shoes, Whitecliff Butchers and Whitecliff Bakery. It was only
as she got older that she realised it was something unique to the
town. Everywhere else had B&Qs, Clarks and Greggs. The
chains had invaded the town much later – but some places, like
the toy shop, were still going.

Millie looked at a smiling Beth, clutching that voucher, and
it was impossible not to see herself at the same age. If there had
been a competition to win a voucher for toys, her eight-year-old
self would have been desperate to win.

Millie was momentarily lost in her own nostalgia before she
remembered what she was supposed to be looking for.

There was nothing else in the online version of the *Journal*
about Beth Parris, nor anything on Facebook or the other social
media sites that was definitely Dean's daughter. There were a
couple of Beths in the UK that seemed to be the right age – but
none who had ever mentioned Whitecliff and nobody with a
photo of Dean.

Millie could feel her excitement fading. She'd felt so sure
that an internet deep dive would give her something.

But then she'd also read something recently about more and
more young people going dark on social media. That followed
from stories about those slightly older losing jobs or opportuni-
ties because of silly things posted when they were little more
than children.

If Dean's daughter had hidden all her accounts, assuming she had them to begin with, it was probably a sensible move.

But it didn't help Millie in her attempts to spy on the family.

She tried Dean+Parris+Whitecliff+wife – but there was nothing online about her death during childbirth. Millie couldn't even find digital versions of the articles Guy had found in his mounds of newspapers. No wonder he'd called his clutter 'the archives'. He likely had a more rounded history of Whitecliff's last four decades than anyone.

It was warm in Millie's kitchen and she opened the window a crack, despite the cold outside. She checked her phone for messages, before remembering that Guy was the sort who called instead of texted, despite the Blackberry he carried.

Millie turned back to her laptop. With little luck on social media, she figured she might as well go broad, so typed Dean+Whitecliff into Google. There was a place named Whitecliff in New Zealand, another in Australia, and at least four in Canada. That was the least of her issues – because nine of the top ten hits was about a Canadian man named Dean Whitecliff who had fallen through an open manhole cover and needed to be rescued by the fire brigade. The other link was to Dean's Google reviews, which she had already seen.

There were so many articles about the manhole man that Millie almost missed the thing she was looking for.

Gino's was a restaurant in Whitecliff to which Millie had never been. It was the sort of place that would dump a pair of scallops on a plate and charge twenty quid. Where chips would be called something like 'chunkily sliced locally sourced potatoes, lightly dusted with sea salt'. They'd cost eight quid and there would be six of them.

It only existed because of foodie tourists, who stuck to the upper part of the High Street, well away from the pier and the surrounding pubs and chip shops.

Millie had already scrolled past the TripAdvisor link to Gino's when she wondered why it had appeared among the pages of articles ridiculing manhole cover man. She went back and clicked, then did a lot more scrolling.

There were acres of gushing over-the-top reviews about how Gino's offered the best fish. The reviewers probably didn't know, or care, they were getting it from the same morning market as everyone else.

She was on the third page of reviews when Millie realised she was holding her breath.

My partner and I went out for a romantic meal for his birthday and, having never visited Gino's, we thought it might be nice to try. I can only say that all the five-star reviews must have been written by family members because it was the worst restaurant I've ever visited.

Due to a mix-up at their end, we had a 20-minute wait to sit, despite arriving on time. We then had to wait 20 minutes for the waiter to take our drinks order, and another 20 minutes for our food. By the time our food arrived, we'd already been in the place for almost 90 minutes. If the food had been good, it might have been OK but it was awful and overpriced. My boyfriend, Dean, is a patient man but even he'd had enough by the end.

To top it all, the cloakroom lost my coat.

Avoid at all costs, unless you hate your coat and love over-paying for steak and chips. I'd give zero stars but one is apparently the minimum.

One star, **Judy Huish**

Millie read the review twice, as well as the restaurant's reply underneath, which denied everything and queried whether she'd ever actually visited.

Millie knew precisely who Judy Huish was. She was one of

the Whitecliff lifers. Long after climate change would have finished ravaging the planet, a Huish would still be living in Whitecliff.

Not that Millie could scoff too much at such a thing. There'd been a Westlake in town long before her great-grandfather and she herself wasn't showing any signs of moving.

Judy Huish ran the bed and breakfast on the hill that was on the way towards Guy's cottage. It was part of the final row of shops, cafés and B&Bs before the High Street ended and the fields began.

Unlike Dean, it was easy to find Judy on social media. She ran a Facebook page for her B&B, which linked to her personal account, none of which appeared to have anything in the way of privacy controls.

There were half a dozen photos of orangey sunsets with things like 'Wish You Were Here!' written underneath, plus one of a coffee pot with 'Coffee first, talk later!' Millie kept scrolling, past the Wine o'clock image, past the Gin o'clock image. She kept going past the ones of overcooked breakfasts until she found one of a large picnic bench being fitted at the front of the B&B. Judy had captioned it 'Eat under the stars!' – but that wasn't what had caught Millie's eye.

The thrill was back because the person bolting the bench into the ground had the same chubby sausage fingers that had squeezed hers when they were outside his house. He was crouched in one photo but standing in the next – and there was no question who he was.

It was Dean Parris.

TWENTY-ONE

It was almost dusk as Millie parked a few doors down from Judy's bed and breakfast. The Peruvian café was pumping sweet and salty meaty smells onto the street in what felt like the ultimate piece of marketing. Millie's mouth watered as she walked past the café, then the small card and gift shop that was closed. Millie wasn't sure she'd ever seen it open.

She pulled her hat down over her ears and straightened the reading glasses she'd worn more in the past couple of days than the year beforehand.

The vacancies board at the front of the B&B had a small slider, which had been pulled back to display 'available'. There were lights on inside as Millie opened the gate, passed the now familiar picnic table, and headed for the door. She rang the bell and waited until there was a sound of someone coming down steps inside.

Millie told herself she was here because Dean had come looking for her. That initial meet on his doorstep could have been the end. She'd asked an innocent question on Ingrid's behalf – but then he'd shown up at the nursing home. Plus, she was sure it was his van that had been parked outside her house. *He* was the one who'd made things strange.

Judy couldn't have been much more than five foot. She was wearing fluffy boots with thick tights, a knee skirt, and a huge woolly cardigan that hung past her thighs. She looked up curiously towards Millie, likely trying to place her.

'Can I help?' she asked.

Millie half-turned and pointed towards the pair of picnic benches at the front. 'I was walking past when I saw the benches. I've been looking for something similar for my back garden and wondered where you bought them...?'

Her breath spiralled up and away in the cold night as Millie realised her chest was thundering. Part of it was wondering if Judy would see through her minimal disguise – but it was more because she wasn't used to winging things in such a way. She was a planner, not a seat-of-the-pantser. Something had changed in the previous few days.

Judy craned in, looking past Millie towards the benches, as if she didn't know what was being asked. 'I didn't buy them,' she said. There was a hint of Scottish in her accent. 'They were made for me.'

'Oh...' Millie milked the moment, turning back to the benches, then Judy again. She'd spent more time thinking about woodwork in the previous minute than she had the rest of her life. 'Was it someone local? I might see if I can give them a call.'

Millie half-expected to be turned away as some sort of nutter; if not that then Judy would recognise her and send her packing anyway.

Instead, Judy stepped to the side and waved Millie inside. 'Let's get out of the cold,' she said, while rubbing her hands together.

Judy closed the door and then headed across to a desk next to the stairs. She muttered something about 'having a card somewhere' and then began hunting through drawers on the other side. They were in a small reception, with a rack of brochures and guidebooks off to one side and a long list of 'house rules' pinned to the wall above the counter. A radiator on the wall blazed hot and Millie reached her hands towards it until Judy grunted her way up from behind the desk.

She offered a business card, which Millie took. 'I knew I had one somewhere,' Judy said. 'He lives in town.'

The card had Dean's name printed on the front, along with 'handyman', then a mobile number and an email address.

'Is he good?' Millie asked.

'He's great at what he does. It says handyman but he does carpentry and he changed a couple of locks for me. I can't say a negative thing about his *work*.'

The emphasis on the final word was impossible to miss, even if Millie hadn't been searching for an opening.

'Sounds like you have negative things to say away from his work...?'

It was undeniably fishing – but Judy didn't need asking twice. It felt as if she'd been waiting for such an opportunity. Either that, or steering any possible conversation around to the same thing. 'You could say that!' She pushed herself up to her full height and then tugged at the cardigan, which had slipped from one of her shoulders. If she'd had a cushion, she'd have plumped it up, ready for story time. 'We went out for a while,' Judy said. 'Lasted about five months.'

'I hope he gave you a discount on the bench.'

Judy howled at that. She laughed for so long that she finished the cup of tea she'd been drinking to clear her throat. 'He got paid in other ways,' he said. 'Don't you worry about that.'

Millie had to fight hard not to cringe. She wanted information but not *that much* information.

'Sorry,' Millie replied, wanting to move on. 'It's none of my business but I got screwed over by someone who was supposed to pave my driveway a couple of years back. Took the money and dumped a load of tarmac – and that was it. I had to pay someone else to do it properly.'

'Dean's not like that,' Judy replied. 'He's got other issues – but he'll do a good job if you want him to build you something.'

'Not such a good boyfriend, though...?'

Millie thought for a moment that she'd gone too far. Judy was pulling at her cardigan once more.

'Are you married?' Judy asked.

'Not any longer...'

Judy didn't react, not in any physical way, but something had changed and it felt as if that had been the correct answer.

'So was I,' Judy replied. 'So was he. We were both widowed. Had been for years. Dean came over and helped fix the guttering after that storm we had the year before last. We ended up chatting and then went out a few times. I can't even remember who asked who. He did a few more little jobs around here, ahead of the season, plus he built those benches. I thought we were going somewhere but then...'

She tailed off, staring towards the window behind Millie and the night beyond.

'He ended it?' Millie asked.

A blink and Judy was back in the room. 'I did. Things got a bit... weird.' The sentence slipped away once more before Judy stopped and scanned Millie. 'Sorry, I feel like I know you but I can't place you. Do I know your parents?'

Millie took a breath and realised there was little point in lying. 'David and Karen Westlake,' she said.

The effect was instant. Judy staggered backwards half a step, as if she'd been pushed. She clasped the counter and then gently shook her head. 'Oh... um...' The moment was gone as Judy started fussing with the papers on the desk, before turning to look up at the stairs. 'Sorry. It was good to talk but there's a room that's not been cleaned yet and, um...'

Judy moved towards the door and had a hand on the latch when Millie decided to go for it. 'Do you think it's OK to call Dean?' she asked.

The reply was brusque and sharp. 'It's fine. He'll do a good job. Don't bother mentioning me, though.' She opened the door and a gust of sharp air poured inside making them both shiver. 'I've got to get back,' Judy repeated, which was a polite way of saying 'sod off'.

Millie didn't bother waiting to be told again. She stepped around Judy and hopped across the step, before continuing past the tables, on the way back to her car. There was one question she'd not managed to ask, though she didn't think she'd have got a proper answer anyway.

When Judy was talking about Dean, what exactly did she mean by 'weird'...?

TWENTY-TWO

As soon as Millie stepped back into her house, it felt as if something was wrong. It wasn't the eerie silence, because it was always like that. The estate where her parents lived, where *she* lived, was *so* soundless that the quiet itself had its own tinnitus. She would sometimes talk to the house, asking where something had been left, or if she'd forgotten to turn something off. Until around ten months before, she had always lived with people – and, despite the time that had passed, she still wasn't used to being by herself.

She was used to it now.

'What's wrong?' Millie asked. Her voice echoed along the empty hall, past the rectangles on the wall where photos of her parents had once been.

There was no answer, obviously, and yet Millie felt a chill as she edged along the hall, past the stairs, and into the kitchen.

The window was open.

Millie relaxed. She vaguely remembered opening it earlier, when she'd been at the kitchen table with her laptop and it was warm. Something *was* wrong at the house but it was nothing major.

She crossed the kitchen and leant across the draining board to pull the window closed. Her fingers bristled momentarily from the chill but then she locked the window and everything was well again.

Or was it?

There was another memory, vaguer than the first, of her *closing* the window before she left to visit Judy. It was the chill on her fingers that triggered the thought... unless that had been another day when she'd opened and then closed the window.

She couldn't remember – except that sense of unease was back.

Millie opened the door to the living room and switched on the lights. The first thing she saw, as always, was the gaps on the walls where her parents' photos used to be. Other than that, everything was as she'd left it. The TV was in the far corner, with all the seats pointing towards it. The jacket she wore if it was *really* cold was still dumped over one of the chairs, along with a scarf. Everything was normal.

It wasn't the first time Millie had felt such a strong sense of oddness when arriving back at the house. She always put it down to living alone in the house in which she'd grown up. She once mentioned it to Jack, and he blamed it on ghosts, before realising what he was implying about her parents and stopping himself.

The paranormal was one of his things. There were at least three books on his toilet cistern about various supernatural sightings in the area. Residents did occasionally pass at the nursing home and, perhaps as his way of coping, Jack would blame strange happenings around the place on ghosts. It was either that, or he'd have to admit he'd lost his own pen, she supposed.

Jack had once met her in the smoking area and asked if there were bags under his eyes. He was convinced his tired appearance was down to the presence of a ghost interfering with the mirror in the men's bathroom.

Millie moved back into the hall, with ghosts on her mind. It couldn't be any worse than Guy's panther. Everyone around her was mad.

She moved onto the first step and told the house she needed different friends in her life, before silently admitting to herself that there wasn't a queue of candidates.

It was as she rounded the banister, about to take the second half of the stairs, that a spinning blue burst through the rippled glass of the front door. Spinning, strobing lights bounced up and around the walls, like a disco ball with a very precise taste in colour.

Millie was frozen for a second but then she moved quickly, hurrying back downstairs and into the living room. She watched through the window as a second police car followed a first onto her driveway. There were no sirens but the whirring lights fizzed silent fireworks into every corner of the house.

The doorbell sounded and then there was a shape of someone at the window, silhouetted against the blue. There was a woman's voice – 'Can you open the door?' – as Millie realised whoever it was could see her through the glass.

It had been ten months since police had turned up at the house. There'd been an ambulance then as well. Millie had long wondered if they'd be back.

And now... they were.

She edged away from the living room, into the hall, where the spinning blue strobe had now stopped. It was dark inside but the security light was on again outside, casting shadows across a couple of figures on the front step.

Millie waited on the other side of the door. 'What's going on?' she asked.

A man's voice sounded through the glass: 'We've had reports of a disturbance at this address.'

It took Millie a moment to process what he'd said. 'Disturbance? There's only me here.'

'What's your name?'

'Millie.'

'Who else lives here, Millie?'

'Just me.'

The shadows shuffled, possibly turning to face each other. It was hard to tell. 'Is anyone inside with you?' the man asked.

'I told you – it's just me.'

'Can you open the door, Millie?'

She didn't like the way he was saying her name. It was the way she spoke to Eric sometimes, when he wasn't doing what he was told.

'Have you got ID?'

There was more shuffling and then some sort of card was pressed to the door. Because the glass was rippled, Millie couldn't easily see what was on it. There was definitely a logo that looked like some sort of seal, and then the word 'police' in large white letters on a blue background. She couldn't make out the number or name that was next to the fuzzy photo but already knew the officers would be genuine. People could forge IDs but they weren't faking a pair of marked police cars.

'We just want to make sure you're OK,' a woman's voice said.

'I'm fine.'

'Once we've made sure that's true, we'll be on our way.'

Millie thought of Jack and the casual way he'd wanted to call the police, as if that would solve all problems. Had he called them anyway and sent them to her house? It didn't feel like something he'd do.

Millie unlocked the door and levered it open enough so that she could see outside. As well as the two officers at the door, there were two more a little further back, standing next to the second car. Four police officers felt like a *lot* for both Whitecliff, and whatever this was. Millie felt the hairs on the back of her neck lift.

She took a moment to take in the pair closer to her. Both were in uniform and holding their hats. The woman was younger than she was by a few years, with a tight bun clamped to her head. The man was a little older and seemed vaguely familiar, as if he might have been in the year or two above her at school. Given everyone in town went to the same place, it was possible. Perhaps even likely.

'There isn't a disturbance,' Millie said, mainly talking to the woman.

'What's your last name, Millie?' she replied.

The woman likely knew but Millie played along anyway. 'Westlake.'

'Can we come in, Millie? We just want to make sure everything's fine and then we can leave you.'

'Everything *is* fine. It's only me here.'

The officer nodded, although it didn't feel as if she was listening. 'Like I said, if you let us in, we can verify that.'

Millie knew there wasn't a lot she could do. There was nothing to hide and yet she'd had enough of the police trampling around and asking questions after her parents had died. Guy might have written that the police said she wasn't a suspect – but it didn't feel like that at the time. They had sat in the living room on two occasions and asked the same questions over and over as if she *was* suspected of something. Someone had taken photos from the street and put them online. Along with Guy writing that she *wasn't* a suspect, there were dozens of photos of officers heading in and out of the house, making it look like she might be.

'We'll be quick,' the woman said.

'Who told you there was a disturbance?' Millie asked.

The two officers exchanged a brief glance but there was no answer.

'Like I said, if you let us in, we'll be as fast as we can.'

Millie considered closing the door, although she knew there would be consequences if she did. Perhaps they'd kick it through, or maybe they'd go away and get a warrant, before *really* turning the house over.

She didn't want that – and there was nothing to hide anyway.

Millie pulled the door inwards and stepped aside, hovering in the frame as the two officers went past her. The other pair waited by the second car as Millie closed the door to keep out the cold.

'Is there anywhere in particular we should look, Millie?' the woman said.

'What do you mean? I told you, there is no disturbance. It's only me here.'

That got a nod, although Millie wasn't certain the officer believed her.

There was something unspoken between the pair and then the man headed for the stairs. His heavy boots clumped up as he called 'Is anyone here?' to the empty house.

'There's really nobody here,' Millie told the female officer, which got only a narrow-lipped smile.

As doors opened and closed upstairs, the other officer poked her head into the nearest cupboard and turned on the lights. When it was obvious there was nothing more than a few coats and a giant pack of toilet rolls from the cash and carry, she closed it again, and headed into the kitchen with Millie. More doors opened upstairs and the man's voice called to ask if anyone was around. Meanwhile, the female officer checked the living room and the small pantry area at the back of the kitchen.

There was momentary quiet upstairs as Millie leant awkwardly against the sink. 'What's going on?' she asked.

The officer was back from her mini tour of the downstairs,

though stood in the doorway into the hall. Millie wondered if she was doing it deliberately to block her in.

'Just doing our checks,' she said.

'If someone called to say there was a disturbance, isn't it a bigger worry that someone's wasting your time?'

The woman smiled with those narrow lips again. It was like a mother placating a child showing her the eleventh rubbish drawing of a rainbow he'd done. *Yes, darling, that's lovely.*

Millie waited.

The footsteps had gone silent upstairs and the man was no longer calling out to anyone who might be in the house. The female officer was avoiding eye contact as if they were in a bar and Millie was some sweaty guy wearing a fedora.

Something still felt off. It had ever since Millie had arrived home. The more she thought about it, the more she was certain she knew the officer who'd gone upstairs. It was the side profile as he'd turned in the hallway. Something about the way his ears stuck out on both sides.

There were footsteps on the stairs getting closer until the man emerged in the hall. Millie couldn't see him properly as the other officer was standing in the way. She turned to face her colleague and, Millie caught what sounded like, 'What is it, Lee?' before she got a mumbled, hushed reply.

Millie knew it was something bad. In the past year or so, since people started recognising her, Millie had a sense for when things weren't right. As soon as she'd seen that boy in the supermarket, she knew why he was there and what he was going to ask. She'd known with other people at other times. That woman with the pram who had shunted it into Millie's ankles and called her a disgrace. The old man who had followed her along the High Street and didn't stop until she was in her car, with the doors locked.

It was a new sense she'd developed across the months – and she was sensing something now.

The female officer suddenly moved further into the hall, past her colleague and towards the front door.

'What's happening?' Millie asked, but there was no answer.

The man took his colleague's place in the doorway, blocking the way, as cold air gushed into the house.

Moments later, the woman was back – along with the other two officers who'd been waiting outside. The trio went upstairs together as Millie shuffled around, trying to see past the officer at what might be going on. He wasn't for moving and, given he took up much of the doorway, Millie had few options.

There was something about his ears, though. It was like he'd played a lot of rugby in his younger days, or perhaps been a boxer. Except, Millie felt she'd seen something like them before.

It wasn't long until three sets of feet made their way back downstairs. The man stepped aside and then her kitchen suddenly felt very crowded as all four of the officers burst through, one after the other, until she was hemmed in next to her sink.

The woman who'd been waiting with Millie before was clutching a large, transparent bag that she held up. 'Do you recognise this?' she asked.

Millie couldn't figure out what was inside the bag at first. It was long and metal, with prongs on one end and a hook on the other. There was some sort of smeared white on it. Paint, or something like that.

'Is that a crowbar?' she asked.

'Do you recognise it?'

'Why would I have a crowbar?'

'Is it yours?' the woman asked.

'No.' Millie felt four sets of eyes on her as she slowly realised what was happening. She pointed towards the front of the house. 'Dad had some tools in the garage but I've not done anything with them. I don't even park in there half the time...'

'Are you saying this *could* be your crowbar?'

Millie looked from the bag to the woman and back again. 'It's obviously not *mine*. It *might* be my dad's. You can check the garage if you want – but I don't know what was already in there...'

'Why was this in the cupboard at the top of your stairs?' the woman asked.

Millie could feel something creeping up her back. She scratched but it wouldn't go away.

'What are you on about?' she replied, although she could see in the woman's eyes that her denials were meaningless. It wasn't the first time Millie felt she wasn't being listened to.

The man who'd first gone up the stairs stepped forward, unclipping the handcuffs from his belt as he did so. He spoke at the same time, everything happening together as the room started to swirl.

'Millie Westlake, I'm arresting you for burglary. You do not have to say anything...'

Millie didn't hear the rest. There was the snap of the handcuff on her wrist but she wasn't even focused on that. Instead, she remembered where she'd seen those ears before.

The woman hadn't asked 'What is it, Lee?' when she was standing in the doorway, she'd asked 'What is it, *Liam*?'.

The man handcuffing Millie, the police officer, was Liam Parris. Millie had first seen those same ears when she was talking to his brother, Dean.

TWENTY-THREE

Everything was a whirlwind as Millie was hustled into one of the waiting police cars and then driven through the streets of Whitecliff. It all seemed to happen in flashes. There were the lights of the seafront and the shops, then the dark of the country lanes, then more light. Two of the officers, though not Liam, were in the front seat were chatting about the takeaway they'd get after shift. Someone mentioned a daughter and the hair straighteners she wanted for Christmas. Then the car stopped and Millie was being helped into a new building, into the police station, where someone said something about her rights and took away her keys and phone.

Then she was in a room with someone she was told was her solicitor. The *duty* solicitor, who was covering that night. Millie couldn't remember what they spoke about, she only remembered how dry her mouth was and how bright the lights were.

And then there was another room. The interview room, someone had called it. There was a camera in the top corner recording everything, and she was on one side of a table with two officers on the other. These were different than those who'd been at her house. They were in suits, instead of uniform.

Detectives, not regular officers. Two women: Burns was older, with greying short hair; the other officer was probably younger than Millie with tight black curls – and Millie instantly forgot her name.

Liam wasn't there.

The crowbar in the bag had gone – but a photo of it was on the table and Burns was pointing at it. 'Is this yours?' she asked.

'I told you it isn't. I said that at the house.'

'How do you explain it appearing in your cupboard?'

Millie looked to the solicitor, who was sitting with his knees crossed and a pad in his hand. He said nothing and Millie felt blank.

'I have no idea,' she replied.

Burglary.

They'd said something about burglary back at the house – and again when Millie had arrived at the station. It must be the one she had heard about at the nursing home that morning. The cook had said someone's dad had chased the burglar out of the house. She had thought it was an *attempted* burglary but perhaps she hadn't been listening properly.

More to the point, the police apparently thought that person was *her*.

'It's been sent away for testing,' Burns said. 'But the colour of the paint on the crowbar is similar to that on the window frame of a house that was broken into last night.'

Millie had no idea what to say – but, luckily, her solicitor shifted in his seat.

'Is there a question in there?' he said. When there was no immediate answer, he continued. 'You've already been told that Ms Westlake has no idea how the tool appeared in her house. She says she invited you to check the garage, where her father used to keep his tools. Even if there is, or is not, a crowbar there, it still doesn't belong to her.'

Burns didn't bother to acknowledge that the solicitor had

spoken – and she certainly didn't turn to look at him. 'Where were you last night?' she asked.

'At home,' Millie replied. 'In bed.'

'By yourself?'

'That's none of your business – but yes.'

'So nobody can attest that you were in bed...?'

'I've had a soft toy frog since I was about ten. He's on the bedroom windowsill, so you can ask him if you want.'

Millie felt the solicitor tense at her side. He'd *definitely* said something about answering the questions concisely and not elaborating unless asked. Technically, he hadn't got onto the subject of snarkiness.

Not that it got anything in the way of a reaction.

'We dusted for fingerprints at the site of the burglary,' Burns said. 'What do you think will happen if they come back as yours?'

'I'd think there's somebody walking around with identical fingerprints to me, because I was asleep last night.'

'What if it's your fingerprints on the crowbar?'

Millie laughed, surprising herself. She'd gone from bemusement to outright annoyance. She held up her hands. 'Look at me. Do you really think I'm going around using crowbars to break into places? I doubt I could lift it properly, let alone do anything with it.'

There was a muffled 'shush' from her side, that Millie realised had come from the solicitor. This was definitely in the realms of 'elaborating'.

This time, Millie's annoyance did get something of a reaction. Burns raised a single eyebrow, which was the most emotion she'd shown since sitting at the table. They must have thought the same thing themselves. Millie wasn't petite as such – but she also wasn't athletic, or brawny up top.

'If it's not your crowbar,' Burns said, 'how did it get into your cupboard?'

It was the one question Millie had anticipated, because she'd been asking it of herself. 'I left the kitchen window open when I went out,' she sad.

'Are you saying somebody broke *into* your house and left the crowbar?'

'I'm saying I don't know. I do know *I* didn't leave it there. I know it's not mine.'

There was a short silence that Millie almost broke by asking if the officer who arrested her was Liam Parris. Perhaps she would have done if it wasn't for the way the solicitor was tapping his toe. She could hear his thoughts. His annoyance. *Don't elaborate.* And so she didn't.

'Why would someone break into your house and leave a crowbar?' Burns asked.

'Why would someone call the police to report a disturbance at my house when I'm the only person who lives there?'

It felt good to be asking questions, even though Millie received no answer. There was a momentary flicker of Burns' eyes in the direction of her colleague, as if they'd spoken about the exact same thing.

'It was an anonymous tip-off, wasn't it?' Millie added. 'You don't know who reported a disturbance.'

The solicitor's toe was bouncing on the floor like a tap-dancer about to leap onto the stage at the Palladium. Millie could sense his silent shouts, telling her to shut up. Or, perhaps that was her own monologue?

But something *had* changed.

Out of nowhere, Burns said she was ending the interview. Both officers stood abruptly and the one whose name Millie couldn't remember said something about being right back. The pair strode to the door and then, almost as quickly as they arrived, they were gone.

The door was barely closed when the solicitor leaned in towards Millie. 'What was it I said about elaboration?'

'Not to do it.'

'Hmm.'

He pressed back in his seat and Millie almost laughed, despite the situation.

'They can't really believe I broke into a house, can they?' she asked.

'It's hard to know. I will say that, in all the years I've been doing this, I've never known someone who looks like you being arrested for burglary.'

Millie wasn't quite sure what he meant by that. Presumably, white, female and middle-class. 'Is that a good thing?' she asked.

'That's hard to know, too.'

'Do you think they know who called to report a disturbance?'

The solicitor uncrossed his knees. A little like Burns, he was another whose expression appeared fixed. There was something permanently weary about him and she could imagine him offering the same droopy-eyed reaction to winning the EuroMillions as he did to finding out he'd run out of Rice Krispies.

'I suspect finding out who made that call is almost as high a priority as getting the crowbar tested for fingerprints.'

'I never touched it,' Millie said. 'I've never even seen it. There's no way my prints can be on it...'

The solicitor didn't reply and she wondered whether he believed her. Whether it mattered.

She thought about telling him about visiting Dean and then finding out he had a brother who she was pretty sure had arrested her. She wondered if he'd believe that and if he'd be able to do anything. Whether there was anything to do.

Millie didn't get the chance because the door opened and the officer with the tight curls was back.

'You can go,' she said. 'You'll get bailed at the front.'

The solicitor stood and packed his notepad into his satchel

with a resigned sigh as if he'd known this was the likely outcome.

Millie found herself standing and looking for her phone, before remembering it had been taken when she'd been booked in.

'This way,' the solicitor said, as he rounded the table. The officer held open the door before the solicitor led Millie through a maze of corridors. They were soon in the same reception area in which Millie had given up her keys and phone.

There was a man in uniform behind the counter who was talking to her – except Millie wasn't focused on him. In the area behind reception, leaning back on an office chair, hands behind his head, was another uniformed officer. His feet were on a desk and he was turned, facing Millie, almost daring her to look.

And she did look – directly into Liam Parris's eyes as his lips curled into the merest hint of a smirk.

TWENTY-FOUR

It was daylight when Millie awoke the next morning. She'd slept in her bed, with the curtains open, not waking once. Her arm was pins and needles from an apparent lack of movement, and her neck was stiff from the pillow that was too soft. It was the first time Millie had slept fully through the night since moving back in with her parents.

She wobbled herself into a sitting position, which wasn't easy with a limp arm that felt as if someone was stabbing it. Her fingers were moving, although they didn't feel like hers – and she watched, enjoying the sensation until she realised she was cold.

Millie wasn't entirely sure why it had taken *this* to make her sleep. If anything, she should have been up all night, worrying and wondering. Regardless of what the police thought, someone had broken into the house to leave the crowbar. They'd picked a good place with the upstairs cupboard. The sort of spot she might use once or twice a week, but was unlikely to check every day.

When she'd got home from the station, Millie had double-checked all the locks before going to bed – and yet it hadn't occurred to her that she could, or *should* be worried. It was all a bit strange – and something she couldn't explain, even to herself.

Millie gathered the quilt and wrapped it around her shoulders as her phone lit up at the side of the bed. She picked it up, to see nine missed calls and forty-nine WhatsApp messages from Alex. She scrolled backwards, to five in the morning, when the messages had begun with a simple 'Everything OK?' Then: 'I heard the police came by'.

The tone started to shift as the messages continued.

Mill?

Shall I come round?

Are you OK?

What happened?

Are you home?

I can come over

The messages continued from there, with varying degrees of politeness, intrigue, and outright nosiness. The most recent message had been sent two minutes before.

Were you arrested?

Millie almost laughed at the speed news raced around Whitecliff. It wasn't even eight in the morning and people knew what had happened the evening before. She suspected neighbours had taken photos of the police cars on her drive and put them up on Facebook. There would be captions like 'Anyone

know what's going on?' underneath – and then endless speculation.

People would have put two and two together, of course.
Being Whitecliff, they'd have made seven. Many would have
assumed the police were there because of something relating to
the death of Millie's parents. If locals didn't think she killed
them before, there was a pretty good chance they would now.

Millie almost ignored Alex's messages, knowing he'd tell
Rachel whatever she told him. If Rachel knew, then everyone
would know.

Except, she couldn't ignore her ex-husband because it
wasn't about him. It was about Eric. If he heard something, he'd
worry about his mum being arrested. Even if he didn't, Alex
would be wary of letting their son spend any time with Millie if
she was in trouble with the authorities.

'It's   fine,'   she   messaged,   before   adding: 'A
misunderstanding.'

Alex's reply was back almost before she'd finished typing.

> Were you arrested?

Millie wasn't sure how best to answer. She *had* been
arrested – but she didn't particularly want Alex knowing that.
Not yet, anyway. She certainly didn't want him knowing she
was on bail.

After a few seconds of thinking about it, she swiped backwards from the thread and instead loaded Jack's messages.

> Ru OK? Rish says u were arrested?

Millie replied with three words – 'Misunderstanding. All
good' – but Jack wasn't having any of that.

> Want me to come over? I'm working til 2 but
> after that?

Millie told him that she was fine and that they'd catch up at some point, before sending three more messages in response to Jack's variations on 'Are you sure?'

There was a message from a number not in Millie's address book that she almost ignored – except it was an enquiry from someone asking if she did same-day grooming as an emergency.

She almost replied that she couldn't but then figured she had nothing better to do around the house. It would be a bit of money, and possibly a new customer, which was never a bad thing. Millie replied, asking for details about the breed, size, and time – and, within minutes, she had an appointment set up for two in the afternoon. It was a strange sense of normality among the madness of the previous evening.

Millie headed downstairs as her phone vibrated in her hand. She ignored whoever it was and yawned her way into the kitchen. If the police *had* done a proper search of the house the night before, they'd either been very tidy about it, or confined themselves to the garage.

She filled a glass from the tap and ambled into the living room, sipping as she fought away the yawns. Millie moved towards the front window. She stared out towards where the police cars had been the night before, where the spinning blue lights had filled the house. It felt dreamlike, as if it had happened to somebody else.

Millie was about to flop into the armchair when she noticed the bird table at the side of the driveway. Her mother had got someone to install it at some point years ago and then, as far as Millie knew, left it without ever bothering to put seed on top. It was more an ornament than anything else. It was now leaning crookedly to the side, suspiciously close to where the second police car had parked the night before.

Still wearing her slippers, Millie headed out to the front of the house, where she inspected the tyre tracks at the edge of the flowerbeds. The mud was unavoidable as she rocked the bird table back into position. She leant on it, squishing it back into the softened ground, where it more or less remained straight.

That's when she realised she was being watched. There was a woman standing at the end of the drive, peering over her glasses in Millie's direction. She was wearing a coat that was bigger than she was, the sort of thing that meant a person was forced to waddle, rather than walk.

Millie couldn't remember the woman's name but knew she lived towards the end of the road. It was in a house that was far too big for one person... not that Millie could talk.

The woman cleared her throat and Millie felt that too-familiar sense that something was about to happen.

'Your mum and dad would be ashamed,' the woman called. She was stuttery yet forceful, with an *in my day*-vibe about her. Give it a minute and she'd be banging on about the war of which she was too young to have been a part.

Millie ignored her and continued straightening the bird table, even though she knew she'd need some sort of mallet to do it properly.

'I know you can hear me,' the woman called. 'I don't know why you stuck around.'

Millie stopped. She straightened and turned very deliberately before striding across the driveway towards the woman. The paving slabs were cold through her slippers and she quickened her pace as she advanced.

'Mind your own business, you old hag.'

The woman started to stumble over something else – but Millie was almost upon her.

'I'll tell you why I stuck around,' Millie said. 'Because this is *my* house. It's not my mum's, it's not my dad's, it's *mine*. Now, how about you turn around and put that new hip to use by sodding off back to wherever you came from.'

The woman stood open-mouthed, her tiny head poking out from the giant coat like a cherry on a barrel.

'Get going, or I'll roll you home,' Millie said.

That was enough for the woman to move backwards and then turn. She huffed and then hurried along the street. It was a guess that she had a new hip. If she did, she was getting her money's worth off the NHS, given the speed at which she was moving.

Millie stood and watched her go, folding her arms across her front as her breath billowed into the greying skies. She was about to turn back to the house when she realised she was *still* being watched.

This time, it wasn't an old woman.

Guy's piece of junk Volvo was across the street, the driver's window down, Barry bouncing around in the passenger seat. Upon realising Millie had seen him, the dog leapt onto Guy's lap and stuck his head out the window, panting for attention.

'How long have you been parked there?' Millie asked, as she reached Guy's window.

'You asking me or Barry?'

Millie nuzzled the dog's nose as he enthusiastically licked her palm.

'We've not been here long,' Guy added. 'I heard you had a bit of an incident overnight. Figured we'd come check on you.'

Millie withdrew her hand as Guy and Barry wrestled over who got the driver's seat. Before long, the dog reluctantly accepted he was supposed to be on the other side. He stumbled across the handbrake and then plopped in the chair, angling his head up to show Millie his huge, dejected-looking eyes. The blackmailing furball had her – and he knew it.

'Give me a few minutes to get dressed,' she said. 'Does your dog eat cheese?'

Barry's ears pricked high.

'You said the magic word,' Guy replied.

. . .

Millie pressed back into the cracked faux-leather bench and curled her knees under herself.

'Poor Barry,' she said.

Guy was across the booth, wriggling to get comfortable as foam spilled from his seat. 'The way that dog looks at people, he'd have you think he's never fed. That nobody's ever shown him any love in his life.'

Millie laughed as she glanced across the diner towards the car park, where Barry was locked in the car with the windows cracked and cheese crumbs to sniff out.

'He's made himself a nest,' Guy added. 'First time I ever left him in the car, he somehow managed to burrow around the back seat and get into the boot. I found him there curled up with a load of blankets I'd left for emergencies. Don't let him convince you that he's got it rough. I was only away for five minutes, paying for petrol.'

Millie settled and listened to the sound of the caff around them. There was the clinking of knives and forks, the vague chatter of talk radio, and plenty of men talking over one another. When she looked back, Guy had slid his Blackberry into the middle of the table. She picked it up; there was a photo of the man who'd arrested her on the screen.

'It's the local police website,' Guy said. 'That's the meet the team page.'

And there he was, halfway down, with a grinning head-and-shoulders shot. His ears took up a good third of the frame and he was listed under the name 'Liam Paris', with a single R. Millie assumed whoever put the site together had spelled his name wrong. No wonder they'd not been able to find him.

'That's him,' Millie said.

Guy took back his phone and dropped it onto the seat. 'What are your bail conditions?' he asked.

'I've got to report back to the station in seven days. They

said someone will be in contact if anything changes between now and then.'

Guy screwed his lips together and made a gentle *hmm* to himself. 'Do you have a solicitor? I can recommend someone. I wouldn't be certain that search was legal. There's all sorts of—'

Millie wasn't sure she wanted to hear it: 'There was a duty solicitor – but he didn't say much at the end. Just that they're waiting for tests to come back on the crowbar and that I shouldn't miss bail next week. Maybe I can talk to whoever you know if I get re-arrested...?'

Guy made the same *hmm* sound to himself once more, not offering the 'it won't come to that' she was hoping to hear.

'Do you have any idea how the crowbar got into your house?' he asked.

'The kitchen window was open, so somebody could have come in through there. You'd have to have gone through the woods to get over the fence and into the house.' She paused, trying to think. There was definitely something else.

'Are you OK?' Guy asked.

Millie needed a moment, trying to remember what she'd read. What she'd heard. 'Dean works with locks,' she said. 'There's a review about it on his Google page. Also, I found out he had a girlfriend. I talked to her – and she mentioned locks as well.'

Guy didn't get a chance to reply because a teenager in a greasy apron had appeared at their table. He placed something close to a dustbin lid in front of Guy. It was piled high with bacon, sausages, slightly burned potato shreds, beans, tomatoes, black pudding slices, a pair of oozing fried eggs and four slices of fried bread.

Millie's plate was more like a coaster in comparison. There were two slices of unbuttered toast, with a pile of oily mini tomatoes on top.

Guy raised an eyebrow at her choice, before accepting a

second mug of tea from the server. He promptly dumped in six teaspoons of sugar and gave it a stir.

Millie surveyed the sight across from her. 'Aren't you worried about a heart attack?' she asked.

Guy took the remark in the spirit with which it had been intended. He laughed to himself and then sipped the tea. He then squirted what felt like half a bottle of ketchup across his food. That done, he stabbed one of the eggs with his fork, creating an orangey goop of yolk, ketchup and bean juice.

'I'm sixty-eight years old,' he said. 'I'd much rather eat this every day, than rattle around some old people's home when I'm in my nineties.' A pause, which came with half a smile. 'No offence to your friends there.'

Millie poked at her tomatoes and started to wish she'd ordered something more... ridiculous. Perhaps he had a point?

Guy cut a sausage into three pieces, dipped a bit into his egg and then waited with it halfway to his mouth. 'You found the girlfriend...?' he said.

'Judy Huish, who runs that B&B on the hill. She reviewed a restaurant where she mentioned him, so I went to have a chat with her. He made the benches at the front of her place, so I said I was interested in buying some. Then she started to tell me about Dean.'

Guy had been chewing but he stopped momentarily and nodded with approval.

'She said she'd broken up with him. She called him "weird".'

Guy had his mug in his hand again. 'What did she mean by that?'

'I didn't get the chance to ask. She recognised me and didn't want to talk after that.'

As Guy sipped his drink, Millie cut into her toast. It was the first thing she'd eaten since... she couldn't remember. Definitely before she'd been arrested. Her stomach gurgled in anticipation and she wished she really had ordered something bigger.

They each ate, not speaking, although Millie found something comforting about that. She ate almost all her meals alone – and, of the ones she didn't, Eric was there, slopping food down his front. Her son, like his father, was a dropper. There was something endearing about it. Maybe not *endearing*. If she spent an hour cooking something, it was more *annoying* when it went down her son's top after one bite. Still, if she was there to see him dropping food down his front, then at least they were together.

Guy was a third of a way through his breakfast when he next spoke. 'You know what this means, don't you?'

'What?'

'You're definitely onto something. Your friends at the home might not have specifically seen *someone* fall from Dean Parris's roof – but they saw *something* that has him spooked.' He pointed at her with his fork. 'The police coming to your house *could* be a coincidence but, considering his brother was one of the officers, I'm not sure I believe in that level of coincidence.'

Millie picked up the remains of her toast with her fingers. Tomato juice had soaked through, leaving it soggy, and she enviously eyed the fried bread on Guy's plate.

'What should I do next?' she asked.

'You've got to be careful, partly because the police are involved but also because you said Dean was outside your house. If he was the one who got into your place and left that crowbar, then it means he's rattled. Perhaps him *and* his brother.' He paused. 'Is there anywhere else you can stay?'

'I'm not going to move because someone's trying to scare me.'

It was the first time Millie had thought about actually being frightened of Dean. She hadn't been before and didn't think she was in the present. Should she be? It hadn't occurred to her that she should leave the house.

Guy was chewing but had that faraway stare that he always

seemed to have when he was thinking. She'd never met another person in whom she could so easily *see* them considering something. When his gaze refocused on her, there was a moment where she thought he might offer her a room at his house – but it wasn't that.

'If it's money, I know someone who runs a B&B. Not Judy. They owe me a favour, more than one, actually. They'd be discreet and—'

'I'm not going anywhere.'

He examined her for a second and then went back to his food. There was only a sausage and some fried bread remaining.

'Did you find anything else in your archives?' Millie asked.

'Only some ads for Dean's handyman business. He ran them every week for six months about a decade ago. Nothing else yet.'

Millie finished her final piece of cursed toast and then watched Guy polish off the rest of his abomination. He gulped it down with a third mug of sugar, infused with a hint of tea.

'How many burglaries are there here each year?' Millie asked.

Guy puffed out a breath. 'Not many. We have one or two in the summer but they tend to be in the caravan parks. It's very rare someone breaks into a house.'

It was what Millie would have guessed. 'Doesn't that make the timing all the stranger?' she asked, already knowing the answer. 'If someone's out to get me – and there are plenty of people who might be – why would they do it with a random burglary? Even if it is Dean, or his brother, what connection would I have? The cook at the nursing home says the house was owned by the parents of someone else who works there – but I don't know her and I don't know them. When I was getting interviewed last night, there was this officer – Burns – and even she seemed sceptical of it all. As if she knew it was nonsense.'

Guy finished his tea and pressed back into the seat. 'That's a good point.' More foam squished between the two strips of duct tape that was holding it together at the side. 'I'll find out what I can about the burglary,' he added. 'I know a few officers I trust.'

Millie looked up to the clock over the door, where, somehow, almost three hours had passed since she'd got into Guy's car.

'I've got work this afternoon,' she said. 'I groom dogs. I can't remember if I told you. I do it from the house.'

'Do you clean up labradoodles who enjoy rolling in fox poo?'

Millie laughed. 'That depends on the price.'

'We might need a different kind of conversation after the next time I let Barry off his lead in the woods.'

They stood and Millie watched as Guy shuffled their plates and cutlery into a pile, before returning it to the counter. The man at the till gave a thumbs-up and a 'cheers, mate', before the two of them headed back to the car together.

In the time they'd been inside, Barry had burrowed his way around the back seat and was curled up in the nest of blankets Guy had described. When the boot was opened, he looked up at them through sleepy eyes, as if to say he was enjoying the snooze, thank you very much. Guy slipped him a strip of bacon that Millie hadn't noticed him pocket – and then the dog bounced his way back into the main part of the car.

Millie was about to clamber into the passenger seat when she stopped and caught Guy's eye across the top of the car. Things had changed.

'I saw something the night after you first came round,' she said. 'I'd gone out and Dean's van was there. He drove off but then, when I went to go inside, there was something at the other end of the road.'

She wanted Guy to push her but he waited.

'Some sort of cat,' she added. 'Some sort of *black* cat. We stared at each other for a few seconds and then it ran off into the trees.'

The gentlest hint of a smile crept onto Guy's face. 'Was it a cat – or a *cat*-cat?'

Millie shrugged and, suddenly, for a reason of which she wasn't sure, it was hilarious. She was laughing and it was only when Barry scratched at the window from the inside that she stopped. 'Let's stick with *cat* for now.'

TWENTY-FIVE

There was a fluttering of curtains from across the road as Millie got out of Guy's car. She stepped onto the pavement outside her house and straightened her top, then gave a polite wave. The curtain immediately flicked back into place, as if it had never moved. From the depths of the night before, there was a defiance she hadn't felt in a long while.

As Guy's Volvo chugged its way around the corner and into the distance, Millie turned her phone back on. There was an almost instant series of buzzes, as if a swarm of furious bees was attacking her hand. There were a few more messages from Alex, who was fishing for information; others from people on Facebook that she hadn't spoken to in years – and one more from Jack asking, again, if she wanted him to come over. Millie thought about caving and saying he should but, for some reason, she wanted to be alone. She told him a client was coming over in the afternoon and that she was fine and would see him soon. She also thanked him for checking on her – and got a love heart emoji in response.

After that, Millie did a tour of the house for the first time properly since the police had been. A few things had moved in the garage but nothing of significance. None of her things were kept in there.

Someone had clearly been in the house to leave the crowbar – but there was nothing missing that she could see. If they had entered the house, it had been specifically to leave it. She found herself wondering if the crowbar had been in that cupboard all the time. Perhaps it was her dad's and she'd somehow missed it through the months the house had been hers. It was a general storage space, filled with blankets, sheets and pillowcases. She went in there occasionally but not often.

Millie tidied up her workspace at the back of the house, ready for the client to arrive with the dog – and it was only as she was finishing up that she realised it was already after two.

She headed through to the front of the house but there was nobody there and no car at the front. She checked her phone but there were no new messages. Millie had accepted plenty of work via text in the past. It was part of her current job – although the timing of the morning's enquiry had been suspicious. It wouldn't be the first time someone had arranged an appointment and then not showed up. Millie wondered what people got from it. She wasn't out of pocket.

Some people had too much time on their hands.

A moment after Millie lowered her phone, it started to buzz with a call from a number she didn't recognise. She assumed it was the potential client – but was met by a throaty-sounding cough as she answered. There was a pair of apologies and then the man introduced himself as the duty solicitor from the previous night.

'I've got news for you,' he said. 'Your bail conditions have been removed.'

Millie hadn't expected to hear from him again and found herself stumbling over a reply. 'Is that good news...?'

'It means you're in the clear. I did some digging and the crowbar tested negative for whatever they were looking at. It wasn't used in the burglary – and I don't think there was any trace of you on it, either.'

Millie asked him to repeat it, which he did with the same weariness he'd spoken with the night before. She couldn't quite believe it. If the crowbar *hadn't* been used for the burglary, then why had it been left at hers? Was it *actually* her father's? And why had someone called the police to report a disturbance that hadn't happened? Was it Dean? Was it his brother? Had Liam smuggled the crowbar into the house and pretended to find it? Wouldn't that be risky in front of his colleagues?

Millie had so many questions.

'Do I need to do anything?' she asked.

'There is one thing.' There was a shuffling of papers at the other end of the line and then: 'What do you want to do with the crowbar?'

Millie wondered if she'd misheard. 'What do you mean?'

'It's not evidence any longer. They took it from your house, so it's yours.'

'I don't understand.'

'I'm not sure I do, either – but they're asking what you want to do with it. I'm not strictly speaking representing you but I can arrange for it to be at the front counter if you wanted to pick it up.'

'They can keep it.'

Something crossed between a yawn and a laugh came from the other end. 'If you're sure. Let's hope you never hear from me again.'

Millie thanked him – and then he was gone. She thought about calling Guy to tell him what had happened but then wondered why *he'd* been her first thought, as opposed to Jack.

In less than twenty-four hours, she'd somehow gone from being arrested for something about which she had no clue – to being exonerated. Even by her own standards of drama, it was quite the effort.

She was brought back to the present by a vehicle cruising across the lowered pavement onto her drive. It jutted sideways, into the space she used to turn around, and then stopped behind the hedge, out of sight from the road. Millie had never seen anyone do that before. Clients would usually park in front of the house and then either reverse onto the road, or into the space where the newcomer's car now sat. The vehicle was newish, one of those crosses between a car and a van. The ones that cluttered up the kerbs at pick-up and drop-off times outside every school in the country. The windows were tinted, giving no view inside.

She was watching from the front window – but nobody got out of the vehicle. Even when it was her parents' house, Millie didn't think someone who'd never visited would have parked like that.

By the time Millie had strode through the house and opened the front door, there was still no movement from the car. She edged across the drive hesitantly, a pace at a time, and when she was halfway towards it, the driver's door popped open a fraction.

But only a fraction.

Nobody got out – and Millie was under the shade of a tree when the driver's door edged open far enough for her to see who was inside. He twisted in the driver's seat and let a leg hang outside as he offered a weak, apologetic smile.

It was no wonder he'd parked in a spot that meant he couldn't be seen from the street. No wonder he'd waited for her to approach, instead of getting turned away. No wonder he'd texted from a number she didn't recognise as some sort of test to make sure she'd be in.

There were three people who Millie blamed for ruining her life.

The first person, the one most at fault, was herself. She'd never tried to pretend differently.

Second was Guy... although recent days had made Millie question whether he'd actually done anything wrong.

Third was the man in front of her.

He climbed out of the car and pushed the door closed, then leaned against it. 'Hi, Mill.'

'Don't call me that.'

He tilted his head and offered another sympathetic smile. She'd seen it hundreds of times before, perhaps thousands. Not only in person but on the news, in the papers, on the internet – and in all those leaflets that littered everyone's doorsteps every few years.

Peter Lewis, Member of Parliament for Whitecliff, was the man with whom Millie had had an affair. She'd lost custody of her son because of what she'd done. Because of what *they'd* done.

And now, after zero contact in an entire year, he was back in her life.

TWENTY-SIX

'You won't believe what I had to go through to borrow this car,' Peter said. He was smiling, as if it was some big joke they were sharing.

'Why are you here?'

He opened the back door of the SUV to reveal a bouncy-looking golden retriever. 'I thought you could do a good job...'

The dog clearly wanted to jump down but was trained well enough to wait on its haunches for permission.

'Are you joking?' Millie replied.

Peter was in a pair of loose jeans and a knit jumper, the sort of thing she knew he wore on weekends. Either that, or if he was posing for an 'at home' piece with the *Journal*. Every election time, he'd be photographed in something similar in an attempt to prove he didn't only wear suits.

'You know I was never much of a joker,' he said – which was partially true. He rarely went out of his way to *try* to be funny.

He snapped his fingers and the dog took the cue, lolloping onto the driveway and then waiting for its head to be scritched.

'You've got some nerve,' Millie said. 'I've not heard from you in over a year – and then you just show up. Different car, different phone number...'

Peter was still close to his vehicle, hidden from the road, but Millie was far enough away that something caught her eye from across the street. The curtain fluttering again – and Millie was suddenly furious.

'Get inside,' she hissed.

Peter didn't need telling twice. He scuttled along the drive, head down, the dog at his side, and ducked into the hall. Millie was a step behind and slammed the door behind them, before turning to fume at him.

Her lives were clashing. Peter had never visited the house before. She had only ever met him in hotels, where she thought nobody could know.

Millie pushed past and muttered 'This way', before leading Peter and his dog through the house to the shed she'd converted at the back. She held open the door for the dog to trot inside and then left it to swing closed as Peter followed.

'What's her name?' Millie asked harshly, as she crouched at the dog's side.

'Penny.'

'I thought you never wanted a dog.'

Peter shrugged, which seemed uncharacteristic and wrong from his shoulders. 'She belongs to an elderly neighbour and I told her I knew someone who specialises in dog grooming.'

Millie grabbed the hose and let the water run, until it was warm. She soothed the dog with a treat and a chin scritch, then crouched again, dampening Penny's fur with the water.

'How do you know what I do?' she asked, not allowing herself to look at the man who was standing by the door.

There was no answer, so Millie repeated herself, adding: 'I didn't do this when I knew you,' she added. 'Are you stalking me?'

That didn't get an answer either – although Millie knew he'd have googled her.

Millie felt the pressure of him watching as she started her routine of wetting, then clipping Penny's fur. The dog sat patiently, with the steady flow of small treats definitely helping. It felt as if turning Peter away would've meant punishing the dog – and Millie didn't want to do that.

She had finished the trim and was about to begin kneading shampoo when Peter next spoke.

'This is a change from what you were doing. I thought you might be...?'

Millie couldn't bring herself to look at him. There was an unfinished question that she wasn't sure she wanted to answer.

Before everything, Millie had been working in events for the local authority. She'd booked singers, bands, comedians, writers, poets, and artists for various gigs and festivals in the area. Not only Whitecliff but the surrounding towns. She had stumbled into the job, really, through a friend of a friend, doing maternity leave cover until she was offered the job properly.

It was only recently that Millie realised it all happened because of her parents' connections. Her dad was a minor celebrity, after all. Her last name had power. Few other people would have fallen into such work. At the time, she'd somehow concluded she deserved it.

Millie had ended up promoting a campaign to get young people registered to vote. As part of that, an event was being hosted at the same television station where her dad presented the news. That was where Millie had met Peter Lewis.

He was the incumbent Member of Parliament for the town and district, and was backing the campaign, alongside his rivals. Millie had argued that the worst type of people to persuade young people to vote were actual politicians. She'd found herself cringing at the back of a studio as three people in suits talked to a pair of teenagers holding skateboards.

After the news segment, the politicians had walked off set separately, congratulating themselves on how well it had all gone. Peter had waited until everyone else was out of earshot and then whispered privately to Millie.

'I think we probably *de*-registered more voters than we gained,' he'd said.

As a single sentence, it summed him up. He'd not meant to be funny and yet there was something about the truthfulness of it all that had made her laugh. Peter was a few years older than her, although he had the air of someone older than that.

He was working as the junior secretary for culture, media and sport at the time and told her he was looking for policy input. He took her out for a working lunch and asked for ideas, based upon her time booking acts for the local festivals.

Of course, they both knew it was never about that.

At their follow-up lunch a week later, one thing had led to another. Peter had told her his marriage was finished and that he was only with his wife for the optics. It was loveless – but so were the marriages of many MPs. They had to remain a couple, preferably heterosexual, otherwise it would turn off voters. He told Millie that he and his wife had an agreement, as long as they were discreet.

Millie knew those were the sorts of things people said, *men* said, when trying to get someone into bed. The problem was, her own marriage was failing – for entirely different reasons. Because of Alex. Because of the thing she'd never been able to tell anyone about.

Back in the present, Millie finished shampooing Penny. She was rinsing the dog a second time when she finally gave Peter a reply.

'I couldn't exactly continue doing what I had been,' Millie said. 'You can't be a face for arts and culture events when you've been on the front page shagging an MP you were supposed to be advising on policy.'

There was deliberate spite in her voice and, when she looked up, Peter was no longer watching her. He was staring aimlessly out the window, one hand in a pocket. Like one of those greying dads in a knitwear advert.

'I was wondering how you've been,' he said.

'Come off it. You didn't even message after everything with Mum and Dad...'

'No...'

He sighed theatrically – and Millie wondered if he'd always done that. It felt put on, but then a lot of what he said and did was like that. She'd learned that, with politicians, it was all performative. It wasn't enough to *feel* sad about something; an MP or councillor had to *look* sad. If not, someone would be taking a photo, or recording them. That performance became so natural, that the line of public and private expressions was barely existent.

'It was a bit too soon,' Peter added. 'I thought it best to keep our heads down.'

'*Our* heads? Or yours?'

No response – but Millie knew the answer.

'Why did you come?' she asked.

'I told you, for the dog.'

'You could have picked any groomer – so why me?'

Peter was staring through the window again and even that felt somewhat rehearsed, as if he was trying to get a good photo for his next leaflet. Something where he wanted to appear thoughtful. There had been a time where it had all felt genuine, of course. Sometimes, Millie wondered if it still was.

'I suppose I wanted to see you,' he said.

Millie grabbed the hairdryer and used the hum to drown out anything more that Peter might want to say.

Penny leaned into the heat, enjoying the brush through her fur as Millie combed her dry. Millie wished all the dogs with which she worked were so calm. Then she also wished this particular one had been brought in by somebody else.

As soon as the hairdryer went off, Millie realised the doorbell was ringing. Peter was surprised, too, as he turned to look back towards the house. Neither of them had heard it.

'Are you expecting someone?' he asked – and Millie enjoyed that niggle of worry in his voice. She had little left to lose by being seen with him – but Peter was still an MP.

Millie told him to wait in the shed with Penny, then returned into the house. She wondered if Jack had decided to pop in after all. He'd ask about the car at the front and she wasn't sure whether she'd be able to lie to his face about who was inside.

She was so busy thinking of a possible reason for the car being where it was, that Millie needed a moment to clock that it wasn't Jack on the other side of the door. It was someone much worse, someone who definitely *couldn't* know that Peter Lewis, MP, was standing in a shed on the other side of the house.

'Hi,' Alex said, when Millie opened the door. He nodded towards Peter's vehicle, parked behind the hedge. 'Whose car is that?'

Millie stared blankly at her ex-husband, mouth half-open, with no idea what to say.

TWENTY-SEVEN

'Test drive for the day,' Millie said. There had been some sort of flyer in the post a couple of days before from a dealership. The banner headline had been about test drives and, moments before Millie tore it in half, something must have stuck.

Alex raised his eyebrows and turned to have another glance at the glimmering SUV. 'I didn't know you were thinking about a new car.'

'I'm not, really. It was a promotional thing...'

That got something of a blink. It was boring enough that hopefully he wouldn't follow it up – and he didn't. There were more pressing things.

'I wanted to make sure you were OK,' he said. 'With the police and everything...'

He took a quarter-step forward, expecting Millie to open the door wider and let him in. She didn't. Instead she stood, blocking the way. He reeled away a little. Probably too used to getting his own way.

'I thought you were at Center Parcs,' she said.

'We're back. It was only a one-night thing. What's going on...?'

'I said it was a misunderstanding,' Millie replied. 'Wrong place, wrong time, that type of thing. It's all been sorted now.'

Alex had always had a way of staring at her which made it feel as if he was trying to read her thoughts. There was an intensity about his brown eyes that felt intoxicating when he was smiling and, if Millie was honest, a little intimidating when he wasn't.

'People are saying—'

'Who cares what people are saying,' Millie interrupted.

Alex was silent at that, although he was still staring. He wanted to know what had happened, probably in part because Rachel was trying to get it out of him.

'You didn't need to come over,' she said.

'I tried messaging!'

'I was asleep – and I replied when I woke up.' Millie held the door firmly, trying to make it clear he wasn't coming in and that she wanted him to go.

Alex took a breath and half-turned. For a moment, she thought that would be it, except he twisted back.

'There's something else,' he said. 'We need to talk.'

Millie felt that *here we go* sinking in her stomach. Nobody ever said 'we need to talk' if what they wanted to talk about was the size of the cake they were buying as a gift. It was never 'we need to talk... here's a winning lottery ticket'.

'What about?' she replied.

'Things... Can I come in?'

Alex motioned forward again but Millie clasped the door tighter, wedging it into her shoulder so that, if he pushed the door, he'd also have to push her.

'Is it about Eric?' Millie asked.

That got a wince. 'Sort of... not really.'

'Is he ill? Hurt?'

A shake of the head. 'Nothing like that.'

'If it's not about him, just tell me.'

Alex did a mini stamp on the spot, like he was in a marching band playing statues. 'It's not really about Eric. I want to talk to you properly. Can I just come in?'

'I'm busy,' Millie said. 'I've got a client's dog in the back. We can talk on the phone later.'

'I'd rather do it in person.'

Alex was stamping some more. It was almost imperceptible and, though he might have been doing it to keep warm, it seemed much more like a mini paddy.

'We'll do it in person tonight,' Millie said.

'I'm here now.'

'I'm *working* now – and you've come over without telling me. Unless it's serious, we'll figure it out later.'

Alex had never been one to take rejection well. Perceived slights at his work would lead to him raging through entire evenings as Millie listened on, offering the odd 'you're so right', or 'I know what you mean'. It was that or an argument.

'He's *our* son,' Alex said, getting louder and going with the nuclear option.

Millie had been ready for it. 'You just said it wasn't about him!'

'It's not... but it is.'

'As long as it's not urgent, we'll talk later. I can come to you, or you can come back. Or we can meet in the middle. Either way, I'm *working* right now.'

The cruellest of smiles slipped across her ex-husband's face and then it was gone. He hadn't said it but he wanted her to know that he thought this business of hers was a *joke*. That she'd thrown away a *proper* career and had now lowered herself to this.

'Fine,' he said. 'I'll come back at seven – assuming you're not *working*.'

'I'll be here.'

Alex finally backed away, although there was a hesitancy to

his walk, as if he was trying to think of something cutting as a send-off. Millie knew that if she gave him a full twenty-four hours, he might come up with something. When he was in court, the witty remarks or fake surprise would appear as if it was off-the-cuff. That was only because the judges, magistrates and jurors didn't see him practising in the mirror the way she used to.

Millie waited until he was out of sight and then closed the door. She hurried through the house to the back, where Peter was still waiting in the shed. Penny was chomping on a chew.

'I thought I'd give her that in case she barked,' Peter said, nodding towards the jar of chews that was on Millie's shelf.

'Why would she bark?'

'I don't know... dogs bark, don't they?'

Millie rolled her eyes as Peter angled towards the front of the house.

'Everything OK...?' he asked.

'You shouldn't have come.' Millie gave Penny a final brush, one last treat, told her she was a good girl, and then stood. 'We're done,' she told Peter. 'Who do I invoice?'

Peter started patting his back pocket. 'I assumed I could pay cash...?'

'Your name on the invoice...?'

'Perhaps we can do this one off the books...?'

'Is that the official party policy?'

Millie left him squirming for a moment, before telling him it was sixty quid. She thought she could have named any figure and he'd have paid.

As it was, Peter began flipping through a slick leather wallet, slipped out four, crisp twenties, and handed them across. He'd either printed them himself, or they'd come direct from a cash machine.

'Keep the change,' he said.

Millie stepped forward, lunged really, and shoved one of

the newly screwed-up twenties into his jeans pocket. She moved away and ruffled Penny's head and back. 'I only did this for the dog,' she said. 'Don't come back. I'm blocking that number you messaged me on, so don't try that either.'

Peter reached for the dog and clipped a lead onto her collar, before opening the door. He paused for a moment, as if he wanted to say something, then stepped through it and moved towards the back door. He was standing in the frame when he finally got up the courage.

'It's not been easy for me,' he said.

It was almost spoken over his shoulder, as if not quite committed to fully saying it.

Millie realised she was standing with her hands on her hips, like her mum used to when there was a chance she could hit the roof. When she could go full Chernobyl.

'*Really?*' Millie replied. 'You still have *your* job. You still see *your* kids whenever you want. I doubt you've ever had anyone call you a slag to your face. There aren't people out there writing Facebook statuses about how you killed your parents.'

Peter twisted a little further, still not quite facing her. 'Do people really think that?'

'It doesn't matter if they *think* that – they say it. To each other, to me.' Millie stopped speaking. She wanted him to go, though there was more to say. 'Do you remember that hotel in Mayfair, when you said you were going to tell you wife you were leaving her?'

A sigh. 'I remember.'

'Why did you tell me that?'

Peter's body slumped a little, something else that didn't quite suit him. 'Because I meant it.'

'When everything came out about us, when we were on the front page, *that* was your chance to do it. Except you blocked my number and went on the BBC to say it was an enormous mistake and that you were staying with your wife.'

'I...' He tailed off and started to mumble something that Millie couldn't make out.

'I told you things about me and Alex,' Millie said.

'I never told anyone.'

In the year since everything had come out, Millie had often wondered if Alex's secret, if *her* secret, was safe. When the affair had started, the only way Millie could justify it was by telling someone – Peter himself – why she was doing it. Only he knew – and then, when he'd had a chance to stand by her, he'd called her an 'enormous mistake'.

'Go,' Millie said. 'I mean it. Don't come back. I don't want to see you again.'

Peter turned, his head slightly drooped, and she wondered why he'd bothered coming. If he'd heard the truthful rumours about her arrest, he'd not mentioned them. And surely, if anything, it was the most dangerous time for him to attempt to see her again?

She followed him into the main house, letting him lead the way towards the front. He patted his pockets, looking for the car keys. Then he opened the front door and left without looking back. It was probably a good job he didn't because, from nowhere, Millie considered asking if he really *was* a cat-puncher. She grinned as the cook's suggestion popped into her mind, imagining the confused expression it would get.

Peter Lewis, MP. Punches cats. Probably. One star. Wouldn't recommend.

There was an almost silent hum as the engine of his borrowed electric car started – and then, unquestionably for the best, he was out of her life.

TWENTY-EIGHT

It was a minute to seven when Millie's doorbell sounded. She hadn't heard anything from Alex since he'd shown up unannounced earlier. She half-thought he wouldn't show, given he'd had to back down and leave the first time.

As soon as Millie opened the door, he moved forward, meaning Millie had to step aside to avoid him walking into her. She was going to invite him in anyway – but the way he was attempting to assert himself over her had been growing. In a general sense, they had been equals when they were together but, since the split, since the public humiliation, that had changed.

When it came to Eric, he had custody and made sure she knew it. If she was early to pick up her son, Alex would leave her waiting outside until it was time. On the single occasion traffic had caused her to be late in dropping him off, Alex had bluntly told her it was a first strike and that he'd be contacting the court if she did it again.

There were a few other occasions, like this, in which he'd stepped into her space, forcing her to move. One time, they'd passed on the street and he'd shoulder-barged her, before stopping and claiming he'd not seen her.

There were many more times when it felt as if he was provoking her into saying something that would look bad if it was reported to the court. Little things like calling it her parents' house. Even sending Rachel to drop off Eric felt like something niggly that he, or they, believed might trigger her.

Pushing past her into her house was one more thing for Millie's mental list, as she wondered if she should start an *actual* list.

Alex got to Millie's kitchen before she did and opened the fridge. He poked his head inside, then withdrew it and shut the door. As Millie watched him, it really felt as if he wanted her to challenge him, which was precisely why she didn't.

'Can we get on with whatever this is?' Millie said. 'I'm pretty sure you have other things to be doing – and it's a Sunday, so nearly Eric's bedtime.'

'We moved that back by half-hour,' Alex replied.

'Oh...'

'Rach can put him to bed anyway.'

Another little poke.

Millie took a breath, not too deep. She didn't want Alex to notice. He was perched on the table now, not sitting *at* it but sitting *on* it.

'I'm sure he enjoys the extra half-hour,' Millie replied, trying not to do so through clenched teeth.

'We're getting married,' Alex said. He spoke so abruptly that Millie almost asked him to repeat himself.

'You and Rachel?'

Millie cursed herself for the dumb question – as Alex relaxed and revelled in it. They were playing a silly game that neither of them acknowledged, even though they both knew they were in it.

'Me and Rachel,' he confirmed. 'I wanted to tell you in

person. Didn't think it was fair if you heard from someone else. We've not gone public yet.'

It sounded genuine but Millie also wondered if he was telling her in person because he wanted to see her reaction. Their own divorce had only been finalised a few months before. Whatever they'd had was long gone but she couldn't help but think about the speed of it all. It was barely a year ago that her affair had been exposed. In that time, not only had he got a new girlfriend, they'd moved in together and were now getting married.

'That's good of you,' Millie heard herself saying. 'Eric said you might be getting a cat, so I should've known it was properly serious.'

Alex laughed, which was probably the first time she'd made him do that since the split. He caught himself halfway through, realising he wasn't supposed to be enjoying whatever this was.

'We've not told anyone else yet,' he added, with a little more seriousness. 'I said I'd tell you, then Eric, then our parents. After that it'll go on Facebook.'

'Thank you...' Millie couldn't think of anything better to say. Perhaps she was too cynical and this genuinely *was* a thoughtful move... 'When's the date?' she asked.

'We're not sure. We don't want to rush it. Rach is only going to get one go at this, so I want it to be right for her.'

Millie couldn't stop the snorted laugh that escaped. *That's what I thought*, she didn't say. She had never pictured herself divorced.

'What does that mean?' Alex replied. Their moment of truce was over. 'It was *your* affair,' he added.

Millie was quiet. Despite the divorce and custody hearings, they'd never really talked about her affair and the reasons. It was always there. Her infidelity was on the divorce papers. It was the reason custody had to be decided in the first place. On the night it had all come out, Millie had been in such shock –

and Alex had been so furious – that she'd left to go to her parents' house. After that, they didn't really have conversations, except through solicitors, or, more recently, back-and-forth texts.

He was right. It *was* her affair but there was more than that. Her private life becoming public meant people thought they knew her. The coverage and venom had become such a tsunami that it sometimes felt as if she was watching her life, instead of living it. She'd gone along with all of it: the divorce, the custody, taking responsibility for it all.

And yet, as Alex stood in her kitchen, taking the moral high ground by talking about *her* affair, Millie felt something swelling within her.

'Does Rachel know?' she asked.

Alex squinted at her. 'Know what?'

It lasted a second at most but Millie saw the twitch of his eyebrow. The momentary tremble of his top lip.

Those three words had him scared, as she knew they would. And she loved it.

For the first time in a year, she had a glimmer of an upper hand.

Except it wasn't a game and she didn't want it to be. Eric was caught in the middle and anything that would harm his father would also hurt him.

Alex rose from the table, standing tall over Millie as he took a step towards her. 'Does Rachel know *what*?' he said.

Millie knew she should back down, she should do it for her son, but she had waited so long to see this. To *feel* it.

'You had the affair!' Alex repeated. He was shouting now, looming over the top of Millie.

'Yes,' Millie replied.

'*You* embarrassed me on the front page. I had to talk to my parents about it. To our neighbours. To people at work. They wanted to pay for me to have therapy!'

'How was it?'

Alex fumed, as Millie knew he would, and his fist clenched. Alex was not the therapy sort. His dad, in particular, was the *pull yourself together*-type, which was something that had been passed down.

'I still have to be in the office,' Alex added. 'People there were passing around those pictures of you on their WhatsApp groups. I'm the one who has to deal with it when kids bully Eric because of who his mum is.'

He was really loud now, flecks of spit gathering in the corner of his mouth. It was the mention of Eric which finally, *finally*, made Millie stop.

'I didn't mean anything by it,' she replied. 'I'm glad you're happy. Rachel, too. I hope the wedding goes well. If you need a hand looking after Eric, to give you a bit of space, or whatever, I'll be around.'

Alex had frozen a pace from her, on tiptoes, fist still clenched. Millie didn't think he'd hit her – and he didn't. He lowered himself and edged backwards, his gaze shooting towards the counter, where Millie realised her phone was buzzing. She ignored it but whoever it was had apparently spooked Alex.

'I should've known you'd be a *bitch* about it,' he said.

He snatched his keys from the table and barrelled along the hall towards the front. As soon as he tried to yank down the handle, Millie remembered that she had absent-mindedly locked it when she'd followed him in. A force of habit that meant her former husband was angrily trying to slam down a handle that wasn't moving.

'The key's there,' Millie said, pointing towards the small side table near the door.

Alex snatched up the key, dropped it, then had to crouch to pick it up. 'People ask me about you,' he said – and there was a snarl to him as he nodded upstairs. 'They ask if I think you killed them.'

Millie shivered involuntarily. Despite everything, she didn't think they'd sink this low.

But Alex was on a roll: 'I tell them I don't know. I say I don't know what you're capable of.'

He jammed the key into the lock and turned it before finally managing to open the door. There was one last glance over his shoulder that was full of fury – although that glimmer of fear remained in his eyes. A moment later and he slammed the door behind him.

Does Rachel know?

Millie had expected a response but, as Alex roared away, she wondered whether she'd started a chain reaction over which she'd have no control.

She headed back through to the kitchen, wondering how long it would be before Alex retaliated. It would be subtle, probably with Eric in the middle. Her son would mysteriously be ill the next weekend he was meant to be with her. Something like that.

Millie picked up her phone from the counter, where a text message from Guy was waiting.

Fancy checking out some cat-cat tracks?

TWENTY-NINE

The pair of light beams stretched deep into the distance, cutting through the dark to reveal the long stretch of muddy grass.

It was uninspiring to say the least. That would have been true even if Millie wasn't wearing three pairs of socks, leggings under jeans, two jumpers, her thickest jacket, gloves and a hat that was pulled down over her ears.

Millie waggled her torch to the side, slicing the light across the moor and out towards the valley in the deepest distance. There was no bright moon tonight, only the vague rustle of the ocean from behind and the eclipsing sense of emptiness ahead.

'If there is a panther out there,' Millie said, 'and it runs at us, what good are these torches?'

Guy whipped his own flashlight from side to side, covering the opposite end of the field from Millie's own beam.

'If it decides we're prey, these torches are no use whatsoever,' Guy replied. He sounded as chirpy as if describing his favourite meal. 'It'll be on us before we even know it's close.'

'That's good to know,' Millie said.

Barry had been left at the house, apparently exhausted after an earlier walk. That left only Millie and Guy to be traipsing across the heath in the middle of the night.

'There's no reason to believe a panther would see humans as prey,' Guy added, still sounding far too cheery for Millie's liking. 'There are plenty of smaller creatures in the woods that a big cat might hunt. In all the handful of sightings, including yours, there's never been any aggression reported. If anything, a panther would likely be more scared of us.'

Millie scoffed. 'How confident are you with that "likely"?'

'Seventy per cent. Eighty.'

Millie wished she could be more certain he was joking.

Her foot slid across a slick patch of mud and, in stopping herself from going over, she slurped her other foot into a different patch of goo. Guy didn't appear to notice as he continued walking.

'How fast are you?' Millie asked.

'At what?'

'Running. How quick do you reckon you could do a hundred metres?'

'Hmm...' Guy took a moment to think. 'I ran twelve-dead when I was in school but it might have been the hundred yards back then.'

'That was fifty years ago.'

Guy made a *pfft* sound with his lips. 'Good point. Why do you ask?'

'Because if a panther *does* come at us, I don't need to outrun *it*, I just need to outrun *you*.'

Guy laughed and so did Millie. It felt good to be in a conversation with someone when they weren't each trying to maliciously niggle one another.

'Tell you what,' Guy said. 'If either of us sees a panther coming, I'll slow down and let you get away.'

'You'll *let* me get away?'

Another laugh: 'I'm being nice!'

'I think I could outrun you anyway.'

'I don't think beating a sixty-eight year-old man in a race is the victory you seem to think it is...'

It was Millie's turn to laugh. 'I'll take any win I can get.'

They continued across the field, with Millie occasionally managing to slurp her way into puddles that Guy was avoiding through either luck, or, more likely, a greater degree of attention.

As they neared the treeline, Guy stopped and swept his light across the barbed-wire fence that lined the edge of the woods. There was a stile in the middle, with deep footprint-shaped puddles leading up to it.

'That's the latest sighting,' Guy said, pointing towards the stile itself. 'Fella told me he was walking his dogs and had come over the stile. He was on the way across the field we've just come over when he said he felt something watching him. When he turned, there was something big and black standing right there.' Guy flicked his light from side to side at a spot a short distance from the stile.

They continued on and then, once they reached the wire, Guy and Millie pointed their torches at the ground and started to walk along the fence line, side by side, looking for tracks.

'Is this what journalists like you do?' Millie asked.

'Not *exactly* this.'

'But people call you up and you go running after whatever story they've told you?'

'More or less. That's what reporting is. Since I left the paper, I get to follow whatever I want.'

'And now you're following sightings of cats?'

'Sightings of a *specific* cat...'

Despite the mud of the field, the verge underneath and around the barbed wire was caked with frost. It would have settled weeks back and likely wouldn't shift until spring. Leaves that had come down in the autumn had crusted together and crunched under their feet. It was even colder in the shadow of the trees and the air was scraping the back of Millie's throat.

'Hard to make prints in this,' Millie said.

'True – but if something *heavy* left a print, it's going to be preserved in this cold.'

Guy stopped and crouched, before flicking away a large stone that Millie hadn't noticed. She wondered what he was doing for a moment, then realised he might have mistaken the shape for a print. They were walking slowly, steadily, making sure nothing could be missed.

'Why did you invite me?' Millie asked.

'I told you before, you're a natural at this. I thought you might enjoy the mystery of it all.'

Millie couldn't remember anyone calling her a natural at anything before. With her previous career, she'd not got the job through any particular interest or ability. A genuine who-she-knew, not *what*-she-knew. Or worse, who her *parents* knew. It felt embarrassing to admit to herself now. She was one of those people who had the word 'privilege' thrown at them – and it was something she couldn't deny. She'd not seen it at the time which, in itself, was more privilege.

As they walked, she realised she was enjoying herself, despite the cold and mud meaning it would usually be everything she hated. She shone her light into the distance, where the barbed wire stretched all the way to the bottom of the valley.

'Did you find out anything else about Dean or his brother?' she asked, realising he had been out of her mind for much of the day.

'There was that, too,' Guy replied. 'I was going to call earlier but I had a lot on and then the email came in about this sighting.'

Guy stopped and angled his torch towards the ground. Millie was a pace away and their chilled breaths met in the middle.

'What?' she asked.

'That attempted burglary you were accused of was at a house that was sold seven months ago. It used to belong to the Long family. Do you know them?'

Millie suddenly remembered what had been said when she was stood outside the nursing home with Jack. The cook had told them that Gloria's mum had been so spooked by the break-in that she wanted to put the house up for sale *again*. She'd missed the key word at the time. They'd only recently bought the place.

'I don't think so,' she replied.

'They lived in town for generations until they sold up. They had a daughter, Stephanie, who'd be about twenty or twenty-one.'

Guy left it at that and Millie wondered what that had to do with anything. Then she realised he wanted her to work it out for herself.

'Beth's age...'

'Exactly. Once I'd heard about the Longs, and *Stephanie* Long, I went back through my archive and I found this.'

He dug into the inside pocket of his patchy coat and then passed a folded-up newspaper to Millie.

'Page nineteen,' he said.

Millie put down her light and Guy angled his towards the page as she took in the 'Top GCSE grades up again' headline. There was a series of photos spread across the page, with teenagers holding up pieces of paper that presumably contained their grades. In the bottom corner, two girls had their faces pressed together, each smiling wide as they held up their results. There was a caption underneath.

Best friends Beth Parris and Stephanie Long celebrate their results. Beth is a keen writer, who wants to study English

Literature at university after doing her A-levels. Stephanie
wants to play hockey for Team GB at the Olympics.

Millie read it three times and then focused properly on the
photo. Assuming the girls in the photo were in the same order as
the words, Beth had long, straight dark hair, while Stephanie was
ginger. They were grinning and happy and Millie felt a twinge of
longing as she looked at their youthful faces. It was barely a blink
ago that she was picking up her own exam results with her best
friend, Nicola, and now she was divorced and approaching forty.
Nicola was something else in her life that had got away. Some*one*
else. Perhaps it had taken everything with Peter the MP for her
to see that she was the destructive force in her own life?

Millie blinked away the thoughts of Nicola, folded the
paper, and handed it back to Guy. He returned it inside his
jacket. Millie leant again one of the posts that separated the
long lines of barbed wire.

'I wonder if Beth ended up doing English Literature,' Millie
said.

'Did you notice the other thing...?'

Millie had but she needed a moment. Things had felt like
too much of a coincidence. Now, from nowhere, it was
becoming clear they weren't.

'Beth's best friend used to live in the house that was broken
into,' Millie said.

Guy replied with something she didn't catch but it was
obvious that's why he'd given her the paper.

'Do you think Dean broke into the house?' Millie asked,
although it was more thinking out loud than an actual question.
'Then he tried to blame me for some reason...?'

'Probably to scare you off... and give the police someone else
to look at?'

'His brother's a police officer.'

It suddenly felt dangerous and far more serious than it had that morning, when Millie had woken up after the best night's sleep in a long while. Assuming it was Dean, he hadn't seriously tried to fit her up for the break-in. It would have taken too much work and luck – plus, perhaps, put himself in the firing line if she'd have mentioned his name. It was only ever about scaring her away.

But from what? Someone falling from his roof? Someone being pushed?

Millie picked up her torch from the ground and was about to continue with Guy along the fence when she spotted something next to her foot.

'Guy...'

She angled her light towards the fence post and the wire attached to it.

Guy crouched, grunting as he went down. He leaned in close, then dug into his jacket again, before pulling out a transparent sandwich bag. He turned the bag inside out, then put his hand inside, before pinching carefully at the wire. When he pulled away, he flipped the bag back the right way and then ran his thumb and finger across the top to seal it.

He offered the bag to Millie, who held it up into her own light.

It was dark and shiny, clumped together by a mix of frost and mud.

'What is it?' she asked, already knowing the answer.

'Fur,' Guy replied. '*Black* fur.'

THIRTY

Millie checked her phone almost instinctively as it buzzed. She was hoping Guy had something about Dean and the break-in – but it was far less important.

'Hot date?' Jack asked.

They were under the shelter at the back of the nursing home as mist swirled around the bottom of the valley. Dean's house was barely a silhouette through the gloom. Millie was still watching it, as if expecting answers to spiral up from the skylight.

She slipped her phone back into her bag. 'Screen time report,' Millie replied.

That got a huff. 'Screen time reports should be like trips to the dentist. The dentist knows you're lying about how often you floss, *you* know you're lying about how often you floss – but you have this mutual pact to pretend everything's fine.'

'What's that got to do with screen time?'

'*I* know I'm on my phone too much, *Siri* knows I'm on my phone too much – but there's no need to keep banging on about it.'

He had a point.

'Is this like smoking?' Millie replied. '*I* know you're still smoking, *Rish* knows you're still smoking – and you obviously do. But we all just pretend you've given up.'

Jack's forehead creased. 'You're so catty today.'

'It's funny you say that...'

Jack obviously didn't know why 'catty' meant something different than he intended but he wasn't listening anyway. He was battling with his sleeve until it was halfway up his arm. 'Nicotine patches,' he said.

There were a pair pressed onto the skin a little above his elbow.

'I didn't know you were supposed to wear two.'

He rolled up his other sleeve – and then turned around and pulled up his top to show her his back. 'Six!'

Below them, something darted out from a gap in the hedge partway down the valley. It was overcast and gloomy, and for the merest moment Millie thought of the dark fur she and Guy had found the night before.

It was only a second later that a man appeared through the same gap, shouting after his dog that was bolting over the dewy grass.

Millie and Jack watched them for a moment, enjoying the relative silence. She was going to ask if they were wise to continue spending time in the smoking shelter if he was giving up nicotine. Except their snatched moments had never really been about anything more than these chats.

'I'm not getting much sleep,' Jack said, out of nowhere. 'There's someone at the back of our flat who's up revving his engine through half the night. He's always bombing around the estate, skidding round bends, doing doughnuts in the car park...'

As if to emphasise the point, Jack erupted into a yawn that he only made a half-hearted attempt to stifle. It didn't feel as if he wanted a reply, more someone to vent at. Millie remained quiet, wondering if there was more to come.

Below, the man had caught his dog and was busy wagging a finger in the animal's direction.

'I had an argument with Rish,' Jack said, quieter this time. Millie knew he'd been building up to it. The talk of screen time and noisy neighbours was his way of getting himself ready to move onto what was really bugging him.

'What about?'

She already knew.

'I finally told him I'm not sure I'm ready for kids.'

'What did he say?'

Jack wasn't ready to answer. He needed to tell the rest of the story: 'We'd been watching Netflix and it was doing that annoying thing where it starts playing something right after the show's finished. You just want a wee but, before you can get off the sofa, it's off again. Rish had paused it and gone off to the toilet and, when he came back, he refilled our glasses... and then I just said it.'

'What happened?'

'Rish froze for a second and I wondered if he'd heard properly. Then he put down the bottle, grabbed his coat and walked out. I've not seen him since.'

'He didn't come home last night?'

A shake of the head. Jack was staring aimlessly across the vast field, where the man had now put his dog on the leash and was heading for the wall on the furthest side.

Millie gently touched Jack's arm and then rested her head on his shoulder.

'That's not a grown-up response,' she said.

'Him or me?'

'Him, obviously. Did you go to the coffee shop?'

'He wasn't due to work today... but yes. He wasn't there. I made a joke of it, saying I'd mixed up the days he was working. They all thought it was funny and I had to go along with it... but I don't know where he is.'

Millie lifted her head away from him.

'Do you think I should call the police?' Jack asked. 'Report him missing?'

Millie took out her phone again and scrolled to find Rishi's name, before pressing the button to call. She put it on speaker and then showed the screen to Jack. It rang half a dozen times before switching to voicemail. Millie hung up without leaving a message. She had barely lowered her phone before a text buzzed through from the number she'd just called.

> Tell him I'm fine

Millie twisted the screen so Jack could see.

He nodded slightly and then turned away. 'I guess it's just me he doesn't want to talk to.' He sighed. 'Where do you think he is?'

'You'd know better than me.'

'Probably his sister's. I thought about driving out there but...'

Millie didn't know what to say. It felt as if much of the conversation had been Jack wanting to talk, rather than listen – which was fine by her. There had been enough times in the previous year when he had been the ear she wanted, especially when it came to Alex's small acts of provocation.

'He *really* wants children,' Jack said.

'The word "he" is quite important in that.'

A pause and another sigh.

Jack was fidgeting and it felt as if he might start fishing for his vape pen. 'I don't know what to do,' he said.

'I think you need to tell him again – and he needs to stay and listen. You can't just walk out because you don't want to hear something.'

Millie hadn't finished her sentence when she remembered closing the door on Guy. It felt like weeks before and she had to remind herself it had been days. She should probably take her own advice.

They didn't get a chance to talk further because the door sounded behind them and one of Jack's colleagues called him through to help deal with a clean-up.

Millie headed inside, too, away from the cold. She drifted through to the rec room, where there was the usual crowd chatting, watching TV, scrolling on their phones, or sitting at the tables towards the back.

Ingrid was sitting by herself at one of the tables near the front windows, a cup of tea in front of her. Millie headed across and asked if she could sit opposite, which got a weary-looking 'of course'.

'Are you feeling better?' Millie asked.

That got a confused, wide-eyed blink, as if Ingrid couldn't remember being confined to her bed. 'I think so.'

'Do you want to play a game?'

Ingrid shook her head. 'Not today, love.' She sounded as tired as she looked and was staring aimlessly out towards the car park. 'Did you find out about the girl who fell?' Ingrid asked. 'It was a week ago now.'

Millie needed a moment to realise that it really had been that long. The hours and days had blended into one another. 'I don't know,' she said. 'I've been trying.'

Ingrid stretched and momentarily placed a cool hand on top of Millie's before removing it. 'I think I want to walk,' she said. 'It wakes me up sometimes. Do you want to come with me?'

Millie didn't answer at first. She was looking around, wondering if one of the staff members needed to agree to this sort of thing. It wasn't as if they were in a prison and, in the summer, the residents were often in the garden outside, enjoying the heat. But there was a difference between that and going for a walk on such a winter's day.

'I'm not a child,' Ingrid said, as if she'd heard Millie's thoughts. 'I'm allowed to walk.'

'It's really cold out.'

'That's why it'll wake me up.'

Ingrid was suddenly on her feet. The last time Millie had seen her, she hadn't got out of bed – and, the time before that, she'd been in a wheelchair. Millie had seen her walking before but it had always been carefully and slowly. Now, she was three paces away before she stopped and turned.

'I'm going out anyway. If you want to come, the company would be nice.'

Millie nearly laughed as she caught up to a seemingly rejuvenated Ingrid. They followed the maze of corridors to the older woman's room, where she almost emptied her drawers of jumpers as she layered up. She finished things off with a thick coat. Millie grabbed her own things from the staff room and then they headed outside onto the gritted, salty drive.

There was an assumption that Ingrid would do a lap of the car park and then they'd be back. But Millie followed as Ingrid led them past the parked cars and out the gate, onto the pavement. Millie checked back towards the home, half-expecting someone to be running after them to say this wasn't allowed.

'Have you heard the latest about Elsie's daughter?' Ingrid asked.

'Not yet.'

'She's taken him back. After she threw out all his clothes, after all that stuff in Harrogate, they're back together. She told him she wanted a divorce, then he said he was sorry and would never do it again. She said he had to prove it so he went and bought her a brand-new car. Some pink thing she's been wanting for years, according to Mick.'

'Does a new car prove he'll never do it again?'

'Doubt it but at least she got a new car out of it.'

Ingrid cackled to herself as they rounded the corner at the

end of the street. Millie hadn't known where they were headed but, as soon as Ingrid started down the hill, she started to get an idea.

'What does Elsie think about it all?' Millie asked.

'Don't know, really. She'll be fine. Do you know about her other daughter's husband and the trip to Dubai?'

Millie allowed herself a little smile. 'Someone mentioned it.'

The slope was covered with small piles of brown salt that had seeped through the frost. Murky water pooled across the pavement. Ingrid was walking more slowly as they continued down, taking her time and stopping to hold onto the fence posts outside people's houses. In her good days and bad days, this was a good one.

As they walked, Ingrid gave Millie a potted history of *her* Whitecliff. She pointed across towards the cliffs and said that a boy in her year had fallen into the sea when taking a shortcut from the school to the farm where he lived. He'd never been seen again and his parents had sold up, unable to live with the grief. It was that land on which Dean's house and a couple of the others had been built.

She talked about riding her bike on the hill where they were walking – and how the boys she knew would race delivery vans from the top to the bottom. When she was a teenager, Ingrid had worked in a sweet shop, predominantly selling sticks of rock in the summers. She talked about 'the Scottish invasion', when large groups of people from Scotland would come south for their summer holidays. Ingrid's dad would go halves on a van with one of his mates, drive up to Scotland and clear out as much haggis and Irn-Bru as they could find – then sell it to the Whitecliff chip shops for twice the price.

It was a different world – but Millie enjoyed hearing about something that was familiar and yet... not.

Millie was barely paying attention to their surroundings and it was only as they reached the abandoned phone box at the bottom of the hill that she realised how far they had walked. The mist had cleared, leaving a clear view up to the nursing home and the newly blue sky above. There was a crispness now; a gentle bite to the most beautiful of days.

Ingrid eyed the phone box for a few seconds and then turned to look across at Dean's house.

'It's very tall, isn't it?' she said.

She stepped into the road without looking, with a more careful Millie following a pace behind. They both shielded their eyes from the sun until the shadow from the house became enough to block the light.

Ingrid led them into the alley at the back of the house, where Millie had found the tile almost a week before. It was still in her house, in the cupboard above the cooker that she needed a step to reach properly.

The old flooring, table, and microwave that had littered the alley had been cleared. There was now only a dusting of frost between the house and the hedge.

Ingrid held her back as she arched and looked up to the full height of the house. 'It's so high,' she repeated. 'That girl would've hurt herself.'

There was no hesitation as she spoke. It wasn't speculation of what could have happened, it was certainty. If anything, now Ingrid was outside Dean's house, she sounded more convinced she'd seen what she said.

'You said "pushed",' Millie replied. 'But did you see who pushed her?'

She was wondering if Ingrid might describe Dean Parris.

'Couldn't see,' she said. 'It was too shadowy.' She waited a moment and then added: 'I wonder how she is?' Ingrid wasn't really talking to anyone but herself.

Millie had no answers but, though they'd only been there for a couple of minutes, it felt as if Ingrid had seen all she wanted. She tightened her scarf and took a step back towards the pavement.

'Shall we go back?' she said. 'It really is quite cold.'

Millie let Ingrid move around her and was about to follow when something caught her eye. It was close to where she'd been standing, almost lost among the gloom of the shadowed verge. She would have likely missed it had it not been for the practice with Guy the night before.

She crouched, leaning in for a better look, and trying to remember what Guy had told her the previous night. Something about prints in the dirt being preserved by the cold.

Two prints *had* been preserved in the icy verge in front of her – but they didn't belong to Guy's mythical panther.

They were too small to be a man's – and, unless Millie was very much mistaken, the small foot and five dimpled toes in the hardened soil belonged to a woman's bare feet.

THIRTY-ONE

Guy took Millie's phone and squinted at the photo of the feet that she'd taken at the back of Dean's house.

'They're about the same size as mine,' Millie said. 'A four or five – but there's no way someone was pushed or jumped off that roof and landed on their feet.'

Guy passed her back the phone. 'Whoever it was could have landed on something and stepped away.'

'Why would she have bare feet?'

'Why would she have jumped? Who would've pushed her?'

They looked to one another. Plenty of questions but still no answers.

Millie pictured the pile of junk that had been at the back of the house. There was the microwave and the old flooring; the three-legged chair and the smashed-up TV unit. If anything, that would have made someone's fall worse. None of it made much sense.

Millie and Guy were in his study. In a house of clutter, the study was king. There were so many piles of books and papers that every movement Millie made felt precarious. As if a rogue elbow might begin a domino effect to send the entire house collapsing. She was in the office chair, trying not to move too much, when Guy indicated the desktop computer at her side.

'Did anyone ever tell you which university Beth went to?' he asked.

Millie tried to remember. It was the neighbour across the street from Dean who'd said she'd been on the street to wave off Beth on the day she left. There was the GCSE photo, which said Beth wanted to do English Literature – but that was taken two years before she'd have had a chance to go.

'I don't think so,' Millie replied.

'I've had no luck finding out,' Guy said. 'I've got a few contacts in the system but was hoping she'd show up with a normal Google search.'

'I had a look, too,' Millie added. 'I couldn't find her. I don't think young people use Facebook.'

Hunting for Beth was one of the things Millie had done the previous evening. She had started with 'Beth Parris university', then 'Beth Parris English literature'. She'd tried with one R, instead of two, then she'd tried more combinations with specific named universities. The only results had been for young women who'd already graduated years before and were too old – or one at Sheffield, who was part of a drama society. That last profile had said she came from Ireland.

'I've got a couple of other contacts but I'd rather not burn them quite yet,' Guy said. 'But I did have one other idea about finding her. I wondered if you fancied a drive...?'

Guy was waiting next to the gate as Millie rounded the car to join him. She slotted in behind him, half-hiding. Past him was the bed and breakfast, with its unused picnic tables at the front.

'I don't think Judy liked me,' Millie said.

'Nonsense! Well, maybe you're right – but I've never been convinced she likes anyone.'

Before Millie could object any further, Guy was through the gate and bounding towards the front door. He didn't bother with knocking, or a doorbell, instead striding through the unlocked door as if he owned the place.

There was nobody at the front lectern, though there was a vague humming coming from the side room. Guy didn't bother knocking on that door, either, brushing it open and leading Millie into a small tearoom. There were half a dozen tables, almost perfectly spaced from one another, with neat place settings and cutlery at each one.

Judy was on the other side of the room, apron around her waist, belting out 'Live And Let Die' with a complete lack of tune, pitch, or knowledge of the words. It was so bad that Millie first thought a goat had got its foot stuck in a blender in the next room.

She bashed an ancient-looking vacuum into the corner and then spun in one movement, pirouetting until she realised Guy was in front of her. Judy screamed and leapt away, dropping the vacuum's handle and almost tripping over a chair. She clutched her heart and then walloped Guy with her free hand.

'What have I told you about sneaking up on old women?!'

Guy leant in and pecked her cheek. 'If you show me an old woman, I'll stop sneaking up on them.'

Millie almost laughed as Judy melted a fraction. *Oh, you...* she almost said.

Guy turned and pointed to Millie, who was still in the doorway. 'I made a new friend,' he said. 'You know Millie Westlake, don't you? We were talking about the best breakfast in White-cliff and I told her she's not lived until my old friend Judy's cooked for her.'

There was conflict in Judy. She trembled a tiny amount, craving the compliment – though there was a frown, too. Millie was more of an unknown quantity.

Guy wasn't done. He nodded across to Millie: 'I said to her, there's only one way to settle this – we'll have to come for breakfast.'

Millie could barely believe the way Guy had switched from cynical, long-in-the-tooth journalist to some sort of charming ladies' man. There was no gruffness now, no rolls of the eyes. Instead, he was twenty years younger, with a twinkle in his eye.

Millie suddenly realised the reason he'd been doing what he had for so long. It was why he *still* had people emailing and calling him, despite retirement. It was all in front of her. He was a chameleon: whatever the other person wanted him to be.

Judy eyed Millie with suspicion, although they all knew what was about to happen.

'Breakfast finished hours ago,' Judy said.

'Oh, come now,' Guy replied. 'What's a few hours between friends?'

'What sort of friend only comes by once a year to be fed?'

It could have been a serious point but not given the way Judy wagged a playful finger in Guy's direction.

Guy laughed. 'Don't forget when I got Dennis Taylor down to cut the ribbon on this place. Told me it was the best fried bread he'd ever had...'

It was done.

'Fine,' Judy replied. 'What do you want?'

'The works, of course.' Guy nodded at Millie and then made a point of loosening his belt. 'The works times two! I've come prepared this time. There's no way you're defeating me again.'

That got another laugh – and another wag of the finger. 'Take a seat, then,' Judy said. 'I'll have to turn the fryer back on. You're lucky I've no guests at the moment.'

Judy set off for the door, flashed another curious stare at Millie, and then kept going.

Guy waited until she was out of sight and then nodded

towards the seat opposite him. 'You're going to have to sit for this.'

'You never said you knew her,' Millie said.

That got something close to a shrug. 'I know a lot of people.'

That already seemed to be true. 'I don't think I like the sound of "The Works",' Millie added.

'Oh, you will. I was serious that this is the best breakfast in Whitecliff.'

'I really can't keep eating breakfasts with you. I've got my blood pressure to think about.'

Millie crossed the room and pulled out the chair, before taking the seat opposite Guy. The tearoom was the sort of thing that had been decorated once and then frozen in time. For Judy's particular tearoom, that year had been around the time of Charles and Diana's wedding. There was a rack of commemorative plates on one wall, with red, white and blue bunting across the top. A china teapot was sitting in a locked display cabinet, alongside six teacups, all of which had Charles and Diana's faces on them.

'Who's going to tell her about Paris?' Millie asked.

Guy smirked and then picked up one of the spoons from the table. 'You're not allowed to joke about that,' he said.

'I don't think she likes me anyway.'

Guy appeared to check his reflection in the spoon, before returning it to the table.

'One thing I've learned over the years,' he replied, 'perhaps the biggest thing, is that everyone likes compliments. You should compliment people widely, freely and often. As long as it's plausible and genuine, nobody is going to be annoyed.' He paused. 'And Judy really *does* do great breakfasts.'

There was a series of sounds from the room beyond. Pots banging and something sizzling. Perhaps a ding of a microwave and a rumble from the pipes.

Millie wondered if life was as simple as Guy made it sound.

He'd been the one doing the same job for forty or fifty years, so it seemed like he had some idea.

As the sounds continued, Guy stood and did a lap of the room. As well as the Charles and Diana shrine, there were a few framed newspaper articles, all about the bed and breakfast. A fading piece had a photo of Dennis Taylor holding a snooker cue in one hand. There was a ceremonial ribbon in the other as he primed himself ready to open the place. Millie wondered where the scissors were. There were a couple of reviews from the *Journal*, plus one from a magazine called 'UK Bed & Breakfast'. Judy had printed out a handful of TripAdvisor reviews and had them framed, too.

On the other side, there were some old, framed photos of Whitecliff itself. One from just after the war, when a bomb had come down on the site of the old docks and blown the yard into the ocean. Millie had learned about that at school – plus done two separate class trips where they'd walked to the dockyard and seen the memorial, even though nobody had died.

When Judy reappeared, Millie was looking at a photo of the pier from the late seventies. It was packed with a barely imaginable number of people. There was seemingly no room to move, let alone do anything.

Guy was back at the table and Judy spoke only to him. 'Almost ready,' she said. 'Do you want white bread or brown?'

'White, of course!'

He replied as if it was the most natural of choices – but it was clearly the correct one as Judy nodded along.

'I'm the same,' she replied. 'I never got into the whole brown bread scene.'

Millie almost laughed at the idea of a 'scene' for bread but stopped herself.

'You must eat with us,' Guy said, talking to Judy.

'I've already eaten.'

'At least sit then. It's been ages since we had a chat. I've been meaning to come in and tell you how that planning application is going up the hill.'

It was, once again, the right thing to say. Judy touched a hand to her chest. 'Oh... I assumed nothing was happening with that.' She was torn, one step towards the kitchen, the other wanting to stay put and listen. 'I've got to get the toast on,' she said.

'Sit with us after,' Guy replied, cheerily. 'We'll talk then.'

Judy disappeared back the way she'd come, again leaving Millie and Guy alone.

'Do you know everyone in town?' Millie asked.

A laugh: 'I've been here a long time. I've covered every election: Local, European and General, for decades. I try to go to the openings of places and events to meet whoever else goes to those things. I go to fetes and fairs and carnivals. I've sat in courts and at planning meetings. I try to respond to every email. Everyone likes to talk about what they've done and what they want to do. If you let them do that, and you actually listen, there's a reasonable chance they'll talk to you when something important happens.'

Millie did remember Guy from some of the events she'd helped to organise. She hadn't known much about him then, certainly not that he'd once been a close friend of her father's. He'd been an old bloke with a notepad. That had all changed when he'd written about her.

She almost replied, to say that it sounded cynical. That if he listened to others, and perhaps wrote about them, then they'd pay it back in the end. Except, she wondered if that was life in a nutshell. Everyone was doing the same thing – helping out others and wondering if it might be worth it in the end. The difference was that Guy didn't call it karma, or spout clichés. He was far more open about it... or, at the very least, he was more open *with her*.

There was a bang from the kitchen and they both turned

together. When Judy failed to appear from the doorway, Millie twisted back and realised Guy was looking at her.

'There's one other thing,' Guy said. 'I've been meaning to bring it up for a few days.' A pause. 'Actually, for a lot longer than that.'

Millie momentarily had no idea what to say, mainly because Guy didn't seem the sort to hold back.

'Do you know who your godparents are?' he asked.

There was another bang from the kitchen.

'I didn't know I had any,' Millie replied.

Guy pressed back and, as he nodded, Millie knew why he'd asked. He saw it in her.

'Your mum and dad asked me and Carol to do it,' he said. 'We did it gladly, of course. We were honoured. I wondered if you knew, or if you remembered. Carol and I used to talk about it before she...'

Millie almost finished the sentence for him. *Before she died.* There was a sudden sense that the woman wearing the white minidress in the photo in Guy's kitchen, this person Millie had never met, was her godmother.

'Carol...' Millie said.

Guy bowed his head a fraction and Millie could almost see the sadness within him. It might have been the gentle twitch of his eyelid, or the way his nostril flared slightly wider. He had told her about the importance of listening and yet, perhaps, the seeing was important too.

'After everything with your dad,' Guy said, 'after I didn't write that story and we fell out, I didn't know where the boundaries were.' He paused. '*We* didn't know.'

Him and Carol.

Millie's eyes ached and she wondered if she'd forgotten how to blink. 'But you wrote that about me anyway. After Mum and Dad, I mean. You said I wasn't a suspect, even though you knew it would make people think I was.'

Guy bowed his head a little lower and he bit his lip. Something had changed – but the moment was obliterated as the doors banged and Judy backed in. She turned, holding a large oval-shaped plate in each hand.

Millie blinked, finally, and the other Guy was back.

'You're in for a real treat,' he said, talking to Millie, but really talking to Judy. He plucked a napkin from the table and tucked it into his collar, before reaching for the knife and fork.

Judy put down a plate in front of each of them – and it made the one from the diner look like a starter. There were mountains of potatoes, mushrooms, black pudding and tomatoes, plus walls of sausages and bacon. Judy hurried out but returned a moment later with a serving platter, laying a crescent of small bowls around each of their plates.

'That's ketchup, brown sauce, salad cream, mayonnaise, Worcester sauce, and baked beans,' she said, as she slotted into an empty chair.

There was so much food. Millie wondered if this was how Guy lived. Whether he travelled from local café to local café, filling himself with this amount of fried stuff every day. His arteries would surely be chucking in the towel and calling a stop to it all any day.

Not today.

Guy munched his way through each of the items, complimenting everything as if it was his first time. Millie said very little, and didn't eat much more. Once Guy was done with the compliments, he moved on to telling Judy about how the developer who had bought the land a little further up the hill was probably going to build flats. He said they were unlikely to get a permit for commercial or leisure use, which got an audible 'phew' from Judy. She touched his arm and asked if it meant talk of a hotel was off the table.

'That's what I'm hearing,' Guy told her, adding, 'but let's keep that between us.'

Judy said how she'd been having sleepless nights worrying that some hotel would appear that would put her out of business. Guy replied that the quality of her rooms and breakfast meant that would never happen.

He really was quite the smooth talker.

Millie was only half-listening when Guy pointed a fork across the table towards her. 'Millie's my goddaughter,' he said.

For more or less the first time since she'd sat, Judy turned to look at Millie, who was in the process of chopping up a sausage. There was a moment of silence, that millisecond of quiet after someone's dropped something.

'Oh...' Judy replied. 'I didn't know.'

And, suddenly, everything made sense. The trip to the B&B, the flattery, the way Guy had asked Millie if she knew who her godparents were. It was all planned, all necessary, because Guy's next sentence was the only thing that mattered.

'Millie had a minor run-in with Dean Parris the other day,' Guy said. He let it hang – but not long enough for anyone else to chip in. 'Nothing major,' he added. 'A misunderstanding, really. Dean said a few things he probably regrets.'

Millie was chewing on the slice of sausage and she waited. The hook had been baited – and there was no way Judy was getting off. Millie was watching a master at work.

'He always did have a bit of a temper on him,' Judy said. She spoke slowly and reluctantly – although it felt as if they were words she'd been meaning to share for a while. 'A bit of a sharp tongue,' she added.

Guy had stopped eating. 'Did he...?'

There was no need to finish the sentence because he'd already opened the gate – and Judy was off.

'We went out for a while last year,' she said. 'Nothing serious. A few dinners here and there. We had drinks at that new wine bar in town. Bit too fancy for me, all Australian this and South African that.'

Guy let it sit. He was somehow almost done with his food but he swirled a bit of bacon into the congealed sauce. 'Only for a while...?'

'Apart from when we were out, we only came here,' Judy said.

'What do you mean?' Guy replied.

'I never saw his house... I mean I *saw* it – but from the outside. He never invited me in. It got to the point that I asked if we could go in – but he said he was redecorating the living room. Then, the next week, he was having a problem with the water. After that, he said there was damp in the roof and he was working on that. There was always something.'

Guy looked across to Millie, though she couldn't read him. She wondered if he wanted her to join in.

'That does sound a bit... *weird*,' he replied.

'Exactly. In the end, I asked if there was a problem with me and he didn't really reply. That was that.'

Millie thought Guy would say something about Judy's breakfasts being too good for someone like Dean – but that would have spoiled the moment. He tilted his head instead, touched her on the arm, the way she'd touched his not long before.

'You don't deserve that,' he said.

Judy sighed. 'I attract them, don't I? Do you remember Mark? He was already married. Then there was Vince, who owed the Inland Revenue a hundred grand.'

'You've never had much luck...'

Judy nodded along, in total agreement.

'Dean's got a daughter, hasn't he?' Guy said, out of nothing. 'I can't remember her name...'

'Beth.'

'That's right.'

'I never met her,' Judy said. 'I obviously saw her around

when she was younger – but she was at university last year when I was seeing her dad.'

It happened so quickly that Millie was left wondering if it had happened at all. Guy's eyes shot to her and away again. A warning that, if she was thinking of interrupting, then it was not the time.

Millie didn't need it. She knew what was going on.

'Good for her!' Guy said. 'It's a shame more young people around here don't get to go. Which one is she at?'

Judy didn't even think before replying. 'Bath Spa,' she said. 'I think she's doing physical education, or some sort of exercise thing. I can't remember.'

Guy didn't react, other than to sweep the final bit of sausage into his mouth. Millie watched him chew, and so did Judy. He had them in the palm of his hand and, even though Millie knew it was happening, she somehow didn't mind.

She almost flinched when he nodded at her. 'Didn't I tell you this breakfast was spectacular?'

Millie's throat was so dry from the anticipation of it all, that she barely got out the reply. 'It really is the best in town,' she said. 'I can't believe I've never been here. I'll have to come back.'

'How much do I owe you?' Guy asked.

The spell broke and Judy shook herself back into the room. 'Don't be silly,' she said. 'You know you're always welcome – especially when it comes with such good news.'

Guy tapped his nose. 'That's between the three of us and the Queen of Hearts,' he said, poking a thumb towards the Charles and Diana memorial. 'You're going to have to seem relieved and surprised when the planners announce their decision.'

Judy stood and reached for Guy's plate. 'I can do surprised.'

She looked to Millie, whose plate was barely a third cleared. 'You done, love? I know it's a lot.'

Millie almost gasped at the word 'love'. Somehow the hostility was gone and even she was in Judy's good books.

'Sorry,' Millie said. 'It was incredible but I'll need to work up to something that big.'

Judy picked up the second plate and then turned and headed off through the doors, towards the kitchen.

Millie was about to ask Guy how long it had taken him to learn such dark arts when she was distracted by a shadow over the road. A net curtain was partially blocking the view but she stood and crossed, pushing it to one side to look properly. As soon as the curtain twitched, the vehicle moved. She'd only had a glance but Millie knew precisely what it was.

'Something up?' Guy asked.

Millie took a breath and watched the white van pull out of sight, before disappearing somewhere up the hill.

'Maybe,' Millie replied.

THIRTY-TWO

Millie and Guy were back in his office when she finally asked the question she'd been thinking about since they left Judy's bed and breakfast.

'Would you have told me you were my godfather if you didn't need Judy to know?' she asked.

Millie was in the office chair, which she'd apparently commandeered for herself. Guy was resting on the edge of the stacked table, next to the giant map. She half-expected a denial – but wasn't that surprised when Guy shrugged.

'I didn't know whether you knew – and I didn't know if it mattered to you. But I *did* need Judy to be comfortable enough with both of us to say everything she did.'

'You could have told me before.'

'True – but I wondered if you already knew. It's been a great little time getting to know you and I didn't want to risk antagonising you. I thought you might be trying to forget it...?'

Millie started to reply but then stopped herself. Saying it was 'great' getting to know her was a compliment – and she now knew exactly how and when Guy threw them about.

But it also sounded true.

And, despite everything she might have expected, it *had* been good getting to know Guy, too. The fact he was her godfather was a bonus.

It still felt cynical. That he had timed telling her to the moment he needed her to know. She wondered if she minded being used? She would've done in almost every other circumstance – though she was using him, too. The story of the girl on the roof wasn't *his* mystery to solve. She'd gone to him.

'We can look for Bath Spa and Beth Parris now,' he said.

It felt like the next logical step, even though Millie wasn't sure it was. Ingrid said someone had been pushed from a roof, then, after Millie had asked questions, Dean had shown up at the nursing home. He'd been at the end of her driveway. If Dean was interested in Millie because of a simple question, and they were trying to find out what was *really* going on with him, was his daughter fair game?

Millie quickly realised Guy meant the computer behind her. She switched on the monitor and waited for Windows to finish with its usual faffing about. Millie loaded a browser window and typed 'Bath Spa' and 'Beth Parris' into Google. She waited as no results appeared. She tried a few other variations, with alternate spellings of Beth's name and then just Beth itself. There was understandably no publicly accessible database of students, past or present. Many of the associated societies and clubs had their own pages, with links to events and certain members. Nothing mentioned Beth.

Guy had been watching as Millie worked and, when she ran out of ideas, he asked if she could move away from the desk. She assumed he had his own plan of what to look for but, instead, he started opening the drawers. As with everything else in the creaking house, the drawers worked in a not working kind of way. The wood was swollen and warped, with Guy battling each one to yank it out.

It was little surprise that each drawer was packed with even more newspapers, notepads and pens. Guy would fight each drawer, pull out everything inside, mumble something to himself, and then put everything back in before wrestling it back into place.

Barry had trotted into the room but was unimpressed by what was going on, and had promptly headed back out again.

Guy finally found what he was looking for in the bottom of four drawers. It was what looked to Millie like a thick paper-back book. It was covered with a floppy leather cover, with many of the pages falling out. Guy laid it flat on the desk and began flipping through the pages, some of which were apparently upside down. Millie wanted to ask what he was doing but didn't want to interrupt whatever form of madness was unfolding in front of her. Guy was intermittently picking up pens and writing notes in the margins, or crossing out what looked like entire paragraphs.

In the end, Millie couldn't hold off any longer.

'What are you doing?' she asked.

He blinked around at her, almost as if he'd forgotten she was there. 'Sorry,' he replied. 'Not used to working with people...' Guy waved her back towards the desk and then handed her one of the loose pages. Millie scanned it and then offered it back.

'Your handwriting is worse than my seven-year-old son's,' she said.

Guy looked at the page himself, before inserting it into the book at what looked like a random spot.

'This is my contacts book,' he said. 'I started it when I began at the paper. I used to take it everywhere and it'd get banged around in the bottom of my bag. Then all the pages started falling out, so I'd stick them back in. Then I ran out of room, so had to start adding extra pages. Carol used to get on at me about putting it all on the computer but I never got round to it.'

Now he'd explained, Millie could see it. The incomprehensible squiggles on the left side of the pages were names, with numbers and addresses dotted around.

'What's all the crossing out?' Millie asked.

'Dead,' Guy replied.

'Oh...'

It sounded blunt and he must have realised it because he momentarily stopped hunting through the book. 'There are names in here who died ten or twenty years ago,' he added, more softly this time. 'I've been to their funerals but was never much good at keeping things up to date. Carol once said she'd help update everything but I suppose...'

He didn't finish the thought because something faraway drifted across him.

Millie had an urge to ask more about Carol, about her *godmother*, but it was impossible to ignore the sense that Guy hadn't coped with the death of his wife. The reason he was still working so relentlessly was because he didn't want to stop and think.

'Here,' Guy said, as he held up a page from the book.

Millie tried to make out the name written across the top – but it was some sort of letter soup.

'It says Graham, UCAS,' Guy explained – although Millie still couldn't see it. Guy's Gs looked more like ampersands.

It was a strange sight to see someone using a landline phone in a house. It had been years since Millie had watched someone type individual numbers into a keypad. Guy was perched on the edge of his desk as Millie hovered, trying not to send any of the paper stacks toppling.

From the melancholy of moments before when mentioning his wife, Guy was a different man once again. 'It's Guy,' he said cheerily, when the phone was answered. 'How's it going?'

And then they were off.

Millie could only hear one side of the call – but that was

enough: 'How's Jen and the girls?' – 'Oh, really?' – 'What did the doctor say about that?' – An enormous belly laugh – 'I could've told you that.' – Another laugh – 'You've got me there.'

Then there was a change.

Guy sat up a little straighter and the smile disappeared. 'I realised I never thanked you for coming to Carol's funeral,' he said. 'I was sorting out a few things and...' – 'No, I'm good. Been keeping busy with the blog.' – A cough – 'That's the other reason I'm calling you actually. I was wondering if you know anyone in the office at Bath Spa.' – 'Oh, nothing serious. Bit of background. If I give you a name, I was wondering if you could check whether they enrolled?' – 'The last three years.' – An even bigger laugh – 'I knew you'd bring that up.' – 'All off the record. Nothing that'll ever be printed, it's just for checking' – 'Sure.' – 'Perfect' – 'OK, it's Beth Parris. That's Parris like the city – but with two Rs.' – A pause – 'I'll be around more or less all day. You've got my number. When are you back, by the way? I've heard rumours of a new real ale pub opening out where the Travelodge used to be. – 'Good idea. Let's do that. Anyway, I'll wait to hear back. Glad to hear the family's well'.

And that was it.

Millie couldn't do anything other than laugh. 'Do you literally know everyone?'

Guy snorted. 'His dad used to be a head of year at the comp. I did a story about them playing father and son cricket in the Whitecliff seconds a few years back. I think there were three pairs of sons and dads in the same team.' He paused and counted on his fingers. '*Thirty* years back. Goodness.'

Millie was beginning to see why Guy had so many contacts, why he knew so many people. Why almost every scenario could be met with a delve through his book of names. It spanned generations.

'I went to the funeral when his dad died,' Guy added. 'Been to a lot more in recent years. I stayed in contact with Graham and his wife. Great couple, great girls. When I was on the *Journal*, I used to do an annual feature about local kids heading off to university. There was one year we had students going to Oxford and Cambridge – and it was quite a big deal. I ended up running a few things through Graham for that.' Another pause. 'He came up for Carol's funeral last year...'

Millie left him to drift into the faraway place he seemed to inhabit when mentioning his wife.

The 'we' he'd talking about when it came to the students was something Millie had almost forgotten. When she was younger, there was an unquestionable local pride about people from the area going off to bigger things. She remembered the feature in the local paper, naming the places students would be going. Someone in her year got a place at Cambridge and the whole street threw a party. When Guy said 'we', he meant the town. She wondered if that pride was still a part of life in Whitecliff, or whether it was only her for whom it felt absent.

Before she could finish the thought, Millie jumped as the phone on the desk began to ring. The piercing *bringggg-bringggg* of a landline was a vague memory of the past – but it brought Guy back to the present, too, as he pounced on the call.

'Graham! That was quick. I wasn't expecting to hear anything 'til tomorrow at the earliest' – 'I can't get reception up here! You know what it's like at the cottage. Lucky to have internet at all.'

After that, there was a long series of 'right', 'oh right', 'oh really' and 'yeah, I bet' replies, until Guy gave a long 'hrmmm', which was followed by: 'That's what I thought.'

The men then promised each other they'd get together some time, Guy said he'd get the first pints in, and that was that.

When he turned to Millie, the jollity was gone and there was a darkness in his expression that she'd never seen before.

'What?' Millie asked.

'Beth Parris enrolled at Bath Spa university fifteen months ago,' Guy said, 'but she's never recorded any marks.'

It took Millie a moment to catch up. 'What does that mean?'

Guy sighed loudly. It suddenly felt as if a weight had been added to him and perhaps her. 'It means she never turned up for classes.'

THIRTY-THREE

Millie tried to think through the timeline.

'Beth applied to university,' she said. 'She was accepted and enrolled on the course for September last year – but she's never turned up for classes.'

'That's what it sounds like. She might have changed her mind about going...?'

Millie was trying to remember what she'd been told. Away from Jack and Alex, and perhaps a few at the nursing home, she wasn't used to having full conversations with other adults. The past week had been quite the change. 'The neighbour said she waved Beth off on the day she went to university. She *saw* her leave.'

Guy closed the pages of his contacts book and wrestled it back into the drawer. When he'd done, he sat and stared at the map for a while as Millie did the same.

'If Beth never made it to uni, where's she been for almost a year and a half?' Millie asked.

They were obviously thinking the same thing – but it was Millie who said it.

'If she's been in that house the whole time, then wouldn't

someone have noticed?'

'He was seeing Judy at the time but didn't let her into the house,' Guy replied. 'You also said it's detached, so no direct neighbours to worry about...'

Guy was showing another side to his personality. He had picked up a newspaper, apparently at random, and was turning the pages with ferocious speed. Millie didn't like seeing him anxious – because if *he* was rattled, then she certainly was.

'I could try asking the neighbour again?' Millie said. 'Ask what she *actually* saw when she waved off Beth. She'd said something about Beth passing her driving test and I assumed she meant Beth was driving when she said goodbye...'

Millie wished she could remember the exact wording of it all. The neighbour had definitely said something about driving test and then Beth going to university. But did that mean Beth had driven herself when she'd left for Bath?

Guy spun in the chair, his expression grave. 'We have to be careful now,' he said. 'Dean already knows you've been looking into him. The crowbar, parking outside your house...'

'I think he was outside the B&B.' Millie wasn't sure about that, either. There were lots of white vans in every town around the country. 'It could have been anyone.'

Guy was quiet, thinking. 'The crowbar...' he said – and then Millie knew what he meant. The break-in had happened at the house where Beth's best friend *used* to live.

'He was looking for Beth,' Millie said. 'She was trapped in his house, kidnapped, or whatever – but she escaped. He thought Stephanie still lived in her old place and he wondered if that's where Beth had gone.'

A quiet sat between them and then: 'Careful...'

There was something in Guy's tone that Millie didn't like. She was right, she sure of it, but now he wanted to hold her back. Except... Millie wasn't sure what to do next. Given *she'd* been arrested so recently, and that Dean's brother was an officer himself, the obvious choice of telling the police didn't feel safe for either her or, more importantly, Beth.

'We need to find out where the Longs moved to,' Millie said, trying to take control. 'And whether Stephanie still lives with them. Beth might still be with her. Do you reckon your mate might be able to check her name, too? See if she went to uni?'

Millie's phone started to buzz, which made her jump mainly because it was the first time she'd had reception at Guy's cottage. She looked at the screen and the one precious bar of signal. Jack's name was flashing but Millie pressed to reject the call.

'I can't ask Graham a second favour so quickly,' Guy said. 'It doesn't work like that. We do things on trust. He trusts I'm asking for a legitimate reason and that he won't get burned as a source.'

'This *is* a legitimate reason.'

Guy shook his head. 'Beth might not have gone to her classes for any number of reasons. Perhaps she drove down and changed her mind when she got there? Perhaps she went to one class and hated it – but she didn't want to come home and lose face with her friends, or her dad. She stayed in the area and got a job. She told people she knew she was still at university. You said the neighbour waved her off. How would it look if Beth was back a week later, saying it didn't work out?'

Millie had been on her feet, primed to leap into action, except Guy was right. *Annoyingly* right. He'd come up with two possible explanations off the top of his head.

Now he'd put the doubt there, put a dose of *realism* there, Millie didn't struggle to think of more. Guy had only asked his friend to look at Beth in relation to Bath Spa – but perhaps she had multiple offers. Even though she'd enrolled at one university, she could have changed her mind and gone with another offer. Maybe she did simply drop out, with or without her dad's knowledge? Perhaps she met a boy and ran off? Or a girl? Or she could have got into drink, or drugs, or any number of other things that caused her to stop going to classes.

'What do we do?' Millie asked.

Guy started to answer but Millie's phone rang a second time, with Jack's name on the screen. She pressed the button to ignore it again.

'I can make a few calls,' Guy said. 'I don't know the Long family but I can usually find someone who knows someone else.' He sounded a little resigned, perhaps even reluctant. 'I don't like coincidences,' he added. 'The coincidence of the break-in being at their old house... Doesn't mean coincidences don't happen. Something feels *off* – but we have to be careful.'

She remembered him telling her that he'd only publish something with two sources. They weren't talking about publishing but, if that were true of whatever this was, they barely had one.

'Leave it with me,' Guy said. 'I'll let you know as soon as I come up with something.'

Millie's phone vibrated once more, this time with a text from Jack.

I need you

Millie stared at it. He had never sent her anything like it in the past. Not want. *Need*.

'I have to go,' Millie said.

She was already on her way to the door when Guy called her back.

'Leave Dean Parris alone,' he said – and there was something familiar about the way he said it. 'I know I'm not your dad, or your mum – and that you're an adult who can do what you want. But it's not a good idea to put yourself in danger. You shouldn't visit his neighbour, either.'

Millie suddenly realised why the tone felt familiar. It had

the same decisiveness as when her father would instruct her not to do something.

That also meant she usually went and did it as soon as her dad's back was turned.

'I'll wait for you to call,' Millie replied, not sure she meant it.

Guy thanked her as Millie said goodbye and rushed through the house. Her phone was drifting between zero bars and one as she held it to the sky, trying to get it to call Jack. She had two calls fail to connect before it finally rang.

Jack answered immediately with a sorry-sounding: 'Mill...'

'What's wrong?' Millie asked.

'Rish is moving out.'

THIRTY-FOUR

Jack and Rishi's flat had only been built four or five years before. An old, abandoned factory had sat unused for a good fifteen years or more before it was finally demolished to make way for hundreds of new apartments. It had turned one of the grubbiest areas of the town into one of the nicest. Predictably, it had also made a bunch of investors and home-flippers rich.

That was one of the few stories Millie remembered reading in the *Journal* from recent times. It was mainly because someone at Alex's law firm had handled the conveyancing on much of that flipping – and Alex didn't understand what the problem was.

The flats were sited near to the old docks, with some of them having idyllic, brochure-worthy views over the bay itself. Jack and Rishi's had a similarly perfect view – but of the car park at the back.

Millie parked at the rear of the block. She was a couple of spaces away from Rishi's car, in which she could see suitcases and bags piled on the back seat. The back door was open, with a pillow having spilled onto the tarmac. Millie picked it up and stuffed it back inside. She closed the door, before heading up the stairs to the first floor. She hurried along the row, to where Jack was blocking the open doorway to the flat. He had his arms spread wide, with his back to her – and he jumped when Millie tapped him on the shoulder.

Beyond him, Rishi was in the hall, a red rucksack in his hands. 'Let me past,' he said.

Jack re-spread his arms to again block the door, with Millie on the outside and Rishi on the inside.

Rishi pushed himself onto tiptoes to see over Jack's shoulder to where Millie was standing on the walkway. 'Tell him, Mill.'

Millie was in the middle, even though she was literally not in the middle. 'I'm not sure barricading him in the flat is a long-term solution,' she said.

'But we've not even talked about it,' Jack replied, though it was unclear to whom he was speaking. 'You can't just have a minor argument and then break up.'

'It's *not* a minor argument,' Rishi called back. 'I fundamentally want one thing from life and you want the opposite.'

If the scene hadn't been so ridiculous, and Jack's text hadn't sounded so serious, Millie would have laughed. Only Rishi would use the word 'fundamentally' as part of what was, at its core, a blazing row.

'I want more than one thing from life,' Jack called back, his voice faltering as he said it.

Rishi was on his tiptoes again, trying to catch Millie's eye. 'Tell him, Mill.'

Millie pressed back against the balcony's railing. She looked both ways, wondering if the shouting was attracting much attention, which it apparently wasn't.

When she looked back, Jack had lowered his arms and turned to face her. Rishi was over his shoulder.

'I don't particularly want to take sides,' she said, talking to them both. 'But I *do* want to point out that Rishi's car is unlocked downstairs. I had to close the door. Maybe you should lock the car and then talk about this?'

Rishi took a step forward. 'There's nothing to talk about.'

Jack thrust an arm across Rishi's front. 'You're not leaving until we've gone through it properly.'

Rishi hoisted his bag higher but Jack grabbed hold of it. Before they could begin wrestling, Millie stepped in between them, which instantly defused whatever was going on.

'How about I lock the car,' Millie said. 'You should go inside and at least have a go at figuring out whatever's going on. No point in rushing off now and changing your mind tomorrow.'

For a moment, Millie thought they were both about to argue – but, somehow, she was the grown-up in the situation. They stepped inside like a pair of puppies scolded for pooping on the floor.

Rishi dug into his pocket and passed Millie a car key. 'Fine,' he said.

'Fine,' Millie replied.

'Fine,' Jack added.

With a trio of fines, Jack and Rishi ducked inside, as Millie headed to the stairs.

She retraced her way to the cars and then plipped the button to lock Rishi's. It was only as she did it that she realised Rishi could have done it himself from upstairs. She wondered how long he and Jack had been peacocking around up there, waiting for her to arrive.

Not that she minded. Not really. They'd been there for her in the past year, Jack especially. Sometimes, when a situation escalated and neither side felt they could back down, a third party was needed to come along and calm it all.

Millie looked up to the row of doors and windows above, wondering if she should return to the flat, or leave them alone to have some time. She was mulling that over when she noticed the man searching through the pile of items which had been dumped next to the giant metal wheelie bin. There was a broken table, plus a mangled mess of electrical cables, alongside a pile of grubby-looking clothes. The man was picking up the clothes, stretching them out, and then tossing them back if he didn't fancy them.

It was a good minute before Millie realised she was staring. She couldn't explain why but it felt as if something more was happening, aside from the obvious.

The man continued hunting through the pile until he had an armful of clothes and what looked like a pillow. He started to limp away from the block, head down, moving quicker and quicker as he reached the lane at the back of the building.

Millie remembered the stories on Guy's website about the fly-tipping, then the pile that had been at the back of Dean's. She'd assumed Dean had left those things there – but perhaps he hadn't. Guy's article had been in front of her the whole time.

Before she knew what she was doing, Millie was following the man at a distance. She had Rishi's car key in one hand, her phone in the other, and her small bag strapped across her front. Her jacket was still on the passenger seat of her car but she didn't want to lose the man, so continued after him without it.

The man was heading in the vague direction of the town centre. He crossed a couple of roads without using the crossing, then headed through a series of alleys until emerging on a strip half a dozen streets away from the promenade. He continued on, now moving away from the centre, following the line of the river until Millie realised where he was going.

Whitecliff had a homeless community, who had set up a camp underneath one of the bridges about half a mile from the town centre. If the local Facebook groups were anything to go by, residents couldn't decide whether they wanted to throw money at them, or to pick every one up and drop them into the sea. There seemed to be very little middle ground between the differing opinions.

After a while, which usually wasn't long, someone would accuse someone else of being a Nazi. That would have another person saying the original accuser was the *actual* Nazi. Then, when people had decided that everyone who wasn't them was definitely a Nazi, it would all get shut down.

The man didn't look back as he followed the river until he reached the bridge. He headed down the bank, towards the series of tents that had been set up underneath the overhang.

Millie couldn't follow any further without being seen, so she crossed the bridge and sat on a bench on the other side of the water. The wood was cold and slightly damp – and she was left blowing into her hands as she had a clear view of what was happening across the way.

The homeless community in Whitecliff – and perhaps everywhere – wasn't the Special Brew-swigging stereotype with which Millie had grown up. There were a handful of men and women in slightly raggedy clothes standing near the tents having a conversation. Two of them were on phones and there was an extension cable plugged into a socket under the bridge. Also plugged into the socket was a string of Christmas lights that zigzagged across the handrails of the bridge, sending off a rainbow of colour.

It was only the coloured lights which made Millie realise it was beginning to get dark. The sky was a gloomy grey, with the merest hint of blue on the horizon. When Millie checked the time on her phone, it wasn't even four o'clock.

Across the water, the man she'd followed was showing off his haul of clothes to the other members of his community. He gave one of the jumpers to a woman in a thick coat, who instantly removed the jacket to put on the newly acquired top.

As he continued displaying clothes, the man put down the pillow he'd taken. He propped it next to a pair of mattresses that were leaning against a wall, underneath the overhang. Millie stood, ready to leave as a creeping sense of shame began to spread. She shouldn't have followed the man, wasn't sure why she had – and this was none of her business.

Something tingled still. As if she was missing something she should've seen.

She was standing next to a community noticeboard: the sort of thing that got plastered with badly designed posters for people's awful bands. Millie knew that more than most, considering the number of emails she used to get sent from local artists, wanting her to listen to some YouTube tracks and book them at the local festivals. They'd have an all-black logo and be called something like VERTICAL DEATH SPLEEN, then wonder why Millie didn't think they were suitable for opening the town's flower festival.

It wasn't the band posters that attracted Millie's attention. There was a sign saying the local rugby club was looking for players. Millie scanned it, because it wasn't only rugby that was played up on the moors outside town.

Before she could finish, Millie's phone started to buzz. Jack's name was on the screen and she pressed to answer, while walking towards the bridge.

'Where are you?' Jack asked.

'Sorry, I got distracted.'

Millie could hear Rishi in the background, shouting to ask whether she had his keys.

'Tell Rish I'm on my way back,' Millie said. 'Have you sorted things out now?'

'Sort of. He wants to get his suitcases back out of the car but you've locked it.'

'I'll be ten minutes. Fifteen tops.'

Millie retraced her steps until she was back at the block of flats. The rubbish pile at the side of the big bin had spread wider following the man's search. Millie ignored that as she continued on to the car park. She was almost at her car when it felt as if her ears had exploded.

A booming, thunderous roar erupted from the furthest side of the tarmac and then a souped-up black car screeched across the parking area. Its exhaust farted smoke as it screamed towards the road and then merged into traffic the way a punch merges into a face. The driver who was already on the road slammed on his brakes, not that it mattered because the black guff machine had swerved across the lanes and was busy charging its way out of sight. The windows were tinted but she'd bet everything she owned on the driver being a bloke. She watched for a moment longer and then headed up the stairs to the flat.

It was Rishi who answered and then held open the door for her.

'Do I need to block the way to stop you leaving?' Millie asked.

Rishi laughed. 'You coming in for a brew?'

Millie handed him the keys and headed inside. She followed him to the living room, where Jack was sitting on the sofa, tapping something into his phone.

'I think I just saw and heard the reason you're not getting much sleep,' Millie said.

Jack looked up. 'That black thing?'

'Some sort of farting twatmobile.'

'That's the guy. Everyone's complaining to the council but nobody's doing anything.'

Millie plonked herself in the armchair next to the sofa as Rishi sat next to Jack. There were a pair of teas on the table and Rishi picked one up.

'Does this mean you're staying?' she asked.

Jack and Rishi exchanged a look, which was hard to miss considering they were sitting next to each other.

'We're going to talk things over properly,' Jack said.

'See if there's any common ground,' Rishi added.

'Does this mean Rish has to start believing in ghosts?' Millie asked.

'Absolutely not,' Rishi replied.

Jack mimed zipping his lips closed as Millie smirked. She didn't know what else to say. Having children was about as black and white an issue as there could be. There weren't a lot of grey areas in wanting to be a dad, or not.

She didn't say that.

'Are you staying for tea?' Jack asked.

'I only came in to make sure the war is over. I've got to get back.'

'To what?' Jack asked. 'Have you got another dog coming over?'

Millie stumbled for a second, probably giving herself away. She didn't have another client coming to the house and, technically, she didn't have anything on.

Except she did.

'Two dogs getting dropped off,' she lied. 'It's going to be a busy night.'

THIRTY-FIVE

Millie was back in her car when she texted Guy to ask if he'd found anything. It was already sent when she remembered reception was hard to come by at the cottage. She called instead, picturing him knocking over a pile of papers as he raced to get to the landline.

If that's what happened, he sounded calm enough when he answered with a formal-sounding 'Guy Rushden'. Millie had somehow forgotten that people used to answer the phone with their own name. Either that or their own number. It felt like something utterly alien, even though her parents used to do it.

She told him it was Millie and asked if he'd found anything. She already knew the answer before he'd replied. There was something that sounded a little like a sigh from the other end.

'Nothing yet,' he replied. 'I'm still working on other things, too – but I promise I'll come back to you.'

She said goodbye and let him go, wondering if he was prioritising the stupid panther story at the expense of something that felt so much more important. Millie didn't like relying on him, on anyone, really. Not since everything had happened with Peter and she'd ended up on her own.

Over the past few days, she'd needed Guy and his ideas and contacts to shunt things forward. If it wasn't for his experience, they wouldn't know anything about Beth Parris, other than that she had passed her driving test and headed off for university.

Millie took a moment, thinking about the poster asking for rugby, football and hockey players, and what she should do next. She set off, driving through the dark, away from the town – but also away from her house. She didn't want to be home alone and yet she also wanted time away from Jack and Rishi to think things through.

Headlights flared across the night on the other side of the road as Millie edged from traffic lights to traffic lights. Out on the ocean, the pier had been lit up for December, as it always was. It looked like a bright, white bulb floating on the rippling black water.

Millie wondered if there was a way to find out if someone had moved. Companies and councils were told about address changes but Millie couldn't think of a way to find that out about the Long family. She felt sure Guy would have an idea, perhaps something he'd kept from her because he was genuinely worried about her delving further?

Millie had still barely had a moment to process the fact that he was her godfather. She wasn't completely sure what it meant, if it meant anything. There was some vague notion that, if parents died while a child was young, the godparents were supposed to step in. That sounded archaic as it was, plus Millie had no idea what a godparent was supposed to be to a grown-up godchild.

The only thing she knew for sure was that she'd likely missed out on years of presents when growing up.

Millie continued driving, fully out of town as the traffic thinned. Guy's cottage was in one direction but she headed the other way, following the route that would eventually lead to the A-road and, ultimately, the motorway.

Millie smiled as she thought about those missing presents. He owed her years' worth of gifts! She believed him unquestioningly about how and why he'd fallen out with her father. Millie had seen that ruthless side of her dad. He was the sometimes serious, sometimes smiling newsreader. The face of the area. And yet, she'd been in the back of the car when he'd knocked the mirror off a parked vehicle and kept driving. He'd snarled for her to shut her mouth when she'd asked if he was going to stop. She'd seen him smile and shake people's hands, or kiss them on each cheek. Then he'd walk away and mutter 'fat bitch' under his breath. There were the other things, too.

Millie was almost out of town when the dark of the country lanes was replaced by bright floodlights pouring through the night. There were eight or nine artificial sports fields that had been built on the edge of town. They were used by schools during the day, and various clubs in the evenings. It had been twelve or thirteen years before that Millie's dad had officially opened them while doing a live broadcast.

Millie slowed as she drove, taking in the huge banners on the fences that were advertising sign-ups for winter football, rugby and hockey leagues. She pulled into the car park and stopped in one of the free spaces, before turning off the engine. Cars were dotted around, mainly under floodlights, as signs on all the fences advised people that there were thieves operating in the area.

Millie waited, staring off towards the lights and the pitches on the far side of the fence. It wasn't only the poster, she'd missed something and couldn't quite place what it was. Something to do with the man and the rubbish and the scavenging...

Millie got out of the car and opened the boot. She removed her big coat, the one that made it look like she'd been swallowed by it, before locking everything and setting off towards the lights.

The air was cold and her breath spiralled ahead. In the

distance, men were shouting over one another as balls thudded into fences. She wondered if the chill would give her memory a nudge. It was like trying to remember someone's name after meeting them once. That sense of knowing something and yet it being slightly out of reach.

Once she got through the gate, Millie emerged into the walkway between a pair of football pitches. Men were charging around, bellowing 'man on' at one another for no apparent reason. Meanwhile, on the sidelines, more men were jogging on the spot and chugging from bottles of luminous liquid.

Millie wasn't sure of her plan. The various teams were after players, and Beth's friend, Stephanie, had once been into hockey. Perhaps someone would know her, or...?

Ultimately, it was better than sitting home by herself.

Millie continued walking, one end of the pitch to the other. There were empty, unlit tennis courts past the football pitches and then a ramp that Millie followed up towards more floodlights.

The sound was quieter away from the football and she found herself at the edge of a hockey pitch. Women were playing on the one closest to her, while men thundered around the pitch on the other side. There was far less shouting, though the *thwick* of stick on ball sounded ferocious every time someone snapped the ball across the field.

Millie continued further, trying to force her thoughts to come together. What had she seen? A bloke with clothes and a pillow... but there was something else.

There were rugby fields past the hockey, though only one was being used – and it was teenagers, not men. Millie stopped to watch as the groups heaved into one another, like stags butting heads. There was a small boy on the furthest side of the field, wearing the same kit as the others but apparently isolated. His sleeves were over his hands and his arms were crossed.

Even from a distance, Millie could tell the poor lad was shivering.

Millie did a lap of field, in which time the ball didn't get near the boy once. She was back where she entered when a shout went up from behind as one of the lads sprinted free from the pack. He clasped the oval ball tight under his arm, swerved away from someone on the opposing team, and then bolted towards the H-shaped posts.

Millie was already at the steps to head back to the hockey field when a second, louder roar went up. She didn't turn to look, partly because it didn't matter if he'd scored. Mainly because being on the steps a second time had left her with a stumbling, stunning sense of déjà vu. The lights and the pitches were now in front of her, stretching far towards the car park in the distance. Millie had seen the view before, even though she'd never been to the fields.

Her father had stood on this spot when he'd opened the place. She knew that not because she was there, but because he'd been on television. Millie doubted she'd watched it live but she must have seen it at some point. The mayor had been there in her massive chain, and there'd been a ribbon and some scissors. The usual. Her dad had talked about community willpower and spirit that day. About working together and probably some more of the regular guff he went on about.

She stopped and watched the women's hockey game below her, trying to clear the memory of her dad. It wasn't helping anything by having him in her head.

One of the teams was wearing green vests and short, matching skirts. Almost every player had tights on underneath, for which Millie didn't blame them. Millie focused on that, on them, anything that wasn't her dad.

And then she saw her.

The ball fizzed across the surface to one of the women in green. She stopped the ball dead with her stick, looked up, and

then fired a pass through the middle of a pair of opposition players, towards one of her teammates.

There was a snap and then the ball sizzled into the air,
towards the goal. A moment later and there was a boom of ball
on hardened board – and then a low cheer.

But Millie wasn't watching the goal. She was watching the
woman who'd played the pass. The one with bright ginger hair
in a high, tight ponytail.

The girl who had been standing next to Beth Parris when
she'd told the local paper she wanted to play hockey at the
Olympics. Stephanie Long.

THIRTY-SIX

If there was any doubt about the player's identity, then it was gone a few minutes later. The red-haired woman was running with the ball when a teammate shouted 'Steph', trying to attract her attention for the pass.

Millie had been lost in the match but realised she was the only person watching. She was still on the steps, raised a short distance over the pitch as if she was some sort of scout watching the talent.

She moved quickly, ducking her head and hurrying back to her car, where she clambered inside and moved it to a different space in the shadows. She was away from the pitches and the clubhouse, cloaked by the dark but with a full view of the car park.

It wasn't long until a steady stream of vehicles began to arrive through the gates. Half a dozen men clambered out of a blue van, all wearing yellow shirts and matching knee socks. Most were in their own cars, with people grabbing bags from back seats and boots, before rushing off towards the warmth of the changing rooms. As they were arriving, they were swapping places with players who'd finished their games and were heading back to their cars.

In among the individuals with wet hair and rosy cheeks from all the running, it wasn't hard to spot Stephanie. Her red hair was almost glowing under the lights of the car park – and she was noticeably taller than her teammates. A small group of women stood close to the changing rooms, chatting and laughing, before they separated and headed to their cars.

Millie half-thought about dashing across the car park and trying to talk to Stephanie under one of the lights, where it might not feel so abrupt and dangerous. She'd opened her own door when Stephanie stopped next to a silver Toyota close to where she'd been talking. The lights on both sides of the car flashed and then Stephanie dropped into the driver's seat. Millie was out of her car but had to dash back because Stephanie already had her headlights on and was starting to follow the one-way system out of the car park.

There was no escaping how uncomfortable it all felt as Millie slotted into the row of cars and began edging towards the exit. She shouldn't be following a young woman, presumably to her home, and yet Millie couldn't think of a better plan. If she could at least find out where Stephanie lived, she might be able to think of a way of initiating a conversation that led around to a question about Beth Parris.

It made her cringe to think about it... but Millie didn't stop the car. She figured she'd try to come up with a plan while she was driving.

Stephanie was thankfully the sort to use her indicators – which wasn't true of everyone in the line of cars. Millie followed her away from the lights of the sports complex and onto the dark country lanes.

The hedges were tall and the verges dark and frosty. There were no street lights on the outskirts of town. The car at the front would fire its headlights up to full beam to light up the entire road, before dipping them down for cars coming the other way.

As they wound their way back towards Whitecliff, cars turned onto various lanes. Millie kept her eye on Stephanie's until there were no other vehicles between them. Aside from a straggler or two far up the lanes behind, Millie and Stephanie were eventually the only vehicles in sight.

It was the sort of thing all young women were warned about. The nightmare of the stranger in the dark... except Millie was the stranger.

They were following the loop across the top of Whitecliff. The lights of the town and the pier were far below, often obscured by lines of hedges and trees.

At the final junction on the furthest side of town, Stephanie turned to begin the winding route down towards the docks.

Millie wondered if Stephanie knew she was being followed. Perhaps she was on the way to the police station to report a stalker. Or somewhere with lights, and people, where she'd be safe. Assuming she lived in town, Stephanie had taken the long way around to get to wherever she was going.

It wasn't any of that.

They were almost back in the town itself when Stephanie indicated, slowed, and pulled into a spot at the front of a short row of shops. Millie continued past the rank and then pulled in past the next junction, next to a postbox. She turned off the engine, letting the lights go dark as she watched in the mirror as Stephanie got out of her car.

The row of shops was the typical sort that flanked most housing estates. There was a Spar, a betting shop, a Bargain Booze, a pizza place at one end and a kebab shop at the other. Stephanie strode along the row, before ducking into the pizza shop. Millie twisted against her seatbelt, trying to get a better view. Fluorescent light spilled onto the pavement behind. The menu board above the counter was so bright that, if Millie's eyes were a bit better, she'd have been able to read it. Stephanie said something to the man behind the counter that made him laugh and then, a moment later, he handed her a stack of pizzas that she carried back to her car. It had taken a minute at most so, presumably, the order had been put in as Stephanie had left the sports complex. If so, it was no wonder she had taken the long way around, while she waited for the pick-up time.

Seconds later and the headlights on Stephanie's car burned once more, before she reversed onto the road. There was a momentary pause as Millie watched the other woman pull her seatbelt across herself – and then Stephanie was away and driving past.

It was the moment for Millie to bail out. She knew Stephanie lived somewhere in the town and that she still played hockey. There was no need to keep following her. Except... she knew she'd keep going. It was partly because she wanted Ingrid to be proved correct and partly because she wanted to know that Beth was safe. But it was also because, after everything from the past year or so, it felt like there was something in her life once again. Something over which she had a degree of control.

She started the car once more and swerved back onto the road. There was nobody immediately behind, though headlights flared further back.

They were soon back in the land of street lights, with Millie trailing Stephanie with what she hoped was enough distance to not make it obvious she was following.

As soon as Millie realised where they were going, she almost laughed. *Almost.*

Stephanie drove past the first exit for where Jack and Rishi lived, then turned into the furthest end of the car park. It was where Millie had been hours before.

On the far side of the car park outside the block where Jack and Rishi lived was a second smattering of apartments. The

Hargreaves Building had gone up a few years earlier and, instead of views of the docks and the water, the flats had sight of a main road on one side, and backed onto the woods on the other. Hidden between the trees was a trail that snaked around the town and up the hill towards where Millie lived. From there, it continued far past that, on into the next county and beyond. There was some sort of annual sea-to-pub walk, where ramblers would begin at the bottom and then walk the twenty or so miles until the trail crossed a road – which just so happened to be the same place that it passed a pub.

Millie vaguely remembered when the flats were built and developers wanted to cut down parts of the woods to create more. There were protests and banners and someone chained themselves to a digger. Her dad had covered it on the news, as one of the times he got out of the studio and went live.

She was almost lost in those thoughts as she swerved off the road into the car park.

Millie found a spot closer to Jack and Rishi's place, then watched across the tarmac as Stephanie got out of her car, balanced her pizzas on one hand, and then locked her vehicle. She strode quickly for the stairs, disappearing momentarily into the shadows before reappearing on the first floor. If Millie was in Jack and Rishi's bathroom, she'd have had a clear view of the window on which Stephanie knocked two or three times with her elbow.

A few seconds passed and then the door opened. There was only darkness within as Stephanie hurried inside and nudged the door closed behind. Millie was left in her car, warm air firing from the vents, as she stared across the car park.

She wondered if she could simply go and knock on the door and ask if Stephanie knew where Beth was. It would take a lot of explaining in regards to what Ingrid had seen – and how and why Millie knew that Beth was supposed to be at Bath Spa University. None of that knowledge painted Millie in a good light – which is one of the reasons why she suspected Guy had told her to be careful.

And then, suddenly, she was doing it anyway. Millie was out of her car and halfway up the stairs, alternating between the shadows and light in more sense than one. Everything about the apartment block was darker and gloomier than the one opposite. On the walls of the stairwell, someone with wasted talent had graffitied an anatomically accurate impression of a sex act that only a gymnast could pull off. The rail itself rattled and felt as if it could fall at any time.

Millie was at Stephanie's door, watching her breath spiral into the air, wondering what to say. There was Guy and his apparently natural ability to talk people into telling him what he wanted. Millie knew she had none of that.

There was a window on either side of the door – but dark curtains were pulled tight, with only the gentle flickering light of a television visible in the very corner. From somewhere behind, headlights flared across the car park, lighting up the block, before disappearing and leaving everything in darkness once again.

Millie rang the doorbell and waited away from the door, giving space and not wanting to seem like any sort of threat.

The hum of the TV went quiet and there was the gentle sound of someone shuffling before a voice sounded through the door. 'Who is it?'

Millie went to answer, although she was so nervous, so out of her depth, that she couldn't quite remember her name. She got there in the end, stammering, 'My name's Millie' through the closed door. She felt watched.

'Who?'

'Millie Westlake.'

'What do you want?' said the voice.

'I'm, er... looking for Beth Parris.'

It was out there now. Guy had said be careful and her she was doing the opposite.

There was more shuffling from the inside and then the door opened. Stephanie stood in the centre, licking her fingers. Behind her, the hall stretched to the kitchen, where the pizza boxes were stacked on a counter.

'Who are you?' Stephanie asked.

'It's complicated and a bit of a long story. Basically, I work at the nursing home on the other side of town. The one that's just up from the school...'

Stephanie gripped the door harder. 'So...?'

'I suppose I don't actually work there, I'm more of a volunteer. I go in and talk to the residents about their days, or play games with them. Some of their families don't visit very often and, um... it's that sort of thing...'

Millie was rambling, unable to get out of it.

Stephanie's frown of confusion was deepening – and Millie didn't blame her.

'Sorry,' Millie added. 'Someone there saw a girl fall off a roof last week. She told me what she'd seen, so I went down to the house. Figured I'd check. That sort of thing.' Something finally clicked in Millie's brain. 'I went to the house and found out it belonged to Dean Parris. I know his daughter is Beth and that you're her friend, so I was wondering if you'd seen her recently...?'

Silence finally settled as Stephanie stared open-mouthed at Millie. It had been a stream of consciousness. In Millie's head, it had sounded reasonable in a roundabout way – but, out loud, it was utter madness. And that was if Stephanie had no idea who she was. If she knew Millie's name from everything that had happened in the past year, that made it worse.

There were so many questions that could've been asked, not least how Millie knew who Stephanie was and where she lived – but Stephanie answered anyway.

'I've not spoken to Beth since we left school,' she said firmly.

'Oh.'

'I don't know why it matters but she went to uni. I sent her a few messages but never heard back. I assumed she had a boyfriend, or something. Maybe changed her number?'

'Right...' Millie found herself saying. 'Sorry...'

Millie wasn't sure what she expected. Perhaps it was this? When she'd been with Guy, it felt so natural and normal when he did his Jedi mind trick thing.

Stephanie motioned as if to close the door but then she stopped and leaned in a fraction. 'Aren't you the woman with the politician and, um...?'

'Yes.'

Millie wondered if this was to be her lifelong legacy. The woman with the politician and um.

'How did you know where I lived?' Stephanie asked.

It was the obvious question, with the only surprise being that Stephanie hadn't asked it earlier.

Millie felt a panic rising, but then found the words 'electoral roll' forming on her lips. It was inexplicable because she didn't think she'd ever thought about such a thing in her life and yet there it was.

Stephanie edged the door closed a fraction, still standing in the gap. 'I've never voted,' she said. 'I don't really *do* politicians.'

Millie tried to laugh it off as a joke but Stephanie's expression didn't change. Millie reached into her bag and held up her phone. 'I've got to take this,' Millie said, still clasping the phone that definitely wasn't ringing.

She took a small step to the side. Stephanie didn't move but Millie did. There were two more sidesteps and then she was off, head down, making a charge for the stairs, the phone clamped to the side of her face, even though there was nobody there.

'Gimme a minute,' she said to the fake caller.

Millie ran down the stairs, taking them two at a time until

she burst back out onto the car park. She walked as quickly as she could without running, bounding across towards her vehicle on the other side of the car park. She dived into the driver's seat and set the engine running – only then daring to angle herself so that she had a view towards Stephanie's flat.

She was still there, her red hair again almost glowing under the orangey security lights. Stephanie leant on the banister and stared down towards Millie, leaving Millie with a sinking sense that this would all be on social media by morning.

THIRTY-SEVEN

Millie couldn't remember the last time she was so embarrassed. When everything had come out about the affair between her and Peter, it was less humiliation, more horror. She wondered if a part of her had expected it to be revealed at some point.

The encounter with Stephanie had, in many ways, been worse. The face-to-face nature of it, combined with her stream of nonsense left Millie half-thinking about continuing on the road out of town and not stopping. Not much point in bothering to hang around if there was a chance she might run into Stephanie at some point. If it wasn't for Eric, getting out and not coming back might have been more of a viable option.

Guy must have been out of his mind when he said she was a natural at this sort of thing. Millie was never going to go anywhere near the sports pitches again. She could picture Stephanie talking to her mates, or getting into the WhatsApp groups. *You'll never guess who turned up at my flat tonight?* Someone would put it on Facebook and then it would be another example of what a nutter Millie was. What a home-wrecking, selfish, parent-killing *nutter*.

She half-thought about calling Guy and talking him

through the disaster. Telling him it was his fault because, if he hadn't said she was a natural, she wouldn't have dreamt of ringing Stephanie's doorbell. But he was also the one who'd told her to be careful.

'You're an idiot,' Millie said to herself.

She had been driving without a plan in the vague direction of her house. It was only as she neared the row of takeaways where Stephanie had stopped that Millie's stomach gurgled viciously. She had given up on Judy's breakfast and then not eaten since.

Suddenly, the thought of a pizza was overwhelming. Not just a pizza but a pizza *to herself*. Partly because she rarely went out in the evening, and partly because she was a fraction outside the Deliveroo zone, Millie only really ate fast food when she was at Jack and Rishi's. Now, she could buy a pizza, drive home, turn off all the lights and hide in a back room while staying off the internet.

Millie parked in the same spot in which Stephanie had been. She was going to get something with tuna, mainly because Jack couldn't stand the smell, so she never got to eat that at his flat.

She had stopped the car and opened the door when she realised what she'd missed. It hit her all at once, that sudden stab of clarity she'd been craving when she was in the cold at the sports pitches.

It wasn't anything Stephanie had said... it was something else.

Stephanie was slim and fit. A young, athletic woman who – at one point not even two years before – wanted to play hockey at a high level. The sort of person who watches what she eats. She might well treat herself here and there, perhaps to something like a pizza after hockey... but it hadn't simply been *a* pizza. There had been three pizza boxes on the counter behind her in the flat. Perhaps she had a boyfriend with a large appetite? Perhaps she lived in the small flat with both her parents for some reason. Or she had an amazing metabolism that meant she could put away a pizza herself...?

Lots of possible explanations.

Except...

Millie restarted her car and set off back the way she'd come. It was a familiar route to Jack and Rishi's and she half-thought about calling Jack from the Bluetooth, asking him to do... what?

She wasn't sure. She could hardly ask him to go knocking on a stranger's door and ask why they had three pizzas. Three large pizzas. That would make Stephanie think two people were bonkers, instead of only her.

Millie slipped into the car park at the back of Jack and Rishi's flat and parked in the shadows. She wasn't even out of the car before she spotted it.

Nestled on the other side on the car park, tucked into one of the spots next to the entrance to the woods, was Dean's white van with the oversized tow bar.

THIRTY-EIGHT

Millie spent a few seconds trying to convince herself it was a different van. She walked towards it, sticking to the shadows, except the closer she got, the more she knew it was Dean's. The same pattern of crusted mud and dirt was clinging to the lower half and she remembered the shape from when it had been parked outside her house.

There was nobody in the driver's seat, no sign of anyone, and Millie felt the hairs on her arms rise. She grabbed her phone and called Guy, though nobody answered his landline. She tried his mobile but that didn't even ring. Millie thought about running across to get Jack and Rishi as some sort of backup – but there would be so much to explain and it was rapidly beginning to feel as if she didn't have time.

Millie was in the stairwell before she knew it. She dashed up at an even faster speed than she'd ran out what felt like moments before. She slowed as she reached Stephanie's flat. There was no flashing lights of the TV shining around the curtains, no hum of a show. Millie wondered if she should knock, or ring the bell – but, as she was considering that, she realised the door was open a fraction.

More chills. More hairs standing up.

Oh no.

There was quiet from the inside and Millie held her breath as she nudged open the front door. It swung quietly inwards and Millie stepped over the threshold onto the carpeted floor of the hall. There was a long bag on the ground, with a hockey stick on top. In front, the light was still on in the kitchen, the three pizza boxes on the counter.

Millie edged forward a pace at a time. If Stephanie was home by herself and had forgotten to lock the door, this was going to take some explaining. Except Millie could hear something now she was further into the flat. There was a woman's voice and...

She stopped. There was a mirror at the end of the hall, just before the doorway to the kitchen. It was tall, almost floor to ceiling, and angled in such a way that Millie could see through the kitchen, towards what looked like the living room on the other side.

Millie held her breath again. Stephanie was sitting on a sofa, more or less facing the doorway and the mirror. If she looked up, she'd see Millie – except she was angled to the side, where Millie could see the back of a man reflected in the glass. Stephanie's eyes were wide and she was pushing back into the material of the sofa, wanting to get away but with nowhere to go.

'Where is she?' the man asked.

Millie would have known it was Dean, even if his van hadn't been outside. The hard R in the 'where' was unmistakably his.

'I know that you know,' he added.

Stephanie craned her neck back into the material of the sofa. 'I've not seen her since she went to uni. I told you that. I thought she was in Bath.'

She was pleading, as if she'd already repeated the same thing more than once.

Dean began to pace, his back disappearing out of view from the mirror as he moved past the doorframe and then back again.

'I went to your old house,' he said. 'Didn't know you'd all moved. I found out you work at the Costa in town but they said you weren't in last week.'

'I've been ill,' Stephanie replied.

'You don't *look* ill.'

Stephanie started sniffing, as if to prove the point – but Dean wasn't having any of it.

'You were well enough to play hockey,' he said. 'I saw that nosey bitch watching you. I saw her come here.'

Millie felt her chest tightening, the hallway shrinking. He meant *her*. Millie had been so focused on finding and following Stephanie that she hadn't noticed Dean was trailing her. That was despite the fact she was certain she'd seen him outside Judy's bed and breakfast earlier in the day.

Oh, no...

'I know you know where she is,' Dean said. 'You can either tell me – or there's no point in keeping you around.'

Stephanie squealed as Dean reached for something Millie couldn't see. She was about to step forward and start shouting, hoping to make enough noise that someone would come to see what was going on – except she never got the chance.

Instead, there was a click of a door from the far side of the kitchen. Millie shrank away, out of sight of the mirror, as she watched someone stride across the kitchen, past the hallway door, and towards the living room. If the newcomer had glanced to her left, she'd have seen Millie standing there – but she didn't. She was thin, with dark hair and pale skin.

And then, out of sight of Millie, she spoke. 'Dad...?'

Millie could no longer see what was happening but Dean's

voice went up when he next spoke. There was a tenderness. 'Beth! There you are, love. I've been hunting all over. Why'd you leave?'

Beth began apologising. 'I'm sorry, Dad. I'll come home. We'll go back to how it was.'

'I've been so worried. I looked everywhere.'

Millie wasn't sure what was going on – but there was unmistakeable concern in his tone.

'What happened?' he added.

'I needed a break,' Beth said. 'It was a mistake. I've really missed you. I was coming home tomorrow anyway – but we can go now.'

Millie tensed as she figured they would head for the hall. There was only one floor. No stairs to escape up, or doors to dive through. If she made a dash to the front door, she'd surely be seen or heard. She craned her neck forward, giving herself a partial view in the mirror once more. She couldn't see much – but she could see Dean holding onto his daughter's wrist. No, not holding, *squeezing*. Beth's skin was rippled and pinched tight.

She angled forward a tiny amount further. Beth was standing in the kitchen doorway, her back to Millie and with her father now facing the opposite way. If Millie could see him, then all he had to do was look up to see her.

Millie stopped moving. Held her breath again. It felt as if everything had stopped because, suddenly, she knew what he was thinking. She could sense the changing atmosphere, like a dark cloud covering the sun.

'We can't leave her,' he said.

Beth's voice cracked. 'Let's just go, Dad,' she said. 'Steph won't say anything, will you?'

'No,' Stephanie replied quickly – but there was terror in her quivering voice.

Dean reached out of sight a second time – but this time Millie saw what for. When he drew back, there was a large kitchen knife in his free hand. He was still gripping Beth with the other. *Crushing* her wrist.

'I'll finish this,' he said. 'Then we'll go home.'

THIRTY-NINE

Not for the first time that day, Millie moved without thinking. She snatched the hockey stick from the top of the duffel bag and launched herself through the kitchen door. She misjudged the space, bouncing off the frame – but had made enough noise that, as she rounded the corner, Dean was turning to see what was going on. He was holding the knife in one hand and his daughter's wrist in the other – but Millie didn't miss. His nose exploded as she thrashed the stick into his face. He staggered sideways, the knife clanging to the ground as he bounced off the other doorframe.

Someone shouted 'no' but it was too late. Millie had already reeled back and slammed the hockey stick at full swing into Dean's cheek.

The doorframe didn't save him the second time.

He slumped forward, falling face-first, unprotected, onto the floor. There was a sticky thud and then a pool of red started to seep from under him. Centimetre by centimetre, it dribbled towards the kitchen counter, on which the three pizza boxes sat.

Everything and everyone had frozen – including Millie. She was standing with the stick still raised as two sets of wide eyes stared from the room beyond. They weren't looking at her, they were watching Dean as Millie realised why. They – like her – were expecting him to pop back up.

Except he didn't.

Millie poked him with the hockey stick, far more gently this time. His eyes were closed, with blood drooling from his mouth. His nose was flat and halfway across his face – but his chest was at least rising slowly.

This time, when Millie looked up, Stephanie and Beth were watching her.

'I'll call the police,' Millie said.

She was trying to remember where her phone was as Beth interrupted. 'No! My uncle's in the police,' she said.

It was suddenly clear why Beth had been hiding for the past week or so. If she called the police, Liam Parris might have showed up – and who knew how things might have gone then. If the police couldn't be trusted, then surely an old friend could.

Millie was still clutching the stick with both hands. The door on the other side of the kitchen led to a small balcony, from which a freezing breeze was skirting into the room. Millie had somehow failed to notice it before.

'Why did you lead him here?'

When Millie looked back towards the living room, she saw it was Stephanie who had asked.

'I didn't mean to,' she replied. 'I can't believe I did. I was so focused on finding Beth, on making sure she was safe...' Millie glanced to Beth – but it was a different girl from the one who'd been photographed getting her exam results. This Beth was so skinny that her cheekbones were almost rectangular. Her arms were bony and lacking definition. She wasn't much more than a skeleton.

Beth turned away, probably self-conscious of what Millie was thinking.

'I know someone,' Millie said. 'He'll know the right person

to call in the police. He probably knows someone high up. Much higher than your uncle.'

Millie was fiddling with her jacket, trying to get the phone from the pocket.

'No,' Beth said – but Millie's cold fingers were already scraping around the screen as she tried to keep a grip on the hockey stick.

'Hey, Siri,' she said. 'Call Guy home.'

'Don't,' Beth replied – but Millie's phone was already doing its thing. She kept eye contact with Beth, desperately wanting to tell her silently that it was safe.

'Guy Rushden...'

She'd forgotten, again, about Guy's ludicrous phone technique.

'It's Millie,' she said. 'I've found Stephanie and Beth – but Dean's here too. I need you to call someone in the police that you trust. Send them to the Hargreaves set of flats. As soon as you can.' She waited a second. 'Have you got that?'

'Yes. I'll do it now.'

That was it. There were no further questions, no stupid to-ing and fro-ing. The line was dead and Millie knew Guy would already be hunting through his shambolic book of contacts.

She almost breathed easier.

'I want to go,' Beth said. She was looking to Stephanie, who was looking to Millie.

'You brought him here,' Stephanie said.

'It was an accident.'

'How did you even know where I live? Were you following me?'

Millie had to look away. 'I just... I wanted to help.'

It sounded pathetic but Millie had nothing else. She had so many questions for Beth about what had happened, even though she had a reasonable idea. Even though it was none of her business.

Millie glanced down to the ground, where Dean's blood was thickening as it spread towards the centre of the room. It was almost black and there was so much of it.

She wasn't the only one looking.

'Should we call an ambulance?' Stephanie asked.

Both women's stares focused on Beth – and Millie knew it wasn't right to ask someone half her age to make such a decision. Someone who had been through whatever she had.

Beth was staring at her father, her eyes narrow, fists clenched. 'Have you got rope?' she asked.

Millie was about to say she didn't – except it obviously wasn't her who had been asked.

'No,' Stephanie replied. 'Who has rope?'

'Anything to tie him up?'

There was a solid stare of fury on Beth's face.

'There's an elastic skipping rope in my gym bag,' Stephanie said. 'I don't know if it will hold...?'

'In the hall?' Millie motioned towards where she'd picked up the hockey stick but Stephanie shook her head.

'Different bag. In the bedroom.'

Millie felt as if she had missed a look or something that passed between the women because, next thing, they were both heading towards the other side of the flat and, presumably, the bedroom. Millie could hear them talking as dark thoughts swirled over what they were saying about her. She was used to people talking about her and this time, perhaps more than any other, she deserved it.

She had visions of being back in the police interview room, trying to explain how she'd come to the flat.

And then the two women were back. They each had a luminous rubbery-looking skipping rope with a plastic handle on either end. Stephanie crossed back into the kitchen and crouched – except with them out of the room, and Millie lost in thoughts of her own self-pity, nobody had been watching Dean.

He moved so quickly that he somehow went from lying flat on his stomach to being on his feet in less time than it took to blink. He elbowed Stephanie under the chin, sending her sprawling head-first into the counter before she bounced backwards and collided with Millie.

Millie barely kept her balance – but Dean wasn't done. He lunged back towards the living room, grabbing the knife from the ground as Millie stared on disbelievingly, wondering why none of them had thought to pick it up.

Dean snarled and sneered in Millie's direction baring his teeth as he grabbed Beth by her upper arm. His daughter yelped in pain as he squeezed hard. He shushed her the way someone might a yapping puppy. The knife was at the side of Beth's head, the sharpest point barely a centimetre from her temple.

'Drop it,' he said.

Blood was still dribbling from his mouth – and Millie needed a moment to understand what he was saying. His nose was pulp, his words a liquid mumble.

Millie dropped the hockey stick – and then kicked it away to the far side of the room when Dean told her to. Her heart was charging. She had no idea what would happen next as the power was now in one place only. Stephanie was on the ground, hunched and leaning against the counter. She was moaning to herself, chin resting on her chest. Beth's eyes were wide, the whites almost burning, as she pleaded silently with Millie. Her voice told a different story as she gave a soft 'let's go' to her dad.

Dean moved the knife away from his daughter, instead holding it in front of him, thrusting it in Millie's direction.

'There's no time,' Beth said. 'She called the police and we have to go.'

Millie didn't know when Dean had woken up, or whether he'd been out at all. Perhaps he'd heard her calling Guy, plus her half of the phone call? He barely reacted anyway. There was a dazed lack of focus about the way he was staring *through*

her, rather than at her. Considering how hard she'd hit him –
twice – it probably wasn't a surprise.

Dean grunted as he shuffled sideways along the wall, using
one hand to keep the knife between him and Millie. The other
was holding a trembling Beth.

Millie had little choice but to move away from the hallway
door, shuffling backwards until she was at Stephanie's side. She
risked a quick glance to the counter, looking for something more
weighty than the pizza boxes. Apart from half a roll of kitchen
paper, the only thing within reach was a sharp-edged wheel
cutter. There was no way Millie could grab it before Dean
could do some serious damage with his knife.

She'd only looked away for a moment but, even in his
confused fug, Dean had seen it. 'Don't,' he said. The fact it was
a slightly gurgled whisper was even more chilling than a
shouted threat. With blood still leaking from his nose and
mouth, he was a horror movie villain.

Dean began backing along the hall, now using Beth as a
shield between him and Millie. The knife was ever closer and,
as Millie made eye contact with Beth, the young woman gave a
gentle, horrifyingly resigned, shake of her head.

It was done.

Father and daughter had backed onto the walkway and
then, out of sight.

Millie crouched quickly and touched a hand to Stephanie's
shoulder. 'You OK?' she asked. The only response was a low
moan.

Not knowing what else to do, while almost crippled from
the sense that she'd brought it all on, Millie snatched the pizza
cutter from the counter. She hurried along the hall, into the
night air, where Dean was disappearing into the stairwell.

Millie had no clue what to do – but following him, while
hoping for the police to arrive, was her only idea. By the time
she got to the tops of the steps, she could hear movement from

the bottom. Millie rushed down but, when she reached the edge of the car park, Dean and Beth were already partway across.

Except they weren't moving.

Dean had an arm outstretched, across Beth, whom he was no longer holding. His van was twenty or thirty metres away, still in the same spot near the cut-through to the woods.

But he was a statue.

Beth took the smallest of sidesteps away. And then a second. Her dad still hadn't moved. He was staring towards his van in the shadows.

...And then Millie saw it.

There was a dark shape clinging to the edge of the gloom. Something sleek and athletic. It was black and yet it was shimmering, as if it had some sort of silver coating. There was yellow in its eyes, like a pair of twinkling Christmas lights.

Millie stared – but Beth was looking the other way. She took a second step to the side, then a third. Her father seemingly hadn't noticed. He was swaying gently on the spot, transfixed by the shape in the shadows.

The roar came from nothing, exploding through the night, obliterating Millie's ears once more. She held up her hands instinctively to cover them, forgetting she was holding the pizza cutter as it clattered to the ground.

It all happened so fast – the roar hadn't come from the shadows around Dean's van.

The black car barrelled out from the other side of the car park, its exhaust thundering like blasting in a quarry. There were no headlights and, if it wasn't for the howling noise, the black of the car might have been lost in the black of the night.

Dean still hadn't moved – but Beth saw what was about to happen a moment before it did. She darted out of the way a fraction of a second before the car smashed into her father. Dean's body almost seemed to hover as he was thrown upwards, before flying backwards and slamming into one of the pillars at the base of Hargreaves block.

The car fell silent and there was a few seconds in which the night was still.

Millie stared across the car park towards Dean's van – but the shape was gone from the shadows.

And then someone started screaming.

FORTY

Millie blew into her hands as she tried to remember where she'd left her gloves. They might be in her car, though they hadn't been in the *actual* glove box. She hadn't had time to go looking for them properly.

And then she appeared, swallowed by a coat that was too big for her and wearing oversized fluffy boots. She smiled as she got closer, though it didn't feel as if there was much behind it. Not that Millie could blame her. There was a scratch around the young woman's eye and another under her cheek.

'Hi,' Beth said, as she reached Millie.

Millie was hovering next to the entrance to the pier: a place so public that she'd have never chosen it herself. Her hood was up which, for the most part, had given her anonymity from the sideways stares to which she was so used. Beth had spotted her, though.

'I wasn't sure you'd come,' Millie said.

The pier entrance was decorated with a string of Christmas lights that looped up and over a series of archways. Thousands more lights were hooked along the walkways and barriers, stretching out into the deep black of the ocean. Families and groups of teenagers were walking up and down the promenade. The arcade machines were dinging and the freezing air smelled of candy floss and chestnuts.

'Do you want to go somewhere else?' Beth asked.

'Sure. I thought—'

'That was Steph. She said somewhere public, just in case...' Beth gave a small shrug and a smile.

She took half a step away before Millie stopped her. 'I hope you don't mind, it's just...'

The younger woman turned and followed Millie's stare across towards the car parked in the bay nearest the pier. An old woman was bundling her way out of the passenger seat, batting away Jack's offers of help.

Ingrid stopped on the kerb and beamed across towards Beth.

'Ingrid?' Beth asked.

Somehow, despite the bustle, it was as if only her voice existed.

'How are you, love?' Ingrid asked.

Beth weaved across the path, sliding around a couple until she was in front of the older woman. Jack was off to the side, hovering awkwardly, not knowing what to say or do, as Millie joined them.

'I can't stay long,' Ingrid said. There was a twinkle to her eye, though the shiver was unmistakable. 'When I heard you were safe, I forced these two to bring me here. Had to see you for myself. Hope you don't mind...?'

Beth was shaking her head and then, in a blink, she had an arm around the older woman. 'I don't know how to thank you.'

Ingrid did her best to hug the younger woman back, though she was using one arm to rest on the car, and the other didn't go the whole way around.

'I wanted to see you for myself,' Ingrid repeated as she stepped away.

'Do you want to sit somewhere?'

Ingrid shivered again. 'Another time, maybe. It's too cold. Too dark. Hate this time of year.' She stretched a hand towards Beth and then lowered it. 'You're real. I told everyone you were real and only these two believed me.'

Beth glanced around to Millie and, by the time she focused back, Ingrid was trying to open the car door. Jack helped but, before Ingrid could eke her way back inside, she managed another 'You're real!'

Millie and Beth watched as Jack shrugged and waved a goodbye and then, as a traffic warden started to cross the road, he was off and away.

'Sorry,' Millie said, when it was only her and Beth. 'She wanted to see you and I thought—'

Beth batted away the concern. 'I'll have to thank her properly sometime. *Talk* to her properly sometime.' She turned and took in the rest of the street and then: 'Shall we go somewhere else? Just me and you?'

The two women turned and walked away from the organised bedlam of Christmas in Whitecliff. They passed the chip shops and the chain pubs; the hotels with their 'no vacancy' signs and work parties raging in the function rooms.

Neither of them spoke – but Whitecliff was alive enough for the both of them. They walked for a good ten minutes until Beth crossed the road and then settled on a bench that overlooked the rippling sea.

Millie sat on the opposite end, as Beth turned to look at the plaque. She sniggered, which had Millie checking it out.

For Robert. He just wanted everyone to shut up.

'I think I'd have liked Robert,' Millie said.

That got a gentle laugh. 'Robert is my spirit animal,' Beth replied.

The bench was cold but the night was colder. The sky was clear and the stars were bright.

'I can't believe I led him to you,' Millie said. 'I didn't mean to. I was trying to help.'

Beth was quiet for a moment. She had every right to be furious. 'You didn't know,' she replied. 'It worked out.'

It was true and yet... it wasn't really the answer. Millie couldn't forget Guy telling her to be careful. She should have listened.

'You're famous,' Beth added.

Millie could sense the younger woman watching her sideways – but she couldn't meet the stare. Instead, she continued looking across the water, back towards the shimmering, winking lights of the pier.

'Not really,' she said. 'Not for good things.'

'I wasn't allowed on the internet when he put me upstairs,' Beth said. 'Dad would let me read a newspaper every day. He must've been one of the last people on the planet still buying one. He'd get the *Journal* each week, too, and I'd read everything cover to cover, even the sport.' A pause. 'I read about you and the politician, then about your parents.'

Millie sagged a little on the bench, as if it was sucking her in. There was a sense that she'd never escape the notoriety she carried.

'What do you do when you're in the middle of it all?' Beth asked. 'When people all know your face and you see them whispering about you. Or they actually talk to you?'

It took Millie a little while to reply. 'I stayed inside a lot,' she said. 'At first, anyway. My friend Jack would stay over sometimes – or he'd take me somewhere away from Whitecliff. In the end, I had to stop caring what people thought. I had to leave my job, so I started again.'

'What do you do now?'

'I groom dogs and do a bit of obedience training. I volunteer at the nursing home where Jack works. That's where I met Ingrid...'

Millie felt Beth breathe in at her side and she knew why. There was that right turn-left turn moment. So many ifs. What if Ingrid hadn't been looking out her window that night? What if Millie hadn't gone in the next day? Or if she had gone in but ended up talking to someone else? So many small things that had created the whole.

They were quiet for a minute or so. Far out on the sea, a pinprick dot of white light had drifted around the cliffs. Some sort of boat chugging its way back towards what was left of the docks.

'I think I want to tell my story,' Beth said. 'Properly, to a real person, not just the police, or Steph, or...' A pause. 'To *one* other person. All of it. Then they can tell everyone else and I never have to say it again.'

She sounded so fragile as she spoke and yet Millie was almost paralysed by the maturity on show.

'I know a person,' she said.

'What about you?'

Two or three softer, red dots had appeared next to the sharp white one as the boat edged closer to shore. Millie turned from it and, for the first time since they'd sat, actually looked at Beth. The young woman was still buried in her coat. A white face lost among a bundle of brown fabric.

'I'm not a reporter,' Millie said. 'I don't—'

'Have you got a voice recorder on your phone?'

'Yes, but—'

'You'll want to record this.'

With little other option, Millie took out her phone and

swiped around the screens until she found the voice recorder app. It was buried away in a folder marked 'Utilities', none of which she could ever remember using.

Millie pressed record. 'Are you sure you want to do this?' she asked.

Beth didn't reply. Not specifically, anyway. She simply started talking. 'Mum died when I was born,' she said. 'It was just Dad and me and he was... *good*. He'd take to me to clubs and things like that. He'd pay for kit and whatever I needed. He went into primary school when some girl was bullying me. He *was* a good dad. I want you to say that. I want people to know.'

Millie wasn't sure quite what Beth meant by wanting her to 'say that' – but she wasn't about to interrupt.

'He wanted me to go to uni,' Beth added. 'He checked over my forms before I sent them in. He'd ask about my coursework. Then I got accepted to go to Bath and...'

Beth stopped and shrank further into her coat. She was barely a set of peeping eyes watching the lights which had morphed fully into a boat that was following the line of the shore.

'I got waved off,' Beth said. 'Dad was driving me to uni in his van. All my stuff was in the back and a few of the neighbours came to say goodbye. They bought me a cake.' She laughed humourlessly to herself. 'We set off out of town and then onto the motorway but Dad was really quiet – which wasn't like him. He'd turned the radio off and we were just sitting there. I asked if he was OK but he didn't reply. Then, when we got to the services, he pulled off, even though we'd only been going about an hour. He said he'd heard something at the back, so he went to check. Then he called me around. He said, 'Come look at this' – so I got out and went to the back of the van and then... I don't know. I woke up in a room I'd never seen before.'

Beth's voice was so fragile that Millie had to lean in to hear.

She wondered if the voice recorder was getting any of it, let alone all of it. Despite her tone, there was an urgency to everything Beth was saying, as if she couldn't get it out quickly enough.

'There was a skylight,' she continued. 'It was dark but I could see the moon. There was carpet on the walls and the ceiling – which I'd never seen before. I didn't understand at first. Have you ever seen carpet on a ceiling?'

It took Millie a second to realise she'd been asked a question. 'No,' she replied.

'I was in the attic,' Beth said. 'Dad had converted it over months when I'd been at school, or out, or wherever. I had no idea until he came up and told me where I was. He said he couldn't let me go, that I was all he had.' Beth sighed and then added: 'That was it. I shouted a bit on the first nights but nobody ever came. I think that's why the carpet was there – so nobody could hear.'

Millie realised she was covering her mouth. Her fingers were freezing but she'd not noticed. Guy had told her about the three-week gap between Dean's father dying – and then his wife in childbirth. He'd gone from having a family to having only a baby daughter. A daughter he'd raised for eighteen years, until, for the first time in his life, he was going to be alone.

That had been fifteen months before.

Millie couldn't speak, even if she wanted to. She was overcome by horror.

'He'd bring me three meals a day,' Beth said. 'Plus snacks. He'd come up and say he was going to the Big Tesco and he wondered if I wanted anything. I had a TV and he'd bring me a newspaper every day – two when the *Journal* was out. I'd never read a paper and then I was reading one every day. He'd get me magazines too...'

'Did you ever get to leave?'

A shake of the head. 'He'd installed a toilet and a sink. They were already there when I woke up. He'd leave me towels and toilet roll. I didn't have a proper shower in over a year. I thought I'd die in there or, worse, that *he'd* die and I'd be left to starve.'

The boat was close to the shore, its spotlight beaming across the black of the water as it slowed to a gentle bob. A man was on the hull and he leapt across to the docks, before hooking a thick rope onto a hook, then dragging the boat towards him.

A part of Millie wished she wasn't the one to hear this. The same part of her didn't particularly want to consider this sort of horror because ignorance provided safety. The other part of her, the larger part, simply wanted to hold the poor young woman.

'Did he...?'

Beth shook her head and Millie wished she hadn't asked.

'It wasn't like that,' Beth said.

Millie didn't reply immediately. It might not have been like that, though it still wasn't right.

'How did you get out?' she asked eventually.

'Dad would come up and open the skylight to let in a bit of air. There was a lock, so I couldn't do it myself. It would get really hot in the summer and I'd have to bang on the hatch to get him to come and open the window. In the winter, there was so much condensation that it would drip from the roof. He'd open the window to try to get rid of it – but that would make it cold, so it couldn't be open for long.'

'Is that how you got out?'

'He'd come up earlier in the day to say he was going to be on a job that night. He always told me if he was going to be out, because it meant he'd bring my food earlier or later. I was on my bed and felt this breeze and then I looked up and realised the skylight wasn't locked. He'd closed it but he hadn't pushed the padlock together properly. It had been like that for hours and I'd not noticed. I couldn't believe it. I thought it might be a test, or... I don't know what I thought. I even called out to him. If Dad had come up, I'd have told him he left the window unlocked. I don't know what I was thinking.'

She shook her head and Millie could understand why Beth didn't want to keep telling the story. She'd have already told it to the police and probably Stephanie. Nobody wanted to keep reliving the same thing over and over. And that's when Millie realised why it was her that Beth wanted to tell.

'I opened the window,' Beth said. 'I had to climb on a chair and pull myself up. I was on the roof and it was freezing. I'd not thought ahead and I was up there in my nightie. It was so cold and, when I moved, a tile fell off and smashed on the floor. I wondered if someone had heard it, or if Dad was home. I was up there shivering and waiting – but nobody came. I looked down but it was so high and I didn't know what to do. I wondered if I could slide down the drainpipe – but it was on the other side and thought it would fall off anyway. I had this giant teddy in the room. I'd had it from when I was little and I guess Dad left it in there for me. I managed to get it up on the roof with me and wondered if I could somehow jump and land on it. Then I looked down and you'll never guess what I saw...'

Millie knew. Her brain had put it together in the end, even though it had taken a while.

'A mattress,' she said.

Beth moved quickly, shrugging off the hood of her coat and gripping Millie's arm. 'How did you know?'

There had been the leftover junk at the back of Dean's house, Guy's fly-tipping story, then the extra rubbish near Jack and Rishi's. Millie had seen the man hunting for something useful, plus the mattresses under the bridge. At some point between Beth landing on it, and Millie visiting the house the next day, the mattress had been dragged away.

When she'd followed the people who'd been hunting through the bins, Millie hadn't quite known why it was important. It had taken time to fester but she'd got there in the end. And it had led her to that poster looking for new hockey players.

'A bit of a guess,' Millie said. 'It was the most confusing thing about Ingrid seeing someone fall off the roof. Nobody could've landed without breaking bones. Whoever it was had to have landed on something.'

Beth thought on that; Millie figuring out that part of it had seemingly thrown her.

'It was a miracle,' she said after a short while. 'Like someone had left it for me. It had all lined up, with Dad being on a job and the window being open – and the mattress being right there.'

'It was still brave to jump.'

Beth didn't react to that – but one more mystery had been solved. When Ingrid thought she'd seen someone *push* Beth, she'd almost certainly seen the giant teddy on the roof. If not that, then simply a shadow that wasn't there from Keith's angle.

Beth stopped for a moment, watching as the four men who'd been on the boat started to unload a series of crates into the back of a white van.

It wasn't *that* van but Millie could see why Beth had stopped speaking.

'I thought about going back for my shoes,' Beth said after a while. 'Warmer clothes, too – but I didn't know when Dad was due back. I didn't even know what time it was. There was no clock in the attic. I just knew it was late – and that he might come back – so I jumped.'

'It's still amazing you didn't hurt yourself.'

'That was the miracle. The mattress being right there – and then I hit it perfectly. I twisted a bit in the air and landed on my back. I thought it would hurt but I tried standing and it was fine. Just cold. *Really* cold.'

Millie pictured the bare footprints frozen into the verge.

The tile, too. If it hadn't been for those things, perhaps she'd have dismissed Ingrid's story.

'What did you do?' Millie asked.

'I hadn't thought that far ahead. When I was out, my first thought was to go back in and look for my phone. Or any phone. I thought about going to the neighbour – but all the lights were off and I wondered if she knew. I wasn't thinking right. I thought about the police, obviously – but I didn't know how to contact them and I didn't know if my uncle would come out.'

She stopped as the white van on the docks growled to life, its headlights searing through the night. All four men were inside and it rumbled away from its spot, edging towards the road, before accelerating up the hill and out of sight.

'There was a phone box,' Beth continued. 'I didn't think it worked. I didn't even know what it was until I was about twelve or thirteen. We did this thing at school about old technology – and none of us knew how those phones worked.' She laughed gently to herself at the memory. 'I picked up the handle – and there was a hum. When Steph and me first got mobiles, we memorised each other's numbers. It was the first one I ever knew. Still is. Someone had left a pound on the box in there – another miracle, I suppose – and so I put it in, called her number, and then we were talking. She came and picked me up. I hid in the hedge for a while and I was sure Dad would come back – but he never did. Steph pulled in by the phone box – and that was it.' She stopped. 'I didn't think anyone could have seen me jump...'

Beth had spoken of miracles – and perhaps Ingrid was another.

'Were you with Stephanie the whole time?' Millie asked.

'She called in sick to work and we ordered in food. She didn't want to risk running into my dad if she went out to get things. We were trying to figure out what to do. I couldn't risk running into my uncle if we went to the police. She said we could tell her mum and dad – but they were in Cancun and weren't due back for another week. She'd only just moved into her flat and hardly anyone knew where she lived. It was safe, so we stayed there and it was... well, nice, I suppose. We'd not seen each other in over a year. She thought I'd gone to Bath and ghosted her.'

'She's a good friend if she thought that but still came to pick you up without question.'

'Yeah...'

Beth was silent for a little while. Across the bay, back towards the centre, the lights were starting to turn off. They were replaced by headlights and tail lights as people in town for the Christmas decorations began to drift home.

'We couldn't stay inside forever,' Beth said. 'Steph wanted to go to hockey practice. She's played since we were kids and never misses a session. She said she'd get pizza on the way back and we were really hungry because we'd run out of food.' A pause. 'I guess that's what led you to us?'

Millie turned away, unable to look anywhere near Beth. It had also led Dean to them. It had put both young women's lives in danger. 'Right...'

It felt as if the story might be over. Millie was ready to answer anything Beth had – but there was nothing. Millie wouldn't blame her for wanting to move on.

Beth was looking past the town, up towards the cliffs in the distance. It was dark but there was a hint of shadowed moonlight cast across the vague outline of what looked like a giant puppet. They'd both grown up in Whitecliff, and both knew what it was.

'It must be the Bay Burning soon,' Beth said. 'We used to go every year when I was young.'

The Bay Burning was one of those traditions that only seemed to happen in one town. A large marionette was being constructed on the cliffs and, in a couple of days, residents would head up to write down their grievances and concerns – and then deliver them to the puppet. After a short ceremony, it would be set on fire and then sent over the cliffs into the ocean, as a way of cleansing the town's problems. For people who grew up in Whitecliff, it was the most natural ceremony imaginable. It was only when they described it to people who *didn't* come from the town that it sounded as mad as it was.

'I know what I'd write down,' Beth said.

Millie had a pretty good idea what she'd write, even though she knew she wouldn't go. It was probably a year too early for Eric. The sight of the fire and the ceremony could be scary for younger children.

'What's happened with your uncle?' Millie asked.

A shake of the head. 'Nothing, really. He says he thought I was in Bath. It's just...'

'What?'

'Before he was a policeman, he was a carpet fitter.'

Millie felt that creeping tingle of Guy's voice in her head, telling her to be careful. There were still unanswered questions about the crowbar in her house and who'd told the police there was a disturbance. Millie wasn't sure she'd get a proper answer about that – but, if she was certain about anything, it's that she would be even warier of the police in future.

'He and dad shared everything,' Beth said. 'I know that he knew...'

There was no answer to that and Millie knew that whatever came of the recording, this particular part would never see the light of day.

'What are you going to do next?' Millie asked.

'I've been referred to a therapist – but I think I want to get away. Somewhere warm. Steph's mum and dad say they know someone in Mexico that could put us up for a bit. I don't know. Maybe I'll go to uni after all? Cut my hair? Change my name...?'

She looked to Millie once more. 'Have you ever thought about doing that?'

'I...' Millie was stuck. The question had come from nowhere but she didn't feel as if she could lie. Not to Beth, of all people. 'I don't think I should have to change my name,' she said. 'Or cut my hair. If other people have an issue with me, that's their problem.'

'Steph said that people reckon you killed your mum and dad?'

'Some do.'

'Why?'

'I think...' Millie sighed. 'It's complicated. There was a thing in the paper that said I wasn't a suspect, except nobody else was named *as* a suspect. That was when nobody believed Mum and Dad could have killed themselves. When it hadn't even been suggested. People said they had no reason to do it. That Dad was still on the telly and looking forward to retiring. That Mum had already retired and was busy with her bridge club and other things. Then everyone on Facebook was asking why I'd done it – and people were saying I did it for the house, or the inheritance. That I'd been left with nothing after the affair. People already thought I was a terrible person – so it wasn't a big stretch. Others were saying there was no proof but it was too late by then.'

It was the first time Millie had ever laid it out so forensically. She wondered if there would be a follow-up question. Perhaps the obvious follow-up. She knew she'd tell the truth.

'I've got something to ask you,' Beth said.

But it wasn't that.

'Do you know why he stopped?' Beth added.

Millie had been bracing herself for the big question that hadn't come. 'Why *who* stopped?'

'Dad. I thought we were heading to his van but then he just... stopped. Like he'd seen a ghost or something. He kept staring into the shadows – and then that car came out of nowhere.' She took a breath. 'Did you see anything?'

Millie had replayed those moments ever since the car had slammed into Dean. She thought there'd been something sleek with bright yellow eyes – except the only other person now alive who'd been there apparently hadn't seen it. The more days that had passed, the more it felt like a dream. Or, perhaps, the more it felt like one of Beth's miracles.

'No,' Millie said. 'I didn't see anything.'

FORTY-ONE

'Can I read you this review?' Millie asked.

Guy was in his kitchen, battling a chicken into the oven. 'What's it for?' he asked.

'The beach.'

'Who reviews a beach?'

'That's kind of the point. Listen to this.'

Millie had been so bemused by the review that she'd screen-grabbed it so she could read if ever she was feeling bad about herself.

Whitecliff Beach

The sand is much too sandy and I lost my flip flop.

One star

Guy laughed. 'Is that a real review?'

'Do you think I'm making these up?'

The oven door was slammed shut and Guy stood, then crossed to the table to sit next to Millie. Barry remained in the middle of the floor, staring at the oven and the chicken beyond. His tail swished across the tiles, like an inbuilt sweeper.

'I had to get a new web host for the blog,' Guy said. 'The site should be back up now – but I wasn't expecting so many visits. The record number of views for a story before now was about six hundred. I had more than a year's worth of hits in under an hour.'

'Are you sure it wasn't the fly-tipping follow-up that took the site offline?'

That got another laugh. 'I said you were a natural.'

'All I did was type up what Beth told me. She didn't want to read it. Said to put it up and that she was going on holiday.'

Many of the thousands of hits Millie's piece had received came from various other news organisations that had taken the story and the quotes to republish. Beth had refused to talk to anyone else – and disappeared to Mexico with Stephanie. Hardly anyone knew that because, after Dean's body was recovered, the police had to make a statement about what had gone on. Since then, the media were infatuated with the story of the father who held his own daughter hostage for a year. The fact his brother was a serving police officer had been left out of everything. When it came to Liam, nothing could be known for sure. Nothing could be proven.

'How's the panther story going?' Millie asked.

'Gone cold. No sightings. No prints. I don't think I'll get to write it.'

It wasn't only Beth that Millie had failed to tell of what she thought she saw a moment before Dean was hit by the car. She hadn't told anyone. She didn't want to be the woman who saw things in the shadows.

Barry started sniffing closer to the oven, before turning to look at Guy. The dog tilted his head, as if to ask when the food would be ready.

'Are you going to keep it up?' Guy asked.

'Keep what up?'

'Poking your nose in around here. I know it's a small town

but you'd be surprised about the secrets people have buried.' A pause. 'After this, maybe you won't be surprised.'

He sounded serious, even though Millie wasn't convinced he was. 'I like working with my dogs,' she said.

'Do both.'

Millie didn't reply to that. In the last year or so, she hadn't thought too far ahead – although maybe that was the problem. Even when she was married, she'd felt alone for a while but now... perhaps that wasn't true any longer.

'Alex is gay,' Millie said. 'That's why I had the affair.'

Guy had been reaching for the bag of sugar to add more to his tea but the spoon had stopped halfway there. 'Your ex-husband?'

'Right. I mean, I guess he's bi technically. I'm not sure it matters. Eric was struggling to sleep through the night and we had these baby monitor things to see if there was a pattern to when he'd wake up. I'd get alerts on my phone and then I'd be able to check the video in the morning. We used to turn it off during the day – but I suppose I forgot one morning. I was at work when I got an alert. I thought there might be a burglar – but it was Alex and... he wasn't alone.'

Guy put down the spoon on the table and turned to face her properly. 'Were they...?'

'Whatever you're imagining is what they were doing. I don't know why they chose Eric's room. I never asked.'

'What did you do?'

Millie couldn't finish the story if she was being watched. She reached for the spoon and heaped half a dozen sugars into Guy's mug, before stirring it for him. He seemed to get the message as he picked it up and spun to watch Barry on the floor.

'I didn't do anything,' Millie said. 'I didn't want to leave Eric without a dad. Ironic, considering what happened, I didn't want kids to pick on him at school. I didn't want to face everyone saying how brave Alex was for finally coming out, as if I was some sort of prop for it all. I carried on as if nothing was different. I'd get tested once a month, just in case – and then I met Peter.'

Guy was holding his mug, not drinking. 'I didn't know.'

'How would you?'

'Does anyone else?'

'Only Peter. I could've said something at the custody hearings but I didn't think anyone would believe me. Even if they did, it would have made things worse for Eric.'

Guy blew out a long, low sigh. 'I've heard some stories over the years...' he said.

'Can you find out who leaked it?' Millie asked.

Guy was looking at her again, confused now. 'Leaked what?'

'Someone must have told the paper or the photographer about Peter and me. They had someone right there. They knew where we were. It wasn't me and I don't think it was Peter. I don't know what he had to gain.'

Guy's eyebrow was twitching and, perhaps for the first time since they'd met properly, it felt as if Millie had him surprised and stumped.

'I can maybe ask around,' he replied. 'But sources are sacred. I doubt I'll get any bites. If it was the other way around, I wouldn't give up my source.'

Millie didn't reply, not right away. On top of everything, she had spent a year wondering if someone had betrayed her.

'I'm going to pop out for an hour,' she said. 'I'll be back to eat.'

Guy didn't ask but Millie answered anyway.

'My friend Jack wants me to go to a haunted ghost tree with him. He read something in a book about it but doesn't want to go on his own. He's back with his boyfriend, who says he's an idiot.'

Guy laughed. 'I did say there were secrets in this town but I've never heard of a haunted ghost tree.'

Millie was on her feet. She crouched to ruffle Barry's ears, though he had eyes only for the contents of the oven.

'I'll be back,' she said.

She was at the kitchen door when Guy called her name. Millie turned but she knew what was coming.

'Did you do it?' he asked. 'Did you kill them?'

Millie had wondered if he'd ever ask. If he'd *really* ask. He knew what her dad could be like, after all. She thought about how she would have answered had Beth asked on that bench.

Guy continued talking before Millie could reply. 'Don't answer,' he said quickly. 'I shouldn't have asked. Of course you didn't.'

He let it hang with the unasked 'did you?' on the end.

Millie waited for a second longer, blew a kiss at Barry, and then she headed off to her car, ready to meet Jack at the haunted ghost tree.

A NOTE FROM THE AUTHOR

Authors draw on all sorts of nonsense from their own lives when they're writing a book. Even though the events and the characters in this *are* fictional, there is one thing that happened to me in a sort of, kind of way.

When I was eighteen, I went to the US to work on a summer camp after finishing my A-levels. It was the first time I'd ever been abroad and the first time I'd been on a plane. None of my family or friends were there and it was genuinely a leap into something new. My first experience of being an individual, rather than a classmate, a friend, a son, a brother, a teammate, or any number of other things.

I was working in the office at a camp in the Pocono Mountains of Pennsylvania. I saw fireflies on my first night there, thought it was the most incredible thing I'd ever seen – and, more than two decades later, I've never seen them since.

I slept in a large wooden 'bunk' full of top and bottom beds that were filled with support staff, such as cooks and cleaners. Because of the way the camp worked, almost everyone in our bunk came from a different country. I spent an entire summer mixing with other teenagers and young twenty-somethings, who'd come from pretty much every European destination you can think of. It was great. I ripped off myself to tell some of those stories (sort of) in one of my other books, *Truly, Madly, Amy*.

Although the support staff were largely European, the camp counsellors – who slept in cabins alongside the children – were almost all American. After the campers went to bed, one counsellor per bunk would remain to look over them, while the others would mix with us in the staff lounge.

What was unquestionably the greatest find about my first week in the United States was that American girls liked my accent. I would very happily sit in the staff lounge and reply to such existential questions like 'How do you say the word cheese?'. I'd reply with the word 'cheese' and, somehow, I had what can only be described as a rapt audience of people my own age. *Girls* my own age.

This was not the sort of attention to which I was used.

It was fair to say that if I'd gone around my old college common room saying the word 'cheese' to girls my age, then I would have received a welcome that was far less warm. And, possibly, a restraining order.

Once per week, we all had a night off to do what we wanted. The senior camp staff – the bigwigs, if you like – would supervise the children in their bunks. That meant every counsellor and the whole support staff would all head off to definitely not drink because the age for alcohol intake in the US is twenty-one and we all very much respected that law and definitely didn't think it was stupid.

As well as showing total respect for the rules, quite a lot of us would be driven on the camp minibus to the nearest mall, which was roughly a fifteen-minute drive.

I had started to hang around with one girl in particular and we'd go to that mall to eat terrible – but wonderful – fast food. I'm talking an actual bucket of fries drenched in that squirty yellow stuff that's half-soggy condom, half-cheese. Against all odds, it tastes amazing, although you can feel it clogging your arteries as it goes down. I also started to eat strombolis – which is basically a Swiss roll pizza. For someone who grew up in a small Somerset town, where prawns were viewed with suspicion, this was quite the change.

After we'd eaten our awful but amazing, life-shortening, food, we'd watch whatever was new at the cinema that week. I'm talking such classics as *Wild Wild West*, *Tarzan* and *Big Daddy* with Adam Sandler. By the time that was finished, all the shops would be shut, so we'd mooch around and wait for the minibus to pick us up to take us back to camp.

And this is the memory I've held for more than twenty years before changing it a bit and writing it into this book.

The two of us were young, so the lack of a chair was no issue as we sat on the low kerb outside the doors of the mall. It was dark and the car park was more or less empty, even though the spotlights around the lot were lit, which made everything easy to see.

We were sitting and talking on that warm July evening – and somewhere in the distance, although not *that* far away, a large black dog lumbered across the tarmac. I can't remember what we were talking about, but I do remember saying: 'That was a big dog'.

Roughly two minutes later, a truck came screeching up to the kerb where we were sitting. One guy was driving and there were two or three in the bed, all wearing uniforms. One of them had some sort of rifle strapped across their front and a woman shouted at us to 'get inside'. I assumed there was some weird rule about not sitting on kerbs in the US – which, in all honesty, wouldn't have surprised me. The rifle definitely felt like a bit of overkill.

It wasn't that.

'What's going on?' one of us asked, to which we got a somewhat unexpected reply.

'Didn't you see the bear?!'

I was wonderfully fast on the uptake, replying to tell her that we'd seen a dog. As I was saying it, I was gradually turning two and two into four. We don't have bears in England.

We headed inside to wait for the bus and, as far as I'm

aware, no bears were harmed that evening. I still think it might have been a dog – even if it was bloody massive.

Anyway, dog, bear, or good ol' British panther, if you enjoyed the read, please do leave a review. And, no, not a one-star that says something like: 'It has words on a page'.

Cheers for reading. There will be more of Millie and Whitecliff to come very soon. Rest assured, I'll likely be plagiarising my own life for that too.

– Kerry Wilkinson, October 2022

KERRY WILKINSON PUBLISHING TEAM

Editorial
Ellen Gleeson

Line edits and copyeditor
Jade Craddock

Proofreader
Loma Halden

Production
Alexandra Holmes
Natalie Edwards

Design
David Grogan

Marketing
Alex Crow
Melanie Price
Occy Carr
Ciara Rosney

Publicity
Noelle Holten
Kim Nash
Sarah Hardy
Jess Readett

Distribution
Chris Lucraft
Marina Valles
Stephanie Straub

Audio
Alba Proko
Nina Winters
Helen Keeley
Carmelite Studios

Rights and contracts
Peta Nightingale
Richard King
Saidah Graham

Printed in the USA
CPSIA information can be obtained
at www.ICGtesting.com
LVHW091922081023
760488LV00050B/426

9 781837 900527